Through Rose Tinted Glasses

Mon A Johnson

**Grosvenor House
Publishing Limited**

This book is published by
Grosvenor House Publishing Ltd
Link House
140 The Broadway, Tolworth, Surrey, KT6 7HT.
www.grosvenorhousepublishing.co.uk

A CIP record for this book
is available from the British Library

ISBN 978-1-83975-641-2

ACKNOWLEDGEMENTS

I wish to offer heartfelt thanks and gratitude to Linda Aldous and Rita Bishop whose artwork is used for this novel.

Using wonderful acrylics, Linda painted Pippa in her rose tinted glasses with a Norfolk wherry and traditional windmill in the background.

Rita kindly provided a beautiful watercolour painted from the top of St James Hill in Norwich. She cleverly superimposed a pair of rose tinted glasses in front of her painting.

DISCLAIMER

This is a work of **fiction**. Names, characters, events and incidents are the products of the author's imagination. Any resemblance to actual persons, living or dead, or actual events is purely coincidental. The inclusion of any business names, brand names or public institutions is purely for the sake of authenticity and in no way reflects an opinion or real event. The author makes reference to the non-exhaustive list below and no inference in relation to them should be made.

Norwich City Football Club
Chapelfield Gardens, Norwich
Memorial Poppy Exhibition at Tower of London
Victoria & Albert Museum
Rod Stewart, You Wear It Well
Carly Simon, Coming Around Again
Keane, Somewhere Only We Know
Mary Hopkins, Goodbye
Fifty Shades trilogy
Dan Brown
Peppa Pig
Babe
Bill and Teds Bogus Journey
Building For The Future

Dedication

For Toby, my greatest confidant, loyal friend,
most wonderful companion and the best dog
anyone could have known.

CONTENT

CHAPTER 1

'Patience is a virtue, possess it if you can,
seldom in a German Shepherd and never in a man.'

Pippa was feeling very happy with her lot.

She was driving home from her Saturday shift at the bank and to top off the good feeling a song she hadn't heard for years started to play on the radio, Rod Stewart's, 'You Wear It Well'.

She turned up the volume and couldn't help but smile as she was singing along. It brought back memories of when she and Matti would sit in her bedroom as teenagers with their acoustic guitars attempting to play and sing the song, without a great deal of success they would both later admit. But here she was a grown woman of fifty-five, where on earth had the time gone?

Thankfully for Pippa the years had been kind to her, she maintained a healthy lifestyle and could easily be taken for younger than her years. This was helped as her mother would say, by her crowning glory, the family trait of thick blonde hair. She would reply with a laugh. 'Thank goodness I didn't take after father.' Father was as bald as a coot!

Her work journey was a bumble of a ride, twenty-eight miles door to door but not too many busy roads on her route, which she saw as a bonus. But that was Pippa, wherever there was a negative she would pull a positive.

She was keen to get home to see husband Karl. Pippa had recently purchased an investment property, a bungalow in the neighbouring village of Bagby. This was a pretty little village, with its own primary school, village hall, doctor's surgery, shops, pubs, two banks and Pippa would say with relish that it even has its very own railway station. Certainly, a great convenience but none the less her enthusiasm could have been seen as a little over the top.

The Bagby bungalow was owned since the 1970's by the same elderly woman and was in the loveliest of settings and as the estate agent Adam Jenner of Wilkinsons informed during his sales pitch, 'you often find with properties owned by the more mature it comes with good gas central heating and double-glazed windows to keep the cold at bay but in need of a complete refurbishment.'

Karl and Pippa were thrilled when the offer was accepted, and they named the bungalow Pride and Joy. Karl wanted to call it Pension Pot but agreed with his wife that wasn't possibly the best of his ideas.

They hadn't done anything like this before, their own cottage was immaculate and decorated to their taste when they moved in. But this didn't hamper their excitement and there was no delay on getting the works completed. They planned on decorating and a few basic things themselves, but that was the limit of their confidence, with the professionals on board for the real work plus they were having a conservatory built to add extra living space. They both understood a few sacrifices with their time now would be worth it, the quicker the works were complete the sooner a tenant could move in.

During her shift Karl sent through an email with photos showing his mornings efforts. He'd laid a laminate floor in the conservatory. She was excited as from the photos it looked wonderful. She loved when an email would ping through from Karl, he would send numerous through on each of her shifts. They were full of humour, interest, and above all her husband would send through flattering comments which made her smile.

Pippa was known for her eBay skills, in particular holding her nerve and not bidding to the very last moment to secure the best price. The kitchen installed at the Pride and Joy was purchased this way, second hand from eBay. It was actually still in situ in the seller's kitchen when they turned up with the van.

Pippa's son Eddie joined them, thank goodness she thought at the time. Whilst Karl was physically big and strong, he sometimes didn't take on board that Pippa's strength did not match his, so Eddie would be a great help. She also thought Karl's fuse was possibly getting shorter and shorter, so again having Eddie's calming happy presence would be very welcome. For Pippa anytime with Eddie was always enjoyed.

As Pippa was driving, she could see their own home in the distance, an impressive looking single storey cottage which had been majorly extended over the years. It was strange as when she was a child it was owned by one of her mother's dearest friends. She loved when they visited Rose Tooke to have afternoon tea in the garden. Back then it was a modest pretty little cottage in a very large garden with beautiful mature trees and deep established boarders. But most of all it was set on the brow of a hill, or 'undulation' as Pippa would say, for anyone that knew Norfolk it wasn't flat, there were large mounds and dips, but it didn't have rolling hills as such to get in the way of the beautiful skyline.

With the rise of property prices in the area and its location with spectacular views there was no way it wouldn't have been bought and extended beyond its original state. Which needed to be sympathetic to meet not only the strict planning permissions required for a conservation area, but also to appease the local parish council members who would have their penny worth of what could and shouldn't happen with a property in any of the Hepton villages.

There was now a red brick wall surrounding the front of the property and large remote controlled iron gates to the driveway. The previous owners Jack and Felicity Phillips went to great lengths to ensure they were totally secure. Karl would say he wondered if Jack was a gangster to require such high security. Pippa couldn't disagree, for the talk in the villages was the Phillips' had to sell up quickly as they were moving permanently to Spain. Their need for a quick sale was music to Pippa and Karl's ears as it meant they were in a good position to purchase the property at a sensible price. The Phillips' had spent a fortune to achieve the look they were wanting, which oozed quality and style.

Pippa was not shy to say she was thrilled they owned it. She even loved its name, The Marshman's, Hepton-on-the-Marshes.

As she pulled on the drive, Dave Spelman was pulling in behind her. Dave was installing the conservatory at the

4

Pride and Joy. She parked in her normal spot, waved and called.

'Hi Dave, all OK with you.'

Dave had a deep booming voice and Pippa often wondered if he had a hearing problem as he never spoke at a normal level, he just seemed to shout. Nonetheless, he was a pleasant chap and she felt she had known him forever, he had been at the same school with her and her late husband Matti. Dave was also with Matti at the cricket ground at Upper Hepton when the fateful accident happened all those years ago, in the summer of 1980.

Dave always liked Pippa and when she and Karl asked him to quote to build the conservatory, he offered a highly competitive figure to secure the job. Unknown to him, his was the only quote they'd sought as Pippa convinced Karl that Dave was the right person for the project and having seen his work Karl fully agreed.

Pippa opened the beautiful oak door to their spacious entrance hall and to her great delight and certainly no surprise Billy her black and tan German Shepherd was waiting for her return. He adored Pippa and she him.

'Hello Billy, have you had a good day? We've got company, here's Dave come to see us. Karl are you there, Dave's just pulled up.'

She called through to the lounge from where she could hear the TV, she assumed Karl was watching the football.

As Dave came through the door, he boomed in his Norfolk dialect.

'You just got in from work, can't believe you'd be in all your black trousers and top with the prospect of Bill's fluffy ginger hairs all over you, love the boots, very nice.'

'Yup you guessed right. Cup of tea Dave, I'll pop the kettle on.'

Dave was rubbing his hands in anticipation.

'Yes please, I'm parched haven't stopped since eight this morning fitting Jim Talbot's windows. You know what he's like, a right tight arse and he wanted me to cut corners, he started putting on his parts, gave me a loada ole squit. Well, I told him, hold you hard either I do 'em proper or not at all. So a cuppa would go down a treat my sweet'

Pippa chuckled he did make her smile and the answer for a cuppa was one of his many sayings. She mimicked Dave as she walked through the hall into the lounge, saying.

'Okey-dokey my sweet.'

Suddenly it was as if the atmosphere were cut with a knife. Pippa looked across the lounge where Karl was sitting on the floor, his back propped up against one of the sofas. He looked awful.

Pippa was concerned, softly asking.

'Hello love, are you alright?'

Karl, exhausted snapped.

'No I'm not. Do I look alright? I'm hungry, I haven't eaten all day and I haven't stopped.'

Pippa embarrassingly asked.

'Why haven't you eaten the lunch I'd left you? Anyway, I'll make you a cup of tea, I'm just going to pop the kettle on to make one for Dave.'

As she was saying this Dave walked through to the lounge and looked down to Karl sitting on the floor. Dave's usual booming voice for once a lot quieter than his norm.

'Hello Karl, cor you do look queer, you alright mate?'

Karl hadn't realised Dave was there.

'Oh, hello Dave, yes not too bad thanks, just a bit shattered what with being away working all week, and then going over to the Bagby property. Not long now though and it will be finished. You well?'

Dave was nodding as Pippa came through from the kitchen. She excitedly asked.

'Well Dave how are things going with our little Pride and Joy, any news on the conservatory?'

'Oooh yes. Cor blast me, it's looking a treat, I'm well chuffed with it. I went down there after Jim Talbot's and I finished off the trims and gave it all a wipe down. I saw you've laid the laminate floor in there Karl, it's gonna look really bootiful by the time we've all finished. I've just come to pick up the final payment if OK with you.'

The revelation that Dave had just come from the Bagby bungalow did nothing to reduce Karl's stress levels. He asked anxiously.

'What, you've just come from there, you didn't go in the bathroom did you? I'd laid the last tiles on the floor just inside the door this morning!'

Dave looked as if all the stuffing had just been knocked out of him, his powering voice was now more of a hush.

'Well yes, I went in to wash my hands, I didn't feel the tiles move underneath me Karl. I'm really sorry mate, I didn't know I shouldn't go in there.'

Karl didn't answer, he just looked in disgust from Dave directly to the TV.

Dave turned to Pippa.

'Just remembered my sweet, I promised to take our Hayley to the Co-Op, I won't be able to stay for that cuppa, perhaps next time.'

Pippa was sitting at the dining room table writing the cheque from her bank account, relieved that the embarrassing situation should soon be over. She handed over the cheque.

'Here you go Dave, I'll see you out. As you say can't keep Hayley from her shopping, even if it is the metropolis of the Co-op.'

She put a laugh in her voice and saw Dave to the door adding quietly.

'I'm sure it will be alright. Don't worry, Karl's just tired, he's overdone it.'

Dave tapped Pippa on the shoulder and mouthed.

'Sorry love, I'm really sorry.'

Pippa went back into the lounge where Karl was now standing.

'That stupid bloke's a hindrance. As if he'd feel anything move under his great hulk, I wouldn't mind betting if there was an earthquake he wouldn't feel it, so he's not going to notice a tile move under him! Half the time I can't understand what he says, he doesn't speak English. Really Pippa, I can't believe you know such idiots, but there again you were at the same school as him so that says it all. I've now got to go back and sort his mess out. What were you doing paying him? He'd cocked up, damaged my floor and you go and pay him without even checking his work. I really can't believe it! Well, are you coming?'

Pippa wasn't keen on getting in the car with Karl in this frame of mind, but knew if she didn't he would see that as a greater affront that the opportunity wasn't grasped to admire the efforts of his labour, so she joined him.

They arrived at the Pride and Joy, Pippa still in her black trousers, top and black patent ankle boots, she thought not a good choice of clothing to be wearing, not only around long-haired German Shepherds but also properties being renovated.

Karl went straight to the bathroom to check the damage and Pippa heading for the conservatory. She could not believe it, calling through to him.

'Oh Karl, it looks really beautiful. From the photos you sent I knew it would look good, whoever rents this will be so happy living here.'

Then she plucked up courage to wander through to the bathroom, asking.

'How's it looking, any damage?'

Karl was in no mood to answer, despite there being no damage to his floor tiles as a result of Dave standing on them.

They got back in the car, Pippa still chattering of how pleased she was with the way everything had come along, it was all so beautiful, and she was proud of their Pride and Joy.

Karl sat and drove in silence. Pippa looked across at him, he looked awful and totally shattered. A few minutes earlier she was on a high, yet now she was looking at her husband wishing they'd never seen the property, let alone bought it. She was concerned that it was all too much and was affecting his health and nothing would be worth that.

They got home to The Marshman's and Pippa made her husband a cup of tea, took his rolls and porkpie out of the fridge, the ones she prepared for his lunch before she went to work.

She gave him enough time to eat his lunch, then went through to run him a deep hot bath, put on some music and called him through to the bathroom to have a nice relaxing soak. As he lay in the bath, she brought him a glass of wine. Within a short while Karl was feeling calmer, his sugar levels were stable, he was content, but most of all he had his wife back in his orbit looking after him. Karl's balance was fully restored.

The following morning when they woke, Pippa went through to make a cup of tea, she gave Billy his morning cuddle, let him out in the garden and stood looking out the kitchen window. Dawn was her favourite time of the day. Her kitchen faced south east, the large skyline was perfect anytime but first thing it was sublime. The new day always seemed to be the turning of a page and with everything being so still it always held the expectation that everything was going to be positive.

Billy came in from the garden and she took the mugs of tea through to the bedroom, gently opened the curtains to allow her husband to slowly come to and they lay in bed drinking their teas.

She was hoping they would not have to go to the Pride and Joy to do more decorating. It had been relentless, and the toll was definitely showing on Karl. Since they got the keys, which was now coming up to four months, they had not had a weekend off. Any hour they could dedicate to get the works out of the way was put in.

As they lay in bed Karl outlined today's plan of action, they would have a well-deserved day off. A trip into Norwich and have their Sunday lunch at Quayside, a new restaurant, near the Cathedral. They would not rush their lunch but as soon as they got back, he would need to spend a few hours in his office to get on with some work. That would leave her free to take Billy for a walk. How did that all sound?

Pippa agreed this sounded wonderful, in fact it sounded perfect. Karl was relieved, whilst he wouldn't have said, he knew his behaviour not only yesterday but of late had let him down. He was not the type of person to admit that upfront, he knew he needed to gain some brownie points he had plans, and these did not include upsetting his wife.

Karl pulled Pippa to him and they kissed passionately, one thing led to another and it was a good while later before Karl got up to make them another cup of tea and a toasted tea cake, all of which were popped on a tray and taken through to his very contented wife.

Karl loved watching Pippa get herself ready, he would lay on the bed watching as she sat at the dressing table run the straightener's through her hair, and then apply her makeup, she would be chattering all the time with such enthusiasm, he adored her sweetness.

When Pippa was ready, they went off in Karl's new black Jaguar. It was a company car, top of the range and he'd made sure it came fully loaded. He spent a lot of time on the road and was going to be comfortable on his journeys. It had nothing to do with the fact that possessions demonstrated status and this car oozed and smoothed his ego. Karl was on a good salary and needed people to be able to see that at a glance.

Quayside lived up to Karl's expectations, he was familiar to eating at good restaurants. For Pippa there was neither a standard nor expectation, as she hadn't ever dreamt that her husband would suggest them going there.

Normally when Karl was home, he didn't want to eat out he wanted to enjoy their beautiful cottage and Pippa was a very good cook, he preferred she entertained him. Plus, she knew he was very careful with his money.

Pippa was enjoying and savouring every minute of the lunch. Not just the experience of the new restaurant and the lovely food, but most importantly to have time to be sitting and having the rare opportunity to be talking with her husband about friends, family, what was going on in the villages. In turn he was updating her with what was happening in his work. She was always interested to hear anything and everything he said, it was a different world than she was used to. She knew all his colleagues so well, even though she hadn't met any of them his descriptions were so clear.

Karl had a nickname for everyone, he would be the first to say that he was rubbish at remembering names, but if he called them something descriptive it would stick. The only downside being the names he gave people were often quite offensive so not something he should call them to their face, but that didn't matter to him, at least he could remember them.

They had just started their main course and Karl was saying that 'Baggy Eyed Steve' was playing away, not only playing away, he had been scoring big style for about two years, but now it was payback time.

Baggy Eyed Steve, known to everyone else as Steve Bedford, was a colleague of Karl's and by all accounts they got on very well. Thank goodness Pippa thought or the name would be far less flattering! Years earlier, Karl took a photo of his baggy eyed colleague as proof to show Pippa. Fair to say once she saw the photo, she couldn't deny that her husband's description was fairly accurate, for Steve did have very baggy eyes.

Karl loved nothing more than a bit of work gossip, in fact he thrived on it. Pippa sat back waiting to hear all the saucy details of what Steve Bedford had been up to.

It transpired that Steve had been having an affair for quite a while with a colleague, Needy Nina. She'd been working at Building For The Future for two years now, which was only a couple of months before she commenced the affair with Steve. Karl saying it was common knowledge within the sales team that Steve and Nina were shagging each other senseless.

When Pippa first heard Karl mention Nina, she thought her husband was worried that his sales position may be threatened as he went on at length that she'd come with a great reputation from one of the competitors.

It turned out that Steve was the one being threatened, but it was his marriage not his job. Nina had said enough is enough, she was fed up being the mistress and she didn't care what dirt or hurt she created in revealing all, she felt it her duty to come clean. She told Steve he needed to get on and tell his fat ugly wife he was leaving her for the new love in his life Nina, or she would be sending evidence of their friendship, and she had been very friendly.

Steve knew the brown stuff was about to hit the fan, big style.

He also knew he had to make a decision between the stability of his wife who was actually very attractive, interesting, good fun and they enjoyed a nice history together. Plus, and most importantly, he loved his wife. Whereas Nina, apart from working for the same company and having sex, they had nothing in common. In fact, there was nothing other than the sex that he liked about her, he was totally bored of her.

It seemed foolish now, but back in October to buy some time with having to make a decision he changed the names on the holiday from his wife to Nina. He'd even sent Nina the confirmation that they were going on holiday together, this placated her all was well. Strangely he'd expected to have everything sorted by the time the holiday came along, but now it was looming, fast! Back in October he'd been pleased that he'd managed to gain extra time as his biggest challenge was damage limitation. This extra time also allowed him to squirrel money away to a secret stash to make sure if it came to divorce, he didn't have to hand so much over to his wife. Steve couldn't face handing over a penny more than he had to.

Pippa sat listened then said.

'Steve's poor wife, I really feel sorry for her. Surely, she can see that her husband is cheating on her. As for Nina and Steve that's not a proper relationship. They both sound very shallow, horrible people and deserve one another. Goodness me Karl, I'm surprised Doug is keeping people like this in the company. I honestly couldn't see Annie my boss at the bank, tolerating any of this sort of behaviour.'

Karl agreed with his wife, saying that Baggy Eyed Steve had relayed not only to him but to the whole sales force that busty Nina, was not only needy but very demanding in the bedroom department. Their trysts had always been away on work in hotels, allowing him to wine and dine his mistress on the company's expenses keeping the costs invisible from his bank account. Doug was not pleased by the blatant behaviour of two of his sales team. Their only saving graces being they gave no indication to clients and always produced results.

Karl started looking at his watch, indicating lunch was over, he settled the bill, and they were on their way back. Pippa loved the rare time she was a passenger as it gave her the opportunity to fully take in the journey. She sat deep in her thoughts, very grateful that her life was surrounded by stability and lovely kind people. She thought, poor Mrs Bedford I hope she comes out of this alright. As for that Steve and Nina they certainly deserve their comeuppance.

They'd only gone a few miles and Karl chirpily said.

'I've been looking at a new car for you. How do you fancy driving around in a brand-new VW estate? There's plenty of room in the back for Billy and your car is getting past its best. And anyway, I don't like that garage you go to. What are they called? That's it, Murray and Son. They ought to rename it to Grease Monkey's R Us, it's a right old dive.'

Pippa's eyes widened with excitement. She couldn't believe she was hearing that her husband was arranging a new car for her. Karl was in full swing and carried on saying.

'I've been to the dealer; they'll knock two grand off for your old heap and if you put down a deposit of eighteen thousand that will make it only two hundred and eighty pounds a month over three years. You can transfer that monthly to my account.'

It took Pippa a little while to take on board Karl's suggestion and finally asked.

'Eighteen thousand pounds deposit and I don't understand why I would need to transfer money monthly to your account?'

Karl didn't take his eyes off the road simply replying.

'Well, the car would be in my name, so the credit agreement would have to be in my name, but as it's a car for you to drive its only right that you pay for it. You don't seem to realise Pippa, if I lost my job tomorrow the Jag would go, and as I've had company cars for more years than I can remember I need to build up insurance in my own name.'

He paused for a few moments and when Pippa didn't answer he lashed out hitting the steering wheel, grumpily shouting.

'Well thank you Karl for taking me for a lovely meal, despite being up to your neck with work and sorting out that bloody property. Give me a broom, I'll pop it up my arse and sweep the floor whilst I'm at it. Pippa you're so bloody tight, I didn't see you get your purse out to pay for lunch.'

Pippa still didn't answer, she was too upset, the lovely day had been spoilt and she was trying to digest the logic of

Karl's reasoning. From what he said his job was secure not least by the dedication, diligence and hours he put in.

Plus, there seemed little or no difference of building up insurance in his own name, be it now or at a time in the future.

But what really upset her was being called tight. To hear Karl speak it was as if he had just treated his wife, but the card he used to pay for lunch was from their joint account.

Pippa was always unnerved when her husband raised the subject of money, she knew he would say things which did not make sense and always resulted in him becoming angry and fly off the deep end which resulted in him sometimes not speaking to her for weeks.

A few months before they were married Karl moved in with Pippa, he suggested and she happily agreed, their salaries would continue to be paid into their individual accounts and they would each transfer £500 a month to a new joint account. This would easily cover all their bills including their annual holiday. Karl emphasised this would allow Pippa to keep her independence as he was keen not to burden her with any of the debts he brought into the marriage, namely a mortgage and maintenance of an investment property he owned in Colchester. Pippa never queried why the rent he received didn't cover the mortgage or any of the associated costs.

The arrangement continued even after they moved to their home, The Marshman's, the money to purchase and furnish it came from Pippa. She funded the recent purchase of the investment property in Bagby, together with monies to cover the renovation work. The money all came from Pippa's inheritance fund. Karl saying, he was loathed to unsettle the tenant at the Colchester property, suggesting it was best if that property was left as it was, to be used in the future as their retirement nest egg.

She was still thinking what Karl had said as he pulled on to The Marshman's driveway. He appeared as if nothing bad happened earlier, saying in a kindly tone.

'I've got to get on with my work now, are you taking Billy for a nice walk?'

Relieved that Karl wasn't in a frame of mind to drag things on Pippa replied.

'Yes, we'll do a circular walk to Upper Hepton and if Eddie and Sophie are about, we'll pop in for a cuppa. Thank you for the lovely meal Karl.'

Karl smiled and gave her a peck on the cheek, casting a disparaging eye towards her car.

'Just give the new car some thought Pippa, it does make sense and I hate the idea of my wife driving around in that old heap.'

Pippa took Billy for a walk. They had only been gone a matter of moments and she started to give thought to the new car and quickly made her decision. She didn't need to change her car; she was content with the one she had.

Murray & Son were a reputable garage and she had full confidence in them. Her parents and Pippa had always used the garage, right back to when it was owned by John senior and in more recent years by his son, also John. Karl had never even been there, how on earth did he form such a negative opinion.

As she walked Pippa thought, Karl may be good at his job, but he really did come out with some crackpot ideas. If he raised the subject again, she would just say the time was not quite right. She knew her decision was correct, not least at every MOT and service John would say it was a cracking car, low milage and had years in it, 'no doubt, due to it never going out of Norfolk'.

CHAPTER 2

'A minute on the lips, a lifetime on the hips.'

On Fridays Pippa regularly attended the local slimming classes, she had been a Diet What Diet target member for years. It didn't cost her anything to attend and she was known as one of the social team, to meet and greet other members which she really enjoyed.

She was popular, she had a kindly reassuring manner and people often would try and confide in her as they knew whatever they said would go no further. But as soon as the confidence was anything to do with their weight or the diet plan Pippa would direct them straight over to Amy Dickens the Diet What Diet consultant.

Amy wasn't your normal slimming consultant; in both personality and body she was larger than life. In all the time Pippa had known Amy, not once had she heard anyone bite back at Amy's comments to 'get yourself sorted, no one ever said this weight loss journey was going to be easy, it's down to you, get your backside into gear'. Quite the opposite everyone adored her frankness, and her knowledge of the programme was second to none. Everyone knew Amy herself struggled with what went past her lips.

Today Pippa was asked to be in the area of the 'Scales of Shame or Fame' as Amy referred to it, which simply was taking people's weight. This was Pippa's favourite area to help. She liked the responsibility, she found it interesting to see and hear people's reactions of what they were expecting their current weight to be and then observe their reaction once their loss, maintain or the horror of all horrors, the dreaded gain had been announced. But above all this gave Pippa an opportunity for a natter.

She could hear and see in the queue her friend Beverley Constance. Bev was proud to be Pippa's friend and knew she took top perch. But she was often irritated by Pippa's niceness and pointed out on more than one occasion over the years that she let people walk all over her. With Pippa saying she saw her niceness as her strength, she wasn't going to be changing now, even if she'd wanted to.

They were firm friends within a few hours of meeting, which had been back in 1974 when they both started at the Head Office of The Eastern England Bank, on Castle Meadow in Norwich, Pippa just sixteen and Bev two years her senior. The first thing that struck Pippa when she met Bev was not her attractive long dark hair, but her Akela, head of scouts' type presence which seemed to be emphasised by the bank's uniform at the time, navy skirt and white blouse surrendering under Bev's very ample breasts. To add to this vision, Bev decided Pippa would be known as Pip and she would always say 'Toodle Pip' instead of saying bye.

When Bev reached the scales, she was very excited to tell Pippa she was throwing a surprise thirtieth birthday party Saturday week for her daughter Lauren. Not only were Pippa, Karl, Eddie and his fiancé Sophie invited, but they would all have a very important role within the surprise and helping out!

'Of course, we'll be there, I can't think of anything else we would rather do, truly Bev I'm looking forward to it already. Let us know how we can help.'

She chuckled to herself as she knew Bev would have no hesitation in providing a list as long as her forearm.

'Will do Pip, mums the word. You're be able to go on eBay tonight and get yourself a new dress.'

Bev looked down at the electronic reading of the scales.

'Good grief how did that happen, safe to say I won't be staying for the class, can't explain that gain to the DWD commandant. I'll ping you an email with all the party details. Toodle Pip.'

As the members were all weighed and had taken to their seats Pippa walked over to join them and thought about Lauren and her pending party. Yes, it was right she was asked to help out. When all said and done, she was Lauren's Godmother. She would definitely look on eBay later for a new dress.

She had just sat down ready for the start of the class, when Bella bloomin' Robertson plonked herself down in the seat next to her. Pippa wasn't keen on Bella, she always made her feel uncomfortable, and she was one of the few people she was at a loss of what to say.

'Hi Pippa, how are things and how's that handsome husband of yours?'

'Yes, all very good thank you, how is life treating Bella?'

'Not too bad, I told you didn't I that I was with a bloke from Sunderland, well I've just finished with him. He wasn't what he cracked himself up to be, didn't even look anything like his photo, I think that must have been from about ten years ago. Plus, I couldn't stand his accent, so I got rid of him. Still, you know what they say plenty of fish in the sea.'

Pippa was taken aback, even by Bella's standards this was below the belt. She would have known Karl had a similar accent as he came from Newcastle and within minutes of meeting anyone, he would let them know that he was a proud and passionate supporter of the Magpies. His accent had softened, well apart from times when he was excited or annoyed and then his speech reverted to his native Geordie. When asked why he moved from Newcastle, he would just look at Pippa and say, 'for this beautiful woman.' Pippa knew this wasn't true. Karl had moved south for work a good few years before he met Pippa.

Pippa was relieved she didn't need to answer Bella as Amy took center stage to a round of applause and they all settled down to the highs, lows and most importantly, the expectations and hopes of each of the members.

The class drew to a close with Amy, oblivious to her new job title of DWD Commandant fresh in the air saying.

'Happy Days People go forth and prosper, both me and my scales hope to see a lot less of you next week. Come on people admit it, those scales need a bit of a rest.'

Without fail everyone would laugh and slowly disband.

Pippa was lost in her thoughts as she drove home, mentally going through her tick list of things to do; take Billy for a short walk round the village and then together they would go in her car to the Pride and Joy, Billy could sit in the garden whilst Pippa would ensure everything was perfect inside. She had been so excited to get to this day. The estate agent, Adam Jenner would be coming at three o'clock to take the Pride and Joy on his books to rent it out. She was also keen to see his impression of the great job that had been done on the property and whilst it wasn't going to be sold, she would be interested to hear his view on how much their efforts had brought.

Adam didn't disappoint, his expression was of true pleasure for it was a great job, and as a result the rent could be higher than he'd previously thought, meaning more commission for him. In anticipation of listing the rental, he had whetted potential clients' appetites that it would be coming on his books. To Karl and Pippa's delight they received a telephone call the following day that a nice elderly couple were keen to pay twelve months' rent in advance for the pleasure of living there.

Saturday night Karl lit the fire pit. It was early May and whilst pleasant during the day the evenings soon chilled and they each sat snuggled with a blanket round their shoulders and a bottle of wine at Karl's side, the iPod playing softly. The good news that they were now landlords helped to relax Karl and he was looking happy.

As the evening pulled in, Karl added more logs to the fire. Pippa was saying about the list of jobs Bev sent through for Lauren's surprise party, which was to be held at the cricket club. She was both pleased and relieved to see the list wasn't too onerous. There was nothing specifically for Karl, and Pippa's tasks were all things she would really enjoy, such as decorating the hall with balloons, banners and ribbons. Bev had arranged with caterers to do the food but asked Pippa to make her famous potato salad, since the caterers' version would pale into insignificance and Bev wanted only the best for Lauren.

Pippa also mentioned that Bella bloomin' Robertson was on the search again for another chap and that she had enquired about her 'handsome husband', which made Karl smirk. She didn't mention that Bella dumped her latest chap because she didn't like his Northern accent! Such a lovely evening needed to be savoured, not spoilt by that damn woman.

Pippa went on.

'Oh, my goodness, no doubt that awful Bella will be at the party, what with Bella's daughter Robyn and Lauren having gone to the same private school. I suppose it would be too much to ask that she had somewhere else to go. You never know she might have one of her new blokes with her.'

Pippa was in full giggles with the vision. Karl said in disgust.

'How does she find all these blokes, that's what I'd like to know. It's not as if she's a looker.'

'She goes on dating sites. Thing is she's having to widen her search area now I think, as from what she's said previously it seems to be the same people on the circuit. I'm sure she's quite attractive in a certain light.'

'Yeh, pitch dark, no Peppa she is not attractive at all and I'm a bloke, so I know what's attractive in a woman or not.'

Pippa thought she misheard her husband but asked.

'Did you just call me Peppa?'

Karl looked lovingly at her.

'Yes, I heard it on the radio the other day and I thought straight away that's going to be the name for my wife.'

'Oh Karl, I think it might have been Peppa Pig you heard, it's a children's programme, I'm not sure I like being referred to as a pig.'

Karl suddenly said very excited.

'I've been dying to tell you, Nina and Steve have both been sacked, the proverbial brown stuff hit the fan.'

'Good job an all.'

Pippa quickly said, thinking I hope Steve's wife is alright and that she comes out OK.

Karl happily relayed the sorry story, and Pippa sat in silence at it all.

On Monday morning the sales team were sitting at the conference table discussing a huge contract. They had been on tenterhooks as they were near the deadline and the printers only delivered the documents on Saturday afternoon to Doug at his home. This was the first time the team had seen the result of their efforts and were now feeling very confident. The courier was waiting in reception to take the packaged documents, by motorbike, to the client for the submission deadline of three o'clock.

No one noticed when Nina marched in, stood behind Steve and tipped a couple of bags of belongings over his head and in the chaos, paper cups of tea and coffee were sent flying all across the table, soaking the tender documents and design drawings.

They all sat in silence, looking at one another and then all looking towards Doug, who stood up and told Nina to leave. She was in no mood to be told what to do, and simply announced that she'd resigned and couldn't work in a place with people like them a minute longer.

Doug phoned the consultant to see if there could be any leeway with the submission of the documents. But he was told he knew the tender specifications, if the documents weren't received by the deadline, they were out of the equation. The team were trying to retrieve the situation, using Steve's scattered clothes to mop up the tea and coffee but all were spoilt in one way or another. Steve was very sheepish, he couldn't take on board what had happened. He was going on holiday the following day and expected to come back with that contract in the bag.'

Pippa finally jumped in.

'I can see why Nina was sacked but did you say Steve was sacked too?'

Irritated by the interruption Karl carried on.

'Yes, I'm coming to that. On Tuesday, Steve and his wife arrive at Gatwick airport and they are walking to check in their bags. She lags behind and Steve calls to her that they need to get a move on, she stands and stares back at him, when this dark haired, tall bloke comes up to her and takes her suitcase. Steve thought he was trying to steal her case, shouts at the bloke who then kisses his wife on the lips, and she turns to Steve announcing.

'Steve, I'm divorcing you and you can thank Nina from me, she's done me a big favour. Three months ago, there was a pair of woman's knickers in your trouser pocket no doubt they were hers. I went on a dating site and met Charles, I'm leaving you for him, he's a proper man.'

With that she walked out of the airport holding this guy's hand. Apparently, Steve stood there wondering how she knew Nina's name as that wouldn't have been on the pair of knickers that were found in his trouser pocket.

Then as Steve was checking in at the five-star hotel in Egypt he received an email from Nina, and everything became clear.

She was furious when Steve told her the week before the holiday, the time was not right, and he was forced to change the holiday back to his wife's name. As her parting shot, she delivered by hand to his wife an A4 envelope full of copies of emails of Steve's undying love for Nina, comments of how his wife was fat and ugly and made him so unhappy, also in the envelope was the confirmation showing that the holiday back in October had been changed to Steve and Nina!

Steve was so upset he took himself into Sharm El Sheikh and went for a session with a hooker and then he was beaten up and mugged. He went to the police station and when they didn't deal with his claims of the theft and assault to his satisfaction, he lost his temper and was arrested for unruly and aggressive behaviour.

Steve phoned Doug on Wednesday relayed the whole torrid tale and begged for his help as he was stuck in a prison in Egypt. Doug being such a nice guy and a happily married man found it really hard to take on board what he was hearing and when he didn't answer quick enough Steve started effing and jeffing and repeatedly saying 'Get me out of here. This place is a shit hole.' Well, that was it, Doug just said 'Steve, you're sacked' and put the phone down.'

Karl was beside himself with laughter, he said he'd found it hysterical when Doug told him the story and even more so now when he was relaying it to Pippa, he felt his sides were splitting. This was totally out of character for Karl as anyone that knew him would say he wasn't a person that laughed hardly often, if at all, and never a good belly laugh.

Pippa didn't find the story funny; she was shocked by it all. Finally saying.

'Well, it sounds as if that horrible Steve and Nina both deserve what they got. I hope his wife is happy with her new man. Steve's karma does seem a bit extreme though to be locked up in an Egyptian prison, I would imagine it's awful. When you said he went for a session with a hookah I thought you meant one of those smoking pipes not a prostitute.'

With that Karl pulled his wife onto his lap and snuggled the blanket round them.

'How come I managed to marry someone as sweet and innocent as you, I love you Peppa.'

She sat snuggled on her husband's lap and they watched the logs on the fire pit spark and crackle, both deep in their thoughts.

Pippa was thinking back to when she first met Karl, it was just a conversation they had at the bar after the bank's annual awards ceremony in Ipswich. Karl's partner Kelly also worked at The Eastern England Bank at a branch in Colchester and had received an invite to the sought-after annual event. The invitation always included a plus one, but Pippa went on her own.

During the meal Kelly overdone the wine and had to take herself to bed, leaving Karl at the bar. When Pippa stood next to him to order her drink they simply chatted for a while, nothing more than that.

Pippa had been surprised when a couple of weeks later, Karl walked into the banking hall of the Castle Meadow branch, she was based at the time in Norwich. When she finished her shift, they went for a coffee before his drive back to Colchester. Karl made it clear it wasn't a chance visit, he'd gone out of his way to make contact with Pippa as he felt it was love at first sight and she was his true soul mate. That was it she was fully and truly smitten, she never thought she would ever meet anyone following the loss of Matti.

She started thinking of the Bagby rental property. When Karl made the suggestion to purchase it, she had been reluctant. But he was determined, he put all the figures on a spreadsheet showing it was win, win they couldn't lose. He reassured Pippa that her inheritance monies, which she saw as Eddie's and any future grandchildren would literally be as safe as houses, she had nothing to worry about. The monthly rental Pippa could return to her savings and the property value would increase nicely and when they decided to sell in the future, the monies she had used to purchase and renovate the property could be returned to the inheritance pot, with any extra equity to be used for their own retirement. Finally, she relented.

She hated all the hours she spent stripping wallpaper, rubbing down and painting, it had been relentless. The project had worried her as she felt the stress had been far too much on her husband. She swore to herself they would never do anything like that again. Thankfully that was all now in the past there were lots of nice things to look forward to and most of all they would have their weekends back again.

She would keep an eye out for the money to hit their joint account and place it in a high interest savings bond. She could see her husband was happy, he was smiling, what a relief.

As she sat snuggled on Karl's lap, his thoughts were very much of the here and now. Yes, he was fortunate his wife was gorgeous, which was important to him as he couldn't have a minger on his arm. She kept everything in his life calm and organised, he could be away all week and when he was home, she doted on him as if he were a god. She didn't put a drain on his income, quite the opposite she was his goose that laid the golden egg.

He was feeling very smug with himself; he couldn't believe how hard it had been to convince Pippa to release monies to buy The Marshman's and then fund the Bagby property.

He knew she saw this as being careful, but he'd say a 'shroud doesn't have pockets', but she wouldn't have any of it. She just saw the monies she'd inherited should be kept safe for that bloody spoilt son of hers and any future grandchildren. She was just plain stupid.

He was smiling broadly with the thought of what he was going to spend the rental monies on. It was music to his ears when he heard that the tenants were paying a lump sum of a whole years rent in advance. He'd keep an eye on the bank account to see when the monies hit and quickly transfer them to his sole account. The last thing he needed was Pippa to get to the monies first and put them where he had no access. He deserved them, he'd worked hard on the Pride and Joy, his pension pot. Karl sighed contentedly, he'd done well, Whey aye, life was good, very good indeed. But mostly his plans were coming together.

CHAPTER 3

'Nothing stays the same.'

Pippa and Karl were up nice and early the morning of Lauren's surprise party. The step ladders were loaded in the car, with the containers of Pippa's potato salad being put in at the last minute to be taken to the fridges at the cricket club, all was ready for Pippa to arrive at ten thirty. Karl would follow her later as he would be popping to the gym first thing.

They had cancelled their membership at the Field View Sports Club while they were busy with the works on the Pride and Joy. Even though it had only been five months, they were both glad and excited to start their memberships again and get back to their normal routines.

The name of the gym didn't exactly reflect the look of the establishment, there was neither a field view and whilst there was a fully equipped gym, a couple of squash courts and a bar, it could hardly be described as a sports club. Pippa had been a member for the twenty-eight years it had been running, Karl for five years now, he joined a year after their marriage. But whenever he felt it necessary, he would remind other members that as he had been a member for a good number of years, he felt it his duty to point out that the Smith's machine or the preachers' bench should not be hogged and needed to be used fairly and respectfully by all, in other words, get off I need them!

The manager was a little lady from Manchester called Janet. Without a doubt Janet put the fear of God into anyone. The fact that she was five foot nothing tall and four foot nothing across was neither here nor there. She used her Mancunian presence to mean no one, and nothing would mess with this girl. Janet took her role of sports club manager very seriously!

Janet was fond of no one, but she spoke kindly to Pippa. When Pippa phoned to say she and Karl wanted to re-join after their break from doing the property works, Janet went through the protocol of the rules. It would be inappropriate if she hadn't, but she was secretly pleased Pippa was coming back to the fold. Pippa had shown Janet kindness on more than one occasion and she was always polite, which Janet liked.

On the morning of the party Karl and Pippa eagerly went their separate ways, Karl to the gym and Pippa to the birthday preparations.

Pippa arrived at the cricket club, the 'Matt Jackson Hall' in memory of her late husband Matti who had lost his life during a cricket match.

Matt had been an only child like Pippa, and they met when she was fourteen and he was sixteen. They were the best of friends, first lovers and genuine soul mates. He had a pleasant easy-going personality and blessed with good looks. He worked at the prestigious Lambast Insurance Company in Norwich. He easily passed the insurance qualifications and been taken on by the Inspection Team. A much-coveted position which also meant his salary had increased accordingly. Anyone who knew him would say he was a lovely chap and adding to all his qualities he was an all-round sportsman.

Sunday 6th August 1980 was a beautiful day. Matt opened the wicket, it was the first bowl of the match, dangerous by any standards, the ball bounced and hit him square on the heart with such force his heart stopped. Dr Newcome was at the match and in spite of his efforts to revive Matt with CPR, the ambulance arrived to find her beloved's life extinguished.

Eddie, their baby son, was coming up to a year-old at the time of the accident and Pippa knew if it wasn't for Eddie, she would not have been able to carry on.

Matt's parents Frank and Victoria were totally devastated at losing their only son but put their energies towards their grandson. Together with Pippa's parents James and Hannah, they all made sure Pippa was fully supported and assistance was always on offer to her and Eddie.

Eddie was the spit and image of Matt in personality, looks and physique but had Pippa's eyes and hair. He was also like his father being an all-round sportsman, studious scholar and had an excellent job. Eddie was a Senior Accountant at Ludwicks and Sheriffs, a respectable Norwich accountancy firm.

Pippa arrived at the cricket club to see Bridget & Harry Fisher, among others being directed by Bev. Oh dear, Pippa thought with a chuckle they'll be thrilled to having been roped in. She quickly set about dressing the hall, with Harry insisting that he foot the ladder. She guessed the real reason for his insistence; Harry was trying to keep out of Bev's way!

At one o'clock they all stopped for a cup of tea and sandwiches that Bridget had brought along, and they sat looking through the hall, it really did look lovely. Bev hadn't skimped on the decorations, they were beautiful. Pippa relished her task of chief decorator. Bev had arranged for someone to fill the balloons with helium, while Pippa positioned and tied them where they were needed. Everything was colour coordinated in a lavender blue. The ribbons and banners were of such a lovely quality.

There was a guy setting up a disco. Pippa wasn't too sure what Lauren would make of 'Ted's Timeout' as the equipment looked a bit early eighties and was obviously a nod to the film Bill and Ted's Bogus Journey.

Pippa was very fond of her Goddaughter, and yes, she was a lovely girl. But Lauren had been a spoilt child, only ever expected the best and her parents indulged her. Even more so in the last few years after Bev and Ashley divorced. A highly acrimonious affair what with Ashley having gone off with someone fifteen years Bev's junior. As a result, they both tried to buy Lauren's affection. Pippa suddenly thought with dread; goodness, what if Ashley is also planning a surprise party for Lauren!

Just at that moment Karl came through the door to the hall, announcing to them all.

'Wow look at all this, how good does this look. Blimey Bev you really know how to throw a surprise party. I don't think you need my help.'

Bev greeted Karl and they air kissed; she was easily flattered.

'Thank you m'dear, yes I was then saying to the Fisher's if Lauren isn't impressed with this, I don't know what she ….'

Stopping mid flow, she turned to the caterers who had just arrived through the doors behind Karl.

'Good about time too, come on there's lots to do, through there, there's the kitchen. Excuse me Karl dear, I need to get on and organise this rabble, see you later.'

With that Bev was away in her element, directing people to their allotted area.

Karl looked at Pippa.

'You about ready to go?'

Before she had time to reply he walked over to Harry giving him a friendly slap on the shoulder and saying with laughter.

'Well done Harry, you took one for the team. I'll buy you a pint later.'

'Yes, tell me about it. What with being the only chap here at the beck and call of all these women, I'll need more than a pint Karl.'

Harry was saying exactly what he felt, he couldn't believe how he'd got dragged into it.

Pippa had finished the party preparations and she was certainly keen to get away, walk Billy, shower, do her hair and makeup. She couldn't wait to put on her new dress, she loved getting prettied up and would always say she liked being a girly girl.

She was well impressed with the new dress, her purchase from eBay. When it arrived earlier that week, she eagerly opened up the parcel, tried it on and it was even better than she'd hoped. It was a midi bodycon dress, black lace overlay, a nude lining, with a halter neck, which suited Pippa's shape perfectly. The dress was new with tags and the seller had sold it for a low starting price as the buttons on the halter neck were missing. Pippa did her usual trick of waiting to the last few seconds to make her offer and secured the purchase. By the time the dress arrived she had been to her local haberdasher and purchased replacement buttons.

So later that evening Karl walked into their bedroom, he himself looking very smart. He'd taken himself to the shops and not skimped, he'd bought a designer pair of dark blue trousers which he teamed up with a pink designer shirt, leather belt and new light brown leather shoes.

As he walked through the bedroom door he was genuinely pleased with the sight before him. His wife looked lovely. Pippa's slim figure, long blonde hair and youthful features were standing before him. He thought how beautiful she was. Pippa looked at Karl and his face said it all, he needn't have uttered a word but felt he had to.

'Oh Peppa, you look lovely.'

A smile came over her face.

'Thank you, my handsome hubby, I have to say you look fairly scrummy yourself.'

As they walked into the cricket club, they were happy and proud to be on each other's arm.

Eddie and his fiancé Sophie were key in keeping everything a surprise from Lauren. They had organised to pick her up, together with her latest boyfriend Oscar, they were all supposedly going for a meal and then on to the prestigious Pasha Night Club. Lauren had been suitably impressed with the plan for her birthday evening as the Upper Hepton restaurant The Spotted Dog Inn, recently received the coveted Jaden Award Restaurant of 2012. And the Pasha Night Club was her favourite place to be seen!

It was through Lauren that Sophie met Eddie. Sophie had also attended the same private school as Lauren and Robyn, Bella's daughter. Sophie felt she would always be indebted to Lauren for introducing her to the love of her life.

Whilst Lauren was a spoilt child, she always felt comfortable in the company of Eddie and Pippa and thought of them as family. Although to Sophie's expressed gratitude she simply replied in the same assertiveness as her mother, 'yes she did indeed owe her and not to worry as she would call on the favour'. Privately she thought it was the least she could do to introduce her best friend to the nicest, kindest people on the planet and you could not get nicer and kinder than Eddie, Pippa and of course Sophie herself.

When Eddie and Sophie organised picking Lauren up on her birthday to go for the meal and on to the night club Lauren had no reason to be suspicious, they were the perfect decoy.

The party was fully underway with, as Pippa put it, so many of the normal culprits in attendance. It was evident why Ted's Timeout had been the DJ of choice as so many of the guests were friends of Bev's and the parents of Lauren's friends, Ted's music was very seventies and eighties.

Dave and Hayley Spelman were there with their sons Tony and Craig. Thankfully Dave either had forgot the embarrassing situation of standing on Karl's tiles or simply chose not to mention it.

Pippa thought how lovely the mix of guests were and how well everyone was blending together when who should walk in, Bella bloomin' Robertson, with her daughter Robyn. Pippa felt a chill go up her spine and told herself, try and ignore her nastiness for Bella had a spiteful tongue to everyone.

Bella caught sight of Pippa and made a beeline for her, enthusiastically greeting her and air kissing her on both cheeks.

'Hello Pippa, goodness me you have polished up well. New dress? Do give us a twirl. Anyone would think you have to work hard on keeping that husband of yours attention.'

Pippa eagerly gave a twirl.

'Why thank you Bella, as Karl says, dress for your shape, so I did and I am pretty pleased with the result, as is he.'

Pippa didn't know where this came from, but it was too late now it was out there. It was a truthful comment, very out of character for Pippa and it had the desired effect, it shut Bella up!

Pippa looked at her and thought she certainly had not dressed for her shape. Bella would religiously attend the Diet What Diet classes most weeks, but it didn't seem to matter what she did, she could not lose weight. Bella always put it down to either her hormones or her natural large frame, obviously nothing to do with what went past her lips.

Bella had come in the exact same design dress as her twenty-nine-year-old daughter and as Bella was fifty-three possibly not a good move. The dress on Robyn looked wonderful. It was a shift style dress, light lemon in colour and size ten. The differences between the dresses were Bella's; a size eighteen and a mink colour! The dresses came to just above the knee which Robyn easily got away with, but Bella, Oh dear!

The evening was underway, and everyone was having a lovely time. Bev came up to Pippa, a little emotional saying how pleased she was that everything had gone so well without a hitch. She went on to say, a little bit slurred, if Ashley had been here how it would have all been a disaster, what a relief she had plucked up the courage to divorce the waste of space. Bev was now into a rant of how useless her ex-husband was. Pippa glanced across the hall and saw Karl coming back from the toilets and Bella Robertson gesturing for him to come and speak with her.

At first Karl seemed pleased that Bella was speaking to him but within no time at all Pippa could see his body language prickle and turn quite aggressive. Whereas Bella was thrilled with whatever she was relaying to Karl, he certainly was not pleased to be hearing it. Oh my goodness, thought Pippa, I hope Bella isn't mentioning about her most recent dating site acquisition, that she'd dumped because she didn't like his accent. Goodness me what a truly awful person that Bella Robertson is.

They were certainly having words and before long Karl stormed off from the conversation and was walking towards Pippa, he caught sight of his wife looking his way, smiled at her and threw his flirty look and everything seemed alright with the world.

When Karl got to Pippa, he pulled his wife to him and she looked lovingly at him. Just at that moment Ted's Timeout started playing Carly Simon's 'Coming Around Again'. Karl steered his wife to the dance floor for a slow dance, and naturally they were looking into each other's faces. Pippa thought what a lucky woman she was to have such a wonderful husband. Karl was holding his wife close, in an all-encompassing grip.

At the end of the song, Karl kissed Pippa gently on the lips, and they walked hand in hand from the dance floor. Pippa was surprised and a little embarrassed to see so many people just looking at them, smiling with affection. She looked across to see Bev who now had tears coming down her cheeks. Oh dear, Pippa thought, the wines had an effect.

Indeed, seeing a couple dancing romantically made Bev very emotional and what with all the energies and her efforts earlier in the day organizing the preparation for the party, resulted in the tears flowing.

Still holding Karl's hand Pippa took the direction towards Bev but was met by Bella coming up to her and singing 'I know nothing stays the same' and then turning her face towards Karl continued 'but if you're willing to play the game, its coming around again' and then looking back to Pippa sung 'there's more room in a broken heart' being words from the song Pippa and Karl had just danced to.

Karl was not impressed, he turned to Pippa and said loud enough for Bella and others around to hear in his true Geordie accent.

'I divvina she's pissed, nothing worse than seeing a mature woman drunk.'

Bella didn't react, she carried on smiling, walking and humming the tune, looking very pleased with herself. Karl was furious and turned to Pippa, grabbing her arm firmly.

'Come on pet, don't let her spoil our evening.'

Pippa and Karl turned to support Bev in her moment of need and Pippa suggested they get lots of helium balloons to pack into the minibus which was already waiting outside. At eleven thirty the minibus would take the true partygoers, namely Lauren, Oscar, Eddie, Sophie, Robyn and many of the birthday girl's friends, to The Pasha Night Club where Bev had arranged for them to be in the V.I.P. seating area. Lauren was thrilled when she heard this.

Everyone went outside to see the minibus off.

Thankfully, it was not long after Pippa and Karl's taxi arrived. They arranged with Bev for Pippa to come back the following morning to help clear and clean the Hall. Karl offering his apologies that unfortunately he wouldn't be able to help as he needed to get on with some work, but Bev was far too oiled to take on or worry about the cleaning of the hall, in any event she would just have thought the reason Karl wouldn't be there was him being uncomfortable at the cricket club, which was named after his wife's late husband.

When they got home, they went directly to the bedroom. As they kissed passionately Karl slowly undressed his wife, he touched her gently and provocatively as he removed each item. He lovingly kissed her neck, pushing her gently on the bed and holding her arms above her head as he continued kissing her breasts, seductively running his mouth over her rib cage and working his way down her body and stood above his now naked wife, and seductively undressed himself.

Pippa loved the look of her husband she thought he was a fine figure of a man. Whenever Karl would kiss or touch her in this way, she would have to catch her breath. They had their time of lust, passion and extreme pleasure, climaxing together. Pippa was fully cradled in her husband's arms, with his legs wrapped around her. As she drifted into a blissful sleep she thought, only if a couple love each other so genuinely could they experience such pleasure, how lucky we are.

CHAPTER 4

'Tis but the truth in masquerade.'

With the renovation works out of the way, life thankfully got back to normality for Pippa, work, gardening, walking Billy, gym, and general chores. She was relieved by the routine and she loved her lifestyle; healthy, gentle and all very familiar. She even liked her job, nice people and the work wasn't difficult, it all came second nature to her having worked at the bank for so long and she adored being based at the small sub-office on Lower Goat Lane in the center of Norwich. She also felt she learnt a lot about life from what she heard from both colleagues and customers alike.

Whilst Pippa liked family and friends and always went out of her way not to upset anyone. Karl on the other hand appeared able to do without friends and family. From what she knew he only had one friend; an ex-colleague called Hew Thomas. He had been Karl's best man at their wedding. Hew was a great character originally from Swansea, a true salesman and total extrovert.

Karl wasn't fussed if his actions were controversial. He didn't care who he upset, didn't hold back on complaining and was tenacious in getting whatever he wanted. When he first met people, he would put them on a pedestal but as soon as he felt they had let him down, as everyone was bound to, they were placed full square in the ditch! Pippa thought that was down to Karl's high expectations of himself.

She knew little about Karl's family. This troubled Pippa in their early days and she would ask about them but never got any further than he was the youngest of six children, with two brothers and three sisters. He had two daughters from his first marriage. If it hadn't been for Karl having to disclose on their marriage certificate his father's name of Stanley, she wouldn't have known that and when Pippa asked his mother's name, he replied 'Mom'. The only person Karl ever made reference in name was Aunt Mildred who when he was a child lived a few doors away and 'was as crazy as a box of frogs.'

She obviously knew that Karl previously had a partner called Kelly. He was keen to emphasise that he was fully divorced before Kelly was on the scene. Pippa certainly had no reason to question or doubt this, not least because their marriage certificate showed Karl's status as 'divorced' and Pippa's as 'widowed.'

From what he said Kelly was a delicate person and she wasn't supported before she had to leave her job with the bank, which was a great sadness, from what Pippa heard it sounded as if Kelly had a mental health issue. Karl relayed he supported her fully during her terrible bouts of depression and periods of darkness and whilst people feel more open to discuss things now, even a few years earlier such a subject would have been taboo, hidden away with little tolerance or discussion.

Karl was very successful in his job and he was thought of well in his profession, he was often being head hunted by various companies and when contacted for a potential new position he would always follow it through and then turn it down. On each refusal Pippa would say.

'Well at least I needn't worry that you'll ever have an affair as you get such a thrill from all these job offers', to which he would agree.

He worked in the area of sales for a modular building firm, Building For The Future. His role was national, so he would be away most of the week staying in hotels but always tried to travel back on a Thursday evening so he could work from his home office on a Friday.

He had a dedicated work ethic which involved very long hours. Pippa wished he could work more normal hours, but the few times she voiced this Karl would get annoyed and frustrated that she couldn't understand the hours he worked were necessary. According to Karl, the reason they had the lifestyle they had was all down to the hours he put into the job.

Pippa did appreciate how hard her husband worked, but she also found it difficult to work out why they needed to be so frugal. From what Karl said he was on a high salary and received good bonuses.

The house he owned in Colchester had a mortgage and was rented out. He was always keen to say this investment was their pension pot to be sold in years to come. Pippa hadn't ever been to Colchester to see it but from what Karl said it was a good property, in a nice area, ideal for renting. She was relieved that he never mentioned of any problems with the maintenance of the property nor any grief with the rental, which she assumed was carried out through a management company. Over the years she had asked a few times if it was on a fixed rate mortgage and would make suggestions of what products were competitive at the time, but Karl would simply say 'all sorted, no problems.' It all appeared to run very smoothly.

When Pippa had her cottage Churchside, she adored living there and she'd been mortgage free since the insurance monies and death in service payment from Lambast Insurance Company following Matti's tragic accident. Admittedly she hadn't changed much in the house, just general decorating, but had worked hard on the garden which she loved.

She had large savings from inheritance monies from the estate of Matti's very wealthy late parents' who had left everything to be divided equally between Pippa and Eddie with 50% of Eddie's share being held in Trust until he turned thirty. She also had monies from the sale of her own parents' modest cottage, which she invested in government bonds again equally between her and Eddie.

Karl was very keen for Pippa to sell Churchside. He never felt comfortable there and would say he felt her late husband's presence.

The cottage perimeter was the church redbrick and flint wall with the garden on one side and on the other the graveyard of Saint John's, where Matt and so many of her family members were buried. Karl especially hated it when he saw his wife visiting the graves of Matt, Fred, Victoria, James, Hannah and her grandparents. He thought at this rate she'll need a wheelbarrow for all the flower arrangements. But Pippa found great solace from visiting the graves and took great care in tending them.

When The Marshman's came on the market Karl saw this as an opportunity and eagerly suggested they look to buy it. He thought her affection for the house from her childhood visits with her mother for afternoon tea at Rose Tooke's would be a catalyst to get her to consider selling Churchside. Karl brought Eddie on board with the suggestion that he buy it from his mother.

'When all said and done Eddie, how wonderful would it be to keep Churchside in the family.'

Eddie was keen to buy Churchside. Yes, it had great sentimental value, but he also recognised it was the most perfect of properties and he could put his stamp on it. His mum looked after it nicely but in time he could make his changes. The location of the house was wonderful, next to the church and on a ridge looking down to the river, and Upper Hepton had become a most desirable area.

The Marshman's would be bought in Pippa's and Karl's joint names outright with no need for a mortgage as all the funds would come from the sale of Churchside and Pippa's inheritance.

However, all did not go entirely how Karl had planned.

He was so happy driving them to the solicitor's appointment to go through the deeds and registry documents for their purchase. The firm Chester and Whelks solicitors dealt in the past with all the legal work for Pippa's wealthy in-laws, also with Pippa's parents' Wills, and Pippa's Will also held in their safe. Karl was looking forward to meeting Theresa Small, the solicitor dealing with the conveyance as Pippa mentioned that in their twenties they both played netball for the same local team.

As he drove, Karl thanked Pippa for being the best wife any man could have and for her consideration ensuring they didn't have to be saddled with a mortgage. He really didn't need the stress of another mortgage on top of the pressure of his job.

'Oh Karl, that's so sweet of you but it goes without saying that The Marshman's would be purchased in our joint names. I've already confirmed to Theresa that's the case, it will be as Tenants in Common with 70% in my name and 30% in yours.'

Karl couldn't believe what he was hearing and nearly crashed the car!

'What do you mean not fifty fifty and what's this Tenants in Common rubbish about?'

Pippa being familiar with the terminology from her work at the bank was unfazed with her reply.

'It means if you die before me your 30% goes to who you stipulate in your Will and if I die before you my 70% goes to who I stipulate in my Will. You need to turn left here, and the car park is on the right.'

How he got through the meeting with the solicitor he would never understand, he'd been looking forward so much to today and again Pippa had spoilt it, she spoilt everything. All he kept thinking was this stupid Theresa Small, no doubt it was her that put Pippa up to this, she wouldn't have come up with it on her own. He considered himself to be a clever person and even he hadn't heard of Tenants in Common. He suspected when that stupid, ugly Theresa had seen that all the monies were coming from Pippa she had poked her nose in where it was not wanted.

A couple of days after their visit to Theresa Small, Karl suggested if it would be a good idea, 'purely out of kindness to Eddie' to assist with his purchase of Churchside that a payment of forty thousand pounds be deferred to be repaid back to Pippa in five years' time. Obviously, it was totally her decision what with the money to buy The Marshman's coming from the sale of Churchside and her inheritance but, 'it just seemed a nice gesture'. What with Eddie due to receive a large sum from his Grandparents' Trust fund when he turned thirty it seemed, 'the right thing for Pippa to do'.

Pippa agreed she thought this was an excellent idea.

Even without his Trust fund Eddie could have saved and repaid his Mum. He wouldn't have the big monthly expense of a mortgage and his position at Ludwick's and Sheriff's was very good, his salary would increase well. He and Sophie were able to have nice holidays and he'd recently bought a new Range Rover, which they proudly called 'Baby'.

Sophie moved in with Eddie after they were engaged and they made many improvements with Churchside, making it very comfortable in a short space of time. The garden was already perfect and with the exception of installing a decking area nothing else needed to change.

Quietly Pippa was relieved that no other changes to the garden would be made as she loved it. Often when Eddie and Sophie were at work, she and Billy would pop over to Churchside. Billy would sit in the garden whilst Pippa would tend to the family graves and have her private thought time. The only other living soul who was privy to Pippa's thoughts was Billy.

Pippa was a walker and she recognised at an early age how fortunate she was to live in such a lovely area. Since a small child she'd always had the companionship of a Labrador Retriever dog. Teddy was the last.

She had been dating Karl for three months when Teddy passed away. Karl agreed the few times he had seen Teddy he was the nicest dog he'd ever known. After a couple of months of mourning she was ready to start to look for another Lab when a friend of hers got in touch to say they were soon to be grandparents, of the fluffy kind. Josie described both parents, who were gorgeous in looks and temperament and Pippa was welcome to come and have a look at them to see what she thought. They had interest and three of the soon to arrive pups had been reserved, did Pippa want to reserve one? Josie knew Pippa was a lover of Lab's but Molly and Davey were both pedigree black and tan German Shepherds.

Pippa was interested and said she'd very much like to see Molly and Davey, arrangements were made for her to go over on Sunday. Pippa asked if she could bring her friend Karl with her as he would be up for the day. Josie happily agreed. Pippa excitedly told Karl of the Sunday appointment and he confirmed German Shepherds were lovely dogs and sang their virtues. As soon as Pippa met Molly and Davey, she put her name on the list. Pippa told Josie she'd always had boy dogs but with changing to a totally different breed she thought she would also change to having a little girl puppy, so if she could be put down for a bitch as her first choice that would be lovely. Josie marked it all down and told Pippa that the other three reservations all requested bitches too but since she had known Pippa for so long and knew she would give the puppy a perfect home, Pippa would have first choice, but she had to keep that quiet.

The puppies were born, and an excited Josie called Pippa announcing that Molly had given birth to five beautiful puppies, three bitches and two dogs. Did Pippa want to come over and choose her bundle of fluff as she had first choice, Josie could then get on to contact the other new parents. Pippa excitedly asked when she could see the puppies and Josie suggested the following evening. Pippa agreed that was perfect as her friend Karl would be up for the night and she knew he would adore to join her at the visit.

They walked quietly into Josie's utility room to look at the puppies suckling at their mother and they were awestruck with the sight before them.

There was no rhyme nor reason, but Pippa asked.

'That puppy, is it a little girl?'

With Josie checking and saying it was a little boy. Pippa looked at Karl and without hesitation he said.

'You can change your mind to a boy if you want, I'm sure Josie won't mind.'

Josie quickly jumped in that girls were more popular and if she wanted a boy that would be great as the others on the reserved list had wanted a bitch as first choice. So that was sorted. Karl took photos straight away and also on their future visits. Pippa collected Billy when he was eight weeks old, a good solid bundle of ginger and black fluff with huge paws out of proportion to the rest of his body.

Billy was the most perfect puppy; she had never known one to be so easy. She knew it was because he was so intelligent, but Karl would disagree.

'No, it's because he's a German Shepherd, you're only used to Labs.'

Either way Pippa found him a delight to train, and Billy was the most pleasurable company. It turned out that no other dog held a spot in Pippa's heart like Billy. He was a gentle soul but also a formidable chap, with his greatest energies and strength always kept for supporting and protecting Pippa.

Billy would sit in the garden at Churchside on the wood decking area Eddie had created and from that slightly elevated spot he could observe the love and reason for his life, Pippa.

Only once did he need to spring into action. Pippa was at her parent's grave and there was a man in his early twenties loitering in the churchyard, she was deep in her personal thoughts and oblivious to his presence. Billy had been watching from his observation spot and when the young man started to creep up on Pippa from behind, Billy leapt over the red brick and flint wall and put himself between the love of his life and the man, who protested his innocence and annoyance at being threatened by such a dangerous dog. Pippa knew Billy had acted appropriately and he wasn't chastised but fully praised for his devoted actions.

CHAPTER 5

'Everyone has an Angel.'

Since they married, every September Karl and Pippa would go to Corfu. The same weeks, the same hotel, the same room, this was their sixth consecutive year. It was their annual luxury. Karl would say they worked hard, they would have the two weeks of spoiling and this was the one time a year they would really indulge. At the Ideal Shore Resort, they certainly did just that.

They weren't the only creatures of habit, other guests did the same, so when Karl and Pippa would turn up, the same staff and guests were there every year. All the guests looked affluent and were ready to be spoilt, at any cost.

Pippa had been looking forward to the holiday so much, Karl had been working far too hard. Normally the modular building industry was always quiet in July and August, so Karl could work from home a few extra days, but this year the pressure continued right through. He was away all week and would often not get back until late on Fridays. He even had to leave Sundays at lunchtime and stay in a hotel overnight and be at whatever site visit was planned early on the Monday morning. Pippa thought this was taking its toll on Karl as he was getting grumpy, tired and very elusive, the holiday could not have come soon enough.

When they arrived at the airport, they both knew they would fully relax and enjoy themselves, for the next two weeks were theirs.

They settled into their routine quickly. The first evening they were reunited with a couple they met the very first year they had been to the Ideal Shore Resort and always enjoyed their company, Erik and Mila from Holland. The first time Pippa saw them she thought what a beautiful couple they made, both very tall, athletic, blonde hair, with the broadest of smiles. And both always had beautifully painted toenails, with each toe a different colour. Karl and Pippa were taken into their confidence and learnt they were not in a relationship together, but the firmest of friends, they lived in different parts of Holland, and were both gay.

Pippa & Karl loved their holidays at the resort. The daytime would be a set routine of Karl securing his favourite spot for their sunbeds. It had to be a frontline view of the sea. Then straight to breakfast in the main restaurant, back to the sunbeds for their tummies to settle. Karl would then go to the gym and Pippa would go to a yoga or an aqua-aerobics class. Afterwards they would go over to the Pino's Bar, looking out to sea, whilst enjoying an alfresco coffee, pastry and fresh fruit. Then back to their sunbeds to read their books, then up to the restaurant for lunch. After a nice stroll back to the sunbeds, read or doze as the moment took them until another little stroll to one of the resort's select beach bars for a late afternoon G&T before heading back to their room to get ready for the evening.

They each took three books and Pippa would need to visit the hotel's library during the second week. She was a very fast reader and her three would be devoured quickly.

This year Pippa bought the Fifty Shades trilogy at the airport and Karl bought the latest Dan Brown book. His other two books had already been chosen carefully and were in his case.

One of the books was a birthday present from Pippa, still wrapped and saved for the holiday. He had seen the book advertised and suggested it would be a good read for him. It was unusual for Karl to express such an interest, Pippa was online without delay and it was ordered. The book explained everyone had a guardian angel.

His third book was a story book but in essence it was saying if people did not apologise for their wrong doings, when they die, they came back in a future life as the victim. Pippa thought it was a very strange choice, but this was one of a series Karl had read and she knew he was keen to read it.

At lunchtime they would go up to the beautiful restaurant where they would always have the same table. The same waiter would have their bottle of rosé wine ready chilling in the ice bucket, and a glass of lemonade, as Pippa liked a token splash to be added. They would make their food selection from the wonderfully presented salad bars and then sitting together they would eat their lunch while Pippa relayed where she was up to in her book.

Karl loved the book choices Pippa made this year. He particularly loved it when she would quietly describe the sex scenes and his wife would smile at him, slowly pull her head down towards her left shoulder in her cheeky naïve way.

Karl loved that his wife was so innocent, it turned him on, big style.

Normally he would never relay what was happening in his book, always saying he could never describe it as well as Pippa, but today he surprised her.

'I have something to tell you about my book.'

She listened intently.

'You know the book, the one about angels. I'd got to a part that said to look out and as long as you were in the right frame of mind there would be an angel in one form or another. So that's what I did. I put the book on my legs, laying on the sunbed I took several deep, slow breaths in through my nose and exhaled through my mouth, and looked out to the sea. I was thinking how lovely the sea, and everything was looking and then that couple that had arrived on the sunbeds behind us piped up talking loudly to the beach boy who'd brought them their drinks. I thought charming, that's all I need listening to you harping on, that's bloody distracted me, thank you for spoiling the moment and I lay there listening to them. The beach boy said his name and asked where they came from. The woman said we come from England, a place called Luton which isn't far from London, this is my husband, well whatever she said his name was I can't remember. Anyway, he's not important but she went on to say. My name is Gab, short for Gabriel. It's an unusual name for a woman it's after the Angel Gabriel. In my family I'm the only girl and all my brothers are named after saints'. She went on to list all her brothers' names then said, 'In fact one of my brothers and his wife are coming here to join us and will arrive tomorrow.'

Karl finished his story looking totally perplexed and went on to pour them both another glass of wine, adding the obligatory splash of lemonade to Pippa's glass.

Sure enough Pippa thought it was a strange story, reading and thinking of angels and then someone called Gabriel is sitting behind them. She didn't think her husband would spin such a yarn, but as they went back to their sunbeds, they passed the couple and she introduced herself and Karl. Without hesitation the woman said she was Gab, short for Gabriel, named by her parents after the Angel Gabriel and her husband was Graham and they were being joined by her brother Paul and sister-in-law Sue the following day.

Karl looked at Pippa and threw her an expression of 'I told you so'.

They carried on enjoying their holiday and loved the days, but it was the evenings when the hotel really came into its own, the entertainment was the best.

There was always a show followed by an after-show party with great music and atmosphere. Erik and Mila were great company and Pippa and Karl always knew they'd be in for a great evening. Pippa loved dancing as did Erik and Mila and the whole evening she would dance with them. Karl on previous years would join in the dancing, but on this holiday, he decided against it. He said it wasn't a good look since he danced like a sideboard, so he stood at the side insisting he got greater pleasure from voyeurism.

Pippa asked what that means, with him replying with a chuckle.

'What you don't know what voyeurism is? It means I like to watch my wife dance.'

Even though English was his second language Erik smiled sweetly at Pippa for he knew exactly the meaning of the word.

Nearing the end of the second week Karl was busy on his mobile phone and work laptop, the latest project he was working on was not going at all smoothly. He told Pippa it was important for him to keep abreast of all texts and emails to ensure any problems were being sorted straight away. He wanted on his return from holiday to just get on and be able to deal with it. He was extra fraught as the contract he was now on was a short turn-around and the pressure was really on him. What with Steve and Nina being sacked the sales team were short of bodies and Doug was really plying on the pressure. Pippa in her naive way thought her husband should be in a better position because Doug couldn't let more people go or there wouldn't be a sales force!

Karl's change in personality was not lost on Erik. One evening at the bar Erik ordered gin and tonics for all four of them, they were brought to their table in large goblets. The waiter handed each of them their glass, and Erik raised his in his normal manner of toast. He would slowly go round each of them, chink each of their glasses, make eye contact and crook his little finger with the recipient's little finger with an obligatory 'chin-chin'. Then in turn each person would go round in the same manner and Erik would say at the end.

'Good, that is very good, if it's not done correctly, we know what that would mean. Bad sex for the recipient', and without fail they would all roar with laughter.

So that night in the normal fashion Erik started the tradition. All of them conformed of what was required, with the exception of Karl, he would not chin-chin or make eye contact with Pippa. Erik reminded Karl of the awful superstition that could befall him and Pippa if it wasn't followed correctly but Karl wouldn't do it. He just shrugged and made eye contact with Erik and Mila but would not look at Pippa.

Later when Karl was at the bar, Erik asked.

'What's going on, why is Karl, so not Karl?'

'I really don't know Erik, as you say he just doesn't seem to be Karl at the moment, I was hoping the holiday would bring him round.'

Erik and Mila returned a couple of days before Karl and Pippa, so she knew it would be a quiet evening. On Sunday's the entertainment team had the day off and there was always a saxophonist in one of the outside bars in the evening. They usually enjoyed listening and Karl was always keen to go, but tonight he was a million miles away and looked very sad.

The following day their normal routine unfolded and after a quiet lunch they were back on their sunbeds. Pippa looked out to the sea, deep in her thoughts of how beautiful the setting was. She looked over to her husband dozing, bronzed from the sun and she thought how handsome he was and how much she loved being in his company, even when he was asleep. Thinking, if only he didn't have to be away so much.

Suddenly it was as if an alarm had just gone off.

She recalled back to when they met, and he was living in Colchester with Kelly. Karl had said what a nice lifestyle he had with Kelly, but he was willing to give it all up for the new love of his life, Pippa. He wouldn't have cared even if she had been penniless, he felt it in his heart he had to spend his life with her.

She remembered him saying how Kelly's family were reasonably well off and she had her own monies from a previous relationship, a chap called Norman who was a barrister. It seemed bizarre to Pippa, but Karl would often say about the times he and Kelly would go and stay for the weekend in Somerset with Norman and his now wife Geraldine. Kelly had a horse called Basil, which she would pay full livery so she could enjoy being a horse owner without the energies and efforts of her maintaining Basil. Karl had polished up on his golf as Kelly's father was the President of the prestigious High Green Golf Club. So, from what he relayed, it all sounded a very nice quality of life.

He'd said how delicate Kelly was, and he would never be able to let her know that he had fallen in love with another woman as Kelly would not have been strong enough to deal with such news. Out of concern for her mental health the break had to be made with the greatest sensitivity. He would buy Kelly out of the Colchester house, giving her a very fair settlement so she could move on, but things could not be rushed. Karl added that tragically Kelly's twin sister had died a few months before from cancer and this loss had totally thrown Kelly into a very dark place. So much so, she handed in her notice at The Eastern England Bank and left her job.

Understandably Pippa agreed the softest approach needed to be shown to Kelly in this time of need. Karl suggested out of kindness he would need to let Kelly think he was either staying overnight at hotels or with his friend, Hew Thomas', who at the time lived at Biggin Hill, convenient for Karl's office in Bromley. The truth was at least three nights a week Karl would be staying over at Pippa's, arriving late Sunday afternoon so they could at least have their Sunday evenings together plus he would stay other nights during the week.

Oh No, please God, please don't let me be the new Kelly and I'll never know what's going on.

Pippa quickly told herself to pull herself together and put such a stupid thought out of her mind, whatever was she thinking, there was nothing wrong with their marriage.

On their return Pippa was pleased to see Eddie, Sophie and of course Billy. She busied herself with her normal routine and was grateful to have the familiarity of friends and family as Karl was away so much now. The flattering flirty emails sent to her at work had long ceased and now when away he wasn't answering his phone, replying to texts or emails. When he was home, he was too tired to even look at her let alone speak with her.

She forced herself to stop asking him to keep in contact while he was away, as he would fly into a terrible temper accusing her of being clingy and she really shouldn't be so miserable. The last thing he needed was to be interrogated, why was she so suspicious? All he did was work all hours God would send, she really did have too much time on her hands, perhaps she needed to increase her hours at the bank and take some of the pressure off of him.

Pippa would always apologise and say she wasn't accusing him of anything she just wanted to either speak with him while he was away or for him to reply to an email, she just wanted to keep in contact. With his reply.

'Really Pippa, some of us are busy, grow up and stop being so bloody needy.'

CHAPTER 6

'Always follow your instincts.'

Since returning from their holiday Pippa was not feeling her usual energetic self, she looked the same, but she had a tiredness that she'd never experienced before. She wasn't doing anything differently, she didn't feel unwell, but when she was at work, the gym, pottering in the garden or walking Billy, everything seemed to take more effort. She hoped it wasn't anything to do with the awful thoughts that had come to her on the last day of their holiday and thought perhaps the tiredness was simply her age finally catching up with her.

Pippa always said she never dreamt, she knew she must dream, but what she meant, she could never recall a dream. Over the years Karl would say what he had dreamt, and Pippa would then decipher its meaning, which usually was to do with something going on at that moment in their lives, she always put the most positive slant on for Karl and normally he would agree with his wife's interpretation.

From the time she was a baby, Pippa's head would hit the pillow and she was asleep. Karl would say she didn't realise how lucky she was as he would struggle with getting to sleep while there she was, blissful in her slumber, oblivious to his tossing and turning. He also thought how fortunate she was not to dream as so many of his dreams were nightmares. Unbeknown to Pippa he wouldn't relay those to her, for fear she would try to decipher their meaning and he dread what she might say.

But for a while now, Pippa was having a recurring dream. On each occasion the dream would get a little further in, and Pippa wasn't sure if she was subconsciously forcing the dream as she was keen, no she wasn't keen, she was desperate, to know what happened. She also wondered if the dream meant she was not sleeping as deeply as she normally did. Was it possible this change in her sleep pattern was the cause of her having less energy?

In the dream Pippa could see herself in a large container, it wasn't a box, and it wasn't exactly a room. Within the container was enough room for a bed, she had water, there was an artificial light from a single bulb, and she knew there was air because she could breathe. But early on in the dream she learnt that if she called out or struggled, the light dimmed to darkness and more frightening, the air decreased so much she couldn't breathe.

As the dreams continued, she learnt not to struggle but to lie still on her bed and go with it as this was the best and only outcome, for there was no release.

The dreams became more and more frequent, but Pippa being Pippa tried to put them to the back of her mind. She had broad shoulders for others, but she never wanted to be a burden or unload to anyone else.

It was late November and as usual on a Friday she attended the morning session of the Diet What Diet class and helped Amy in the area of 'Scales of Shame or Fame'. She was looking forward to the rest of her planned day and drove home, picked up Billy, the birthday card and present for Ruth her cousin and then drove the four miles over to East Beesley to celebrate Ruth's birthday.

Ruth and Pippa were very close, with affection, calling each other Ru and Pip.

Often Pippa cheekily reminded Ruth that she was completely and totally responsible for her. Ruth knew this responsibility wasn't due to them being double cousins, which in itself was unusual as their mothers were sisters and their fathers were brothers, and they shared both sets of grandparents thereby having twice the degree of kinship of ordinary first cousins. The responsibility was simply because Pippa was conceived after the wedding reception of Cousin Ruth and her husband Geoffrey.

Pippa's parents had tried to conceive since they were married but to no joy and despite all their efforts, they had long given up on ever being parents. So, when Pippa came along, obviously after too many sherries at the reception, Pippa was the most cherished child but also the most unexpected surprise. In fact, Hannah, Pippa's mother, had ignored the lack of periods as she thought she was going through the menopause at the age of forty-five.

Billy loved going to Ruth's. She had a Springer Spaniel, Pip, and a black Lab, Henry. The three dogs would rejoice in their reunion, play in the garden and then lie down content with their lot.

Ruth had a holistic healing center which she ran from Cherry Farmhouse and as soon as Pippa pulled on to the large horseshoe driveway, she could feel the peace, which she knew was all generated by her cousin Ru.

Ruth always made a lovely lunch for her guests, but she always made an effort when Pippa came. Not with quality or quantity as that would always be the best, but Pippa was a vegetarian and Ruth being a traditional Norfolk country girl and a carnivore at heart had to focus on what she put on the plates.

Ruth and Pippa were both similar in personality they were both calm, kind, hardworking, humorous and neither easily took offence, but where they differed Ruth was assertive; a trait she wished Pippa could have inherited from the family genes.

They sat in the kitchen and all was at peace, the dogs dozing in the sitting room while Ruth and Pippa nattered at the table. Ruth loved hearing the humour and enthusiasm of Pippa's tales, which normally involved Eddie, Sophie, Billie, her job, things about Pippa's friends and occasionally, very occasionally, Karl.

Often when Pippa said something Ruth could tell it was because it was playing on her mind. Ruth always thought that Pippa was quite naïve for a grown woman, a description Pippa would agree with. This was no doubt due to her sheltered and cherished upbringing. Pippa would say with a giggle she'd only ever kissed two men and she'd married them both.

Likewise, Pippa always sat enthused listening to Ruth, hearing how she had recently helped certain people and even animals had benefitted from her healing. Pippa thought while both the cousins were totally different, how similar in personality they were, but the only thing she would wish herself was to be more assertive like Ruth.

During lunch, Pippa relayed that Jasmine Spalding had phoned to invite her to go along to a Ladies Evening and Christmas Fair, the first week of December at the Bagby

Village Hall. Jasmine was keen that Pippa didn't miss out like she had the year before. She was thrilled to say as the psychic had been so popular, she'd booked him again.

Pippa took a deep sigh, continuing.

'I couldn't think of anything worse, as soon as she told me that, well I thought I'll most definitely come up with some excuse. I know so many people hold great store by it. Well as you know, Karl went to that one before he left the woman he was living with in Colchester and that psychic told him I was his genuine soulmate, and he wouldn't be happy if he stayed with Kelly and he was reassured by what was said to him. But for me, well I can't see myself ever going along and listening to it, let alone have an audience with one. As you've always said Ru, everything happens for a reason and you should never force it, and that for me sums it up. So even if someone is supposed to have the gift of second sight, if they tell you to do this or that, then you are being steered in that direction, so surely you are forcing it?'

Ruth sat with her elbow on the table with her hand slowly stroking her chin, which she always did when in deep thought, and asked.

'Pip, I know this sounds strange and while I haven't thought of this for a few years now, but what I wondered, when Karl was told by that psychic chap that you were his soulmate, how did he know he was speaking of you, did he have a photo of you?'

'Ru, that's not a strange question at all, I asked the same thing and Karl said he didn't have a photo of me, but I'd brushed my hair in his car, and he picked the hairs up that had fallen on the seat and the psychic held the hairs and could tell from them.'

Ruth said with an astonished tone.

'Goodness me dear, who needs a DNA test when you can just pop over to see the local psychic. I think I'll make sure I wear a hairnet permanently; I don't want to run the risk of being the adornment of any passing stranger.'

To which the cousins burst out laughing. When the laughter began to fade the kettle had to be put on for another pot of tea.

Ruth knew Pippa didn't get out much these days, in fact if it wasn't for her job at the bank, attending the Diet What Diet classes on a Friday morning, walking Billy, popping over to see Eddie, Sophie, Bev or herself, she really didn't know who else she would see, and Karl was away so much. Even Pippa's oldest school friend Stella and her husband Maxwell who used to come up from London every year to visit Pippa pre-Karl, but in the last six years they only visited twice and both times when Karl was away. It appeared Karl didn't like company. Ruth suspected things weren't quite as rosy as Pippa tried to make out.

Like Pippa had said, Ruth was a great believer everything should happen naturally and shouldn't be forced, nonetheless Ruth would try and gently steer Pippa in the direction of having an evening out and go to Jasmine Spalding's Ladies Evening.

Ruth also knew Pippa did not like psychics or mediums, she put this down to so many of Pippa's precious people having left this world, with Pippa insisting people should be left in peace and when she leaves this world, she didn't want anyone to disturb her.

Ruth eventually said.

'Well, I think you would really like the Ladies Evening dear, there'll be enough going on and no one would drag you into anything you wouldn't want to do, for my dear little Pip everyone loves you far too much.'

As Pippa was about to leave, Ruth handed her a gift.

'Here you go dear, it's a crystal especially for you, here's a book too, all about the energies from crystals.'

At first Pippa protested, it was Ruth's birthday, and she was the one to receive gifts, not give them. But Ruth insisted. Pippa stood looking at the crystal. It was beautiful and as she was admiring it Ruth relayed a story involving Pippa's father.

James was an engineer, and he had the earliest type of radio, a Crystal Radio and the source of the energy was simply that from the crystal. He'd explained to his niece Ruth when she was only a little girl the principles of how it all worked, but Ruth could remember him saying at the end of the 'crystal tutorial' that in life there are many things that we can't explain and sometimes we all have to go with our instincts, as without someone originally following their instincts that the crystal had energy, then they wouldn't be listening to the radio now and those simple words, 'follow your instincts' had stayed with Ruth forever.

Ruth cupped Pippa's hands gently in hers cradling the crystal in between.

'So, my dear little Pip this is my gift to you, not only the crystal but to remind you to follow your instincts.'

With that she kissed Pippa on the cheek and turning to the dogs in the sitting room called.

'Come on Billy, time to go.'

When Pippa got back, she put the crystal under her pillow, but while the dream, or was it a nightmare of her in the container continued she didn't feel so panicked.

CHAPTER 7

'A lie by any other name is still a lie.'

Familiarity was key in Pippa and Karl's lives and they regularly attended the Bury St Edmunds Christmas Market. They would buy each other's Christmas presents. Pippa loved all the little bespoke shops and also the German market stalls where they both indulged in a glass of Gluhwein to warm themselves inside and out.

The idea for visiting the Christmas Market came from Hew Thomas, Karl's best man.

As Hew and his partner Jeanette bid their farewell to the newlyweds, Jeanette offered for Karl and Pippa to come to theirs in Thetford for a meal, this was possibly out of politeness. With Hew in his normal exuberant manner jumping in, suggesting they should visit the Christmas Market and were more than welcome to stay over at theirs the night before. So that's what they did, and another annual event was formed.

Hew had been with Building For The Future for a number of years when Karl joined in 2007. They were colleagues for only two months when Hew was offered a position as Director of Sales for a high-quality reproduction furniture company. This resulted in him being placed on garden leave until his three-month notice period was completed. This made it even more strange to Pippa that Karl was precious not to lose the friendship of Hew, but in any event, she was grateful that Karl had at least one friend.

With Hew's job change, he and Jeanette moved from Biggin Hill to Thetford. Their house was beautiful, Pippa loved staying there overnight. They were both wonderful hosts and made sure their guests were totally spoilt and Jeanette was a fabulous cook, with everything cooked from scratch.

There was an embarrassing moment at their first visit. Jeanette asked Hew to check with Karl of any dietary requirements so she could plan the meals and Hew messaged Karl to check if there was anything that Jeanette needed to be aware of, such as allergies, vegetarian or vegan. The text reply came straight back to Hew.

… No problems with eating anything, no one under my watch would be a vegan or any of that crap...

Jeanette prepared beautiful homemade steak pies and was planning on offering their guests full English breakfast before they left for their trip to the Christmas Market.

When they sat down for their evening meal Pippa just stared at the plate in front of her, with Jeanette asking if there was a problem?

'Oh, Jeanette I'm so sorry you've gone to so much trouble but I'm a vegetarian, we should have said.'

Hew was furious with Karl, who for some unknown reason found it all hilarious. Jeanette could see Pippa was embarrassed and said it wasn't a problem, there were plenty of vegetables which hadn't gravy poured over them and earlier she had made a leak and mushroom quiche for hers and Hews lunch for Saturday, would she like a piece of that?

If Pippa thought Hew was furious with Karl, it was nothing to what Karl was with Pippa and before she could answer, Karl shouted at her.

'Stop being so childish and get on with your dinner.'

Hew stood up removed Pippa's plate, apologising that her husband was such a pratt with such a warped sense of humour, she really deserved better.

Pippa was surprised that the meal and the rest of their stay went well and was relieved that they were invited back, not least as Karl would never have let her live it down. What she didn't know, future invitations were sent as Jeanette enjoyed Pippa's company, pointing out to Hew with concern.

'I know we found it strange when you were asked to be Karl's best man but having spent some time with him, I think you were the only person he had to ask. I can't put my finger on it, but there's something not quite right.'

Hew couldn't disagree with anything Jeanette said. When Karl contacted totally out of the blue nearly five months into Hew's new position, he assumed Karl was on the lookout for a new position or possibly a job reference. The last thing he expected was to be asked to be his best man!

With their Christmas Market tradition set, 2013 was to be their sixth consecutive year, Pippa had been looking forward to this trip since the year before. There was one difference this year, due to Karl's heavy workload they would not be able to have their usual stay at Hew and Jeanette's. Pippa was disappointed but didn't go stamping her feet in protest, she was just grateful to have some time with her husband.

Pippa was relieved that Karl had been more relaxed and less grumpy for the past couple of weekends. They had a lovely day at the Christmas market and even though Karl's phone kept beeping with messages, he didn't seem pressurised by them, he'd look at the messages now and again, totally unfazed and very satisfied to delete them.

Following their day out they picked Billy up from Eddie and Sophie's, joined them for a quick cup of tea, listened to what they had been up to and got back to The Marshman's. Karl packed a case ready for his week away. Pippa was always impressed with how organised he was. Yes, she had everything laundered and ironed for him to grab and put in his case but nonetheless he was very neat and never forgot to take anything with him.

This week he would need his dress suit for the firm's Christmas meal. She was convinced this would be yet another year he would receive the top salesperson award. Whilst Karl always emphasised it was the team that had brought in the contracts and downplayed his input, Pippa knew it was purely down to her husband's dedicated efforts that deals were secured.

Following their baths and bedtime cup of tea their lovely day drew to a close with Karl having to leave first thing Sunday morning with a difficult drive to Brecon, Wales.

Sadly, Karl reverted to recent form and did not contact Pippa, the first she heard from him was the following Friday evening.

Again, he wore a face like thunder. He came through the door begrudgingly said hello to Billy and then looked at his wife as if she were a leper. Pippa tried to greet her husband, but to no avail. She enquired if he'd had a good week away and excitedly asked how the awards ceremony had gone and Karl would not answer. So, she didn't ask anything further.

The next couple of weeks passed in the similar frame, Karl working away during the week with no communication and on the weekends acting tired and very grumpy, not wanting to converse with his wife.

Pippa was still feeling out of sorts. Not only was she feeling very tired, but also had developed the most horrendous pain in her left side, around the kidney area. She read up on her symptoms and her research found it may be a stone in the kidneys, she was proactive in making sure she drank plenty of water.

Pippa loved everything about Christmas and always booked two weeks annual leave to ensure she enjoyed every moment of it. They didn't have much company over the Christmas period, just Eddie and Sophie from late afternoon Christmas Eve through to Boxing Day, when late morning they would all go over to Sophie's parents, the Carters, for lunch.

Karl always made sure they did not skimp on what was on offer over the festive period, and he enjoyed the Christmas food shop. Pippa had the shopping list in hand, carrier bags ready and off they went.

The supermarket was heaving, she thought it was a good job they were getting it out of the way a good few days before Christmas or there wouldn't be anything left. They were in the final aisle, the alcohol, and Karl was studying the wines. He had a decent wine collection, but that was for his consumption, he never gave any of that away, but he wanted a couple of impressive bottles, at a good price to take to the Carter's for Boxing Day lunch. While he was reading the labels, he was unaware that his wife had come over ill.

Pippa had the most frightful pain in her stomach, she was leaning on the trolley for support and thought she was going to pass out. She wasn't sure if she would prefer to pass out due to the awful pain. She looked along the aisle to Karl, and he was taking his time focused on the labels of the bottles.

As the pain got to a manageable level, Pippa steered the trolley towards him.

'I feel a bit unwell. Can I have the car keys I think I need to sit in the car. Are you alright if I leave you to sort all this, and I'll meet you back at the car?'

He looked at her puzzled but passed her the keys and carried on reading the wine label.

Pippa walked towards the exit and as she was next to one of the tills the pain came back with greater intensity, before she knew it, she had passed out. When she came round, she was on the floor slumped against one of the counters of the tills with people all speaking in muffled voices, asking if she was all right. She laid still, the pain in her stomach and on the left side was horrendous, she had ringing in her ears, and she couldn't understand what was going on.

One of the members of the supermarket was a trained First Responder and he took control of the situation, and she soon found herself on a chair, still with people round her asking what her name was, was she on her own, over and over again. Finally, she managed to say.

'Pippa Taylor and my husband Karl Taylor's here, I felt unwell and wanted to get back to the car.'

A tannoy announcement was made.

'Would Mr Karl Taylor please make himself known to a member of staff.'

It seemed within seconds Karl was standing in front of Pippa, asking if she was alright and what was happening. Pippa didn't know what was happening, but she did know she wasn't alright.

'Oh Karl, I feel awful, I've got the most awful pain in my stomach, I think I need to get to the hospital.'

The First Responder assessed the situation.

'If I was you Mr Taylor I'd get your wife home, I'm sure she doesn't need to go to hospital, if she is put to bed in a nice fluffy dressing gown and hot water bottle she will be feeling better straight away.'

The shopping was rushed through.

Pippa was grateful to get back and to be lying flat on the bed, and yes, her fluffy dressing gown and hot water bottle did help.

The following day, Saturday Pippa took things slowly and Karl was enjoying the switch off and looking forward to the evening. Sophie's parents, Harold and Sally Carter, would pick them up in a taxi at seven thirty to go round to Eddie and Sophie's.

But at six o'clock Pippa was lying on the bed, she wasn't feeling at all well. She was oblivious to the time when Karl walked into the bedroom reminding her, she needed to get ready.

Pippa pulled herself together, drank another glass of water and put her make up on, ran the straighteners through her hair and got dressed. By the time the taxi arrived no one was the wiser that she was not feeling her normal self, she didn't want to discuss that and spoil the evening.

As the taxi pulled into Churchside, Sophie's sister Clare and her husband Dave also pulled on the drive. Eddie and Sophie had decorated outside, and Churchside looked beautiful, Pippa thought it looked like a gingerbread house. Eddie had put icicle lights on the eves of the cottage, taking his time to get them positioned correctly as he wanted everything to look perfect, and it did. The evening was wonderful, plenty of fun and laughter. Sophie was a very nice cook and put on a lovely spread.

Since the moment Eddie had been placed in Pippa's arms, she had always been proud of her son but tonight she felt even more so, and that pride extended to everyone there. The Carter's were a very nice family and they put great energies in bringing their daughters Sophie and Clare up well. Pippa felt very blessed.

Several times she had to go to the bathroom and lay on the floor as she felt poorly, but by the time she'd open the bathroom door she had put on extra makeup and pulled herself together. Karl said she could have driven as she hadn't had a drink; she'd only been drinking tonic water and of course her cups of tea. When the taxi arrived, she'd never been so grateful to see a cab in her life. She went through the motions of kissing and saying goodbye to everyone and willed Sally to hurry up as she desperately needed to lay down. Finally, they were in the taxi and she was soon in the safety of her bed.

Pippa was exhausted and asleep within minutes. She could only have been asleep for about an hour when she woke with a stabbing, twisting pain in her stomach she knew this didn't feel right. She looked at Karl who was snoring next to her. She gently shook Karl's shoulder and said quietly trying to wake him without panicking him.

'Karl, Karl, I don't feel very well.'

But Karl was out for the count.

She thought she'd go through to the kitchen and get a drink of warm water, that might be better than the cold water she had on the side. She popped the kettle on and was standing holding her side and before she knew it, she was on her knees, she was now screaming as the pain reached a crescendo. Poor Billy was panicking as Pippa was in such a bad way. Neither of them could do anything she was doubled up on the floor sobbing, Billy lay next to her whimpering and willing his mummy to be OK.

Pippa wasn't sure how long it was before she was able to get herself back to bed. Karl was still in a deep drink induced sleep and oblivious that she'd not been lying next to him.

She collapsed on the bed she got as close as she could to his body and the warmth helped her feel calmer and supported. She was exhausted and despite not feeling well she fell quickly to sleep.

In the morning when they woke, she told Karl what had happened. He was upset to hear that his wife had been unwell on the kitchen floor. He made them a cup of tea and they slept in to allow her to rest fully.

CHAPTER 8
'Hindsight's a wonderful thing.'

Monday morning couldn't come soon enough for Pippa she phoned the local doctor's surgery and managed to get an appointment for later that day. She was relieved when she walked in to see the doctor on call was Dr Newcome. Greg Newcome had retired three years before, but he helped out at the surgery on a locum basis. In practice he was there as much as when he was a partner, much to all the patient's relief as he was a kindly doctor.

Pippa was pleased to see Greg, she always thought he looked like a big teddy bear, he had a mass of hair on his head and also on his big smiley face, these days it was a light grey colour and his beard seemed more unkempt since his retirement.

Greg was always pleased to see Pippa, but without fail as soon as he saw her, he would think of that awful day when he administered first aid to Matt and though he knew there was nothing anyone could have done to save that young life it was a moment that would always stay with him.

He greeted Pippa and she explained the awful pain she was having, pointing to the kidney area and that it had been so bad she'd even passed out with the pain. She'd taken a urine sample with her and he examined both the sample and her.

He said her tummy was a bit swollen, possibly she needed to have a pee, but there was no evidence in her urine of an infection. But with them being so close to the Christmas period and the surgery not being open he would give her some medication to treat an infection. As always, better to be safe than sorry.

But he agreed with Pippa's research that she probably did have kidney stones and as she was Norfolk born and bred chances were, they would be sizable as history had shown for Norfolk to be the worst area for them.

She asked what if she got the pain again as she really didn't think she could bare it. With Dr Newcome looking at her in surprise, saying.

'Pippa if a pain is that bad you shouldn't be taking pain killers you need to get to hospital.'

Pippa collected the prescription from the pharmacy and as soon as she got home took one of the tablets and some paracetamol and continued with drinking the water to try and flush out her kidneys.

She then gently prepared everything ready for the next day, which would be Christmas Eve, possibly her most favourite evening of the year. She set the dining room table, not only did it put her mind at rest that there was one less thing to do, but it made the room look so pretty.

Christmas was perfect and they all had the most wonderful happy family time. Pippa did have to mention to Eddie, Sophie and also the Carters when they went over on Boxing Day, that she was not feeling herself, not least it was obvious for she couldn't sit, walk or do anything without holding her side. She said she might have a kidney stone, adding with a laugh, as she was Norfolk born and bred Dr Newcome said it could be a stonker!

A couple of weeks later she was back at the doctor's surgery asking if they could arrange a CT scan for her. The locum on duty this day was not known to Pippa and she had a battle on her hands for it to be organised, but in the end, he confirmed that an appointment would come through the post for her. She was surprised and relieved when she had the scan the following week and at the scan, she was instructed to contact her surgery for the results in five days' time.

Pippa went back and thankfully Greg Newcome was on duty.

'Well I never Pippa, you haven't got kidney stones, you've got a huge ovarian cyst the size of a melon. I'll arrange for you to have an appointment with one of the Gynae team and they'll get that sorted for you.'

Two days later Pippa asked Annie her manager if she could use up some holiday so she could leave early. Annie had no hesitation in agreeing the time off. Pippa had already told her of the passing out and horrible pain and she was surprised Pippa had come to work.

Pippa drove straight home, she was keen to get to her bed, desperate to lie down, she felt so unwell.

She got through the front door and the phone was ringing, she rushed to answer it and it was the hospital. The receptionist introduced herself, she was Amy, and she said the name of the consultant, Mr Manx and asked if there was a chance Pippa could pop over that afternoon as they had received her referral and Mr Manx had a free slot when he could see her.

Pippa was taken aback by the speed of the appointment, saying she'd just got in from work and where she lived would take her a while to get to the hospital, would he still have the slot? Mr Manx must have been standing next to the receptionist as she heard Amy speak quietly to someone and heard a man's voice in the background, Amy was back on the phone.

'Yes, that's fine. Mr Manx will be here he's on duty tonight so needs to be at the hospital anyway.'

Pippa went through to Karl who was in his office and she said about the appointment. Karl seemed pleased that the appointment had come through quickly, but he needed to get his report out within the next hour so would not be able to accompany her. She freshened up and took herself to the hospital.

She'd received clear directions from Amy where to park and where to go. When she arrived at the Gynae Department, Amy the receptionist was still there, and she directed Pippa down the corridor to Mr Manx's consultancy room.

Pippa was surprised to see she was the only person in the waiting room. As she sat, she looked up at Mr Manx name plate and read his title, he was Gynae Oncologist, Head of Department. Part of Pippa felt reassured that she was being seen by someone so knowledgeable as Head of Department but the other part of her felt concerned that she was being seen by an Oncologist.

The door was opened by a nurse who smiled at Pippa.

'Hi, you must be Phillipa Taylor come on through.'

Pippa could tell straight away she was in the presence of kind people. Mr Manx introduced himself and the nurse as Liz and he then explained that Pippa had a very large ovarian cyst and the pain she'd experienced was the weight of it twisting the fallopian tube and possibly that was one of the worse abdominal pains anyone could have. He reassured her it couldn't move any more, due to the size of it. It was well and truly wedged, but even though it was huge it could still grow, and they needed to get it out.

Mr Manx examined Pippa with Liz kindly helping her on and off the examination couch.

He showed her the CT scan on his PC. It was indeed huge; it filled her whole tummy. She said with horror.

'How on earth is that in there? I know Dr Newcome said it was the size of a melon, but I was thinking cantaloupe not a watermelon, its blinken huge!'

Thankfully her comment of fruit comparison made them all laugh.

He then explained what would happen. She would need a Laparotomy and that involved being cut from the pubic bone right up to her rib cage, a major operation. He pulled a kindly face and went on to explain that at the time of the operation the microbiologist team would be on hand to take the mass and samples away to do their checks. Unfortunately, they couldn't tell whether she had ovarian cancer or not until the results were back six weeks after the operation.

She would be put straight away on the Cancer Pathway, which meant she would have the operation within a certain time frame. She would be given a named senior nurse who she could contact should she have any queries or problems. The next step was for the hospital to book her an MRI scan and then there would be a meeting to discuss her case and results from the scan and he would see her again to discuss their findings and explain fully the operation. She was handed a leaflet and Mr Manx gave her hand a squeeze. Liz saw her out and Pippa took herself to the car in a bit of a daze.

When she got home, Karl was sitting on the sofa watching TV, she sat down and explained what she had been told.

She was exhausted, had a bath and took herself to bed. In the darkness she started to sob. The reality hit her, what if it was cancer and she wouldn't be at Eddie and Sophie's wedding later on that year or see her grandchildren born.

Karl came to the bedroom, sat on the bed, and scooped his wife up in his arms to try and comfort her.

'Ssshhhh it will be alright, don't take on so, I'm here, we'll get through this.'

Pippa couldn't be sure, but she thought Karl was also sobbing because she could feel his chest keep taking in deep breaths, but she felt reassured that he was holding her in his arms. She gained strength from his comments and was determined they would get through, not only her illness but back to being a loving couple again.

Karl continued to cuddle his wife. Softly saying.

'I don't think you should go to work tomorrow.'

Pippa still sobbing nodded in agreement, he went on.

'It might be an idea to book an appointment at Chester and Whelks, obviously it wouldn't be your friend Theresa we see, what is the name of the solicitor who deals with your Will?'

Pippa didn't answer, in fact trying to focus on breathing was a hard enough task. The shock of Karl's callous comment stopped her sobbing and she tried to pull herself away to lie back down on her pillow, but Karl was holding her too strongly and he went on to say.

'It's only fair to me, I need my mind put at rest that I'm going to be alright, especially with only having 30% shares in this place.'

With that he lessened his grip and she lay down bringing the duvet over her head so she could cry in private. Karl left her to sleep.

The following morning, he brought her a cup of tea to drink in bed and asked if she could remember the name of the solicitor who dealt with her Will or should he just phone Chester and Whelks and get an appointment with whoever they suggest?

Pippa sipped her tea and replied.

'Everything is in order, no problem, I don't need an appointment as nothing needs to change.'

The next few weeks went by with the mass in her tummy getting bigger and bigger and within three weeks she was in maternity jeans and tops.

She apologised to Billy that she didn't feel up to walking, and he would have to make do with going round the garden. She now looked heavily pregnant but as the mass was not in the uterus, it felt like it was taking over everywhere, which it actually was. The weight of the mass was pushing everything through every orifice down below and everything else up into her rib cage. She managed to do her chores, but at a much gentler pace than she was used to and spent most of her time sitting in the orangery reading, with her feet raised on a stool.

They were all relieved when the operation was out of the way and the cyst was no more. They were even more relieved that the mass was benign and that horrible scare and time was out of the way.

Well, everyone seemed relieved apart from Karl.

CHAPTER 9

'Thoughts become words, words become actions.'

Pippa hadn't expected the recovery from her operation to take so long. She assumed, or rather hoped, the mass would be removed, and after a few weeks she would be back to her energetic self.

Yes, Mr Manx had explained it was a major operation, but the mass had caused a lot of internal adhesions and nerve damage and she was told by both Mr Manx and Dr Newcome that she needed to try and be a patient patient, these things simply needed time to heal. She was doing her part by trying to do a little more and more each day and she was given tablets to help with the pain.

One evening on his way from work Eddie popped in to see Pippa and looking uncomfortable went on to say Karl had contacted to remind him that the five years was up. Eddie needed to repay the deferred payment of forty thousand pounds, and it was needed by the beginning of July at the latest! Oh, and don't tell your mum, we don't want to worry her what with the operation and her recovery, she's had enough to deal with.

Pippa listened in disbelief.

'What and for me not to know?'

Eddie went on to say he and Sophie had discussed whether they should tell Pippa as she was still recovering from the effects of the operation but reluctantly, they felt it was something she needed to be made aware of. They had the money, that wasn't the problem, they knew it was to be repaid to Pippa in November they were all organised, it was how Karl was demanding payment seemed strange and quite disturbing. Also, they were concerned as he was asking for it to be transferred to the account in the name of Karl and Pippa and they knew the money was Pippa's, did it need to go to her sole account?

'Too true I need to be aware of it. I really can't believe all this rubbish.'

Pippa sat, taking her time to digest what she had just been told and was not happy with the monies going to the joint account, but she was even more uncomfortable to say for Eddie to transfer them to her sole account as this would put him in a very awkward position with Karl. She confirmed to transfer the monies over to the joint account.

Eddie transferred the monies and that evening much to Pippa's surprise Karl was home and after tea she raised the money transfer.

'Oh, have you checked if the money from Eddie is in our joint account.'

Karl was surprised that Pippa knew about the transfer, but it was his reply that came as a shock to her, with him aggressively shouting at her.

'Why are you so obsessed with money!'

'I'm not obsessed with money, but anyone who works in a bank knows things can go astray. As you know I can't access the bank account from my iPad. I was just double checking that it had landed in our account, that's all.'

He didn't answer.

The following day was the first day Pippa drove since her operation and she took herself and Billy over to see Cousin Ruth. She didn't return directly home but went via the bank. She asked for a breakdown of transactions and the forty thousand pounds had already been transferred over to Karl's personal account.

She came through the front door, and Karl was standing in the hall waiting for her, he looked quite emotional and very strange. She was disturbed by his oddness, and asked if all was OK, she didn't get a reply. She went through to the kitchen to put the kettle on and tried to work out what to say to him. She knew he would fly into a rage, but she couldn't let forty thousand pounds vanish. She'd let him get away with taking the lump sum of the rental monies the year before, that couldn't happen in the future as she told the agent the renewal contract needed to show for the rent to be paid monthly.

Before she knew it, Karl was standing behind her, he made her jump. He was looking very sheepish and then his face changed, to an aggressive, crazed expression. He waived an A4 sheet of paper in the air and slapped it on the kitchen table. Scowled at her, saying.

'You've brought this on yourself, you always do.'

And with that he was off, he'd left her.

Pippa read the letter, it was obvious it had been typed a good few months before and she wondered if he'd stayed waiting for her to be up and about driving again, or most probably he was waiting for the money from Eddie to hit their account and immediately transfer the funds over to his sole account. She thought some may call this squirreling but most would see it for what it was, stealing!

Yes, indeed Karl's letter did inform her that she had brought everything on herself, even the health scare from the huge ovarian cyst in her tummy had been of her making. She had brought this on herself as she was a vegetarian! The letter was clear Karl had warned her of the dangers she would bring on herself by not eating meat, but she hadn't taken notice until it was far too late, she really ought to head the warning and stop being so stupid, she was asking for trouble following such an unbalanced diet. She read though from start to finish, but the whole letter was no more than a disjointed ramble. This was probably her saving grace, the letter being complete rubbish meant she wasn't upset, she was just furious.

Later in the afternoon she sent Karl an email asking if he would be back that night and if she hadn't heard by eight, she would lock up for the evening. Her gut instinct being he had already moved in with someone else, so wasn't expecting a reply.

Eight o'clock came and nothing, so she locked up. She patted Billy on the head and gave him a kiss.

'Do you know what old chum I'm going to have a glass of wine. I won't ask you to join me as I don't think wine is your thing but there's some chicken in the fridge, you can have that.'

Pippa enjoyed her glass of white wine, which she drank from one of the best wine glasses and Billy relished in having some lovely chunks of chicken in his bowl.

The following afternoon she received an email from Karl saying that he would be back at six. He came in through the door, as if he were suffering a bereavement; emotional, sensitive, delicate and unable to speak, taking himself straight to his office.

She'd mentally worked out what to say. He finally came out of his office to join her in the lounge, she turned the television off to have his full attention. Looking him straight in the face, said.

'The forty thousand pounds needs to be sent straight to my sole account or I'm going to the police.'

He in turn looked her straight in the eyes.

'Do what you like, I didn't take the money if you want to involve the police it's up to you, but ask yourself, what wife does that to her husband?'

Without hesitation Pippa said.

'Probably a wife that had six and a half thousand pounds of rental monies taken last year and the money taken yesterday. What do you mean you didn't take the money, both sums were transferred to your sole account?'

Neither sums were ever acknowledged as having been received or gone anywhere by Karl. He had called her bluff; he knew she wouldn't go to the police.

The following week Pippa was sitting in the garden reading her book, Billy lying by her feet and Karl came home, she hadn't expected to see him until the following evening. She smiled and without taking a breath he announced he wanted them to go to a marriage counsellor.

Strangely and despite the enormity of what her husband was saying Pippa couldn't concentrate on what he said, she was just looking, staring at his tie.

He always made a big thing about his Windsor knot and when he'd left the house that morning his tie had the customary knot, but here he was four hours later and his collar was disheveled and his tie looked rushed and while Pippa could not say what knot was on the tie, she knew it did not have her husband's Windsor knot.

Eventually she replied.

'Actually, I don't think we need a counsellor do you, what good would a marriage counsellor do?'

Karl replied in a kindly reassuring tone.

'Things haven't been the same since your operation I think it might help, it couldn't do any harm could it? Just give it a thought Pippa, our marriage is so important, don't you agree?'

Pippa sat and quickly came to her senses, she thought I don't know what your game is Karl Taylor, but if this is financially motivated you may get a shock as it is well documented where all the monies to buy both The Marshman's and the Bagby bungalow came from, my inheritance monies, not one penny of yours. Looking disinterested she finally answered.

'OK if you think it would help, I'll go online and find someone suitable, or have you looked already and got someone lined up?'

Karl confirmed, yes, he had given the marriage guidance counselling a lot of thought and he had already researched online and found someone to meet their needs and she was local. He knew it was important that Pippa wouldn't want to drive far, and he didn't want to cause his wife any discomfort, so distance was a crucial factor. The counsellor was called Amber Strumshaw, and as luck would have it Amber had a slot in her diary and could see them quickly. Karl thought it was important, so rather than creating any delay he snatched up the appointment slot, so they could have their discussions and get back on track with their married bliss.

Three days later they had an appointment for five o'clock. Pippa arrived, but she was on her own as Karl hadn't managed to get back as he was needed to be in Nottingham.

Amber was a strange mix of hippy and headmistress. Being very patient and kind, then there was the other side of her being confident and opinionated. She explained what her role was and then asked.

'So, what do you think, will your husband turn up for any future sessions?'

Pippa didn't take much time to answer.

'No, so many things I do on my own as they're out of Karl's comfort zone, so I suppose it seems only right that the marriage guidance classes are too. I don't think these are his scene.'

Then Pippa just relayed what was on her mind. Until she came up for air, she didn't make eye contact with Amber, choosing to keep focus on her hands and her comments came thick and fast as if she were a greyhound out of a trap, all her thoughts, opinions and even fears were set free.

She said, when they were in different company Karl would morph into whatever the company was, she knew everyone tried to make people comfortable by conforming, but this was different, it was as if he would shape shift. When he first met people, he liked them, if Pippa had any opinion other than Karl's to fit this perfect view of someone, he felt she was being negative. But within a short period of time, he was derogatory and couldn't believe she had put him in a position of knowing such disgusting people.

She realised she knew so little about him. Yes, she knew the name of the company where he worked, he told her he owned a property somewhere in Colchester, but she'd never seen any evidence of it. She had very basic knowledge of his family, but apart from his father's name on their marriage certificate the only other name she knew was Aunt Mildred who apparently lived a few doors away when he was a child, and she was as crazy as a box of frogs.

Pippa knew her husband was spoilt by his company and she had always enjoyed hearing his stories of things that happened in his world. She was the first to say that his world was in a totally different orbit than the calm gentle world she was part of. But disturbingly she had worked out that so many of the stories Karl told, had never actually happened. He would forget what he'd said and contradict what he had told her previously. There had been numerous times when she would listen to him and it was as if Karl wanted these things to happen. But she knew within a period of time, even minutes he would have forgotten what he had told her.

Amber asked why she thought Karl had suggested the sessions and Pippa answered with a frank reply.

'No doubt it has a financial motive, everything with Karl usually has something to do with money or possessions. Strangely, I'd never given it thought until recently, but now I'm convinced that Karl targeted me at the beginning. I'd let it slip I was comfortably well off, obviously his smooth manner flattered me and with me having an unaccustomed glass or two of wine, loosened my tongue. Let's be totally honest how odd that is, someone turns up in a banking hall professing their love to someone they met at a bar and had a conversation lasting no more than half an hour!

'I now think it had nothing to do with him falling in love with me at first sight, but more the fact that when we were speaking at the bar, I'd relaxed and when he'd asked, how horrible it must have been to have been widowed at such an early age, how on earth had I coped financially, it must have been so hard for me to get on with my life and bring up a little boy. I remember answering way outside of my normal reserved manner, I was fortunate that I'd had the full support of both sets of parents and also been looked after very well financially as the benefactor from their Wills.'

She knew for some time now Karl had been a different person. She had ignored it for so long, but in the past year he was a completely different chap than the Karl she knew. He would belittle and undermine her in front of anyone, even if they were in the supermarket, he would have to make a derogatory remark, he couldn't help himself, it was as if it had to happen. She had been his princess and now she felt like a leper. Pre-nasty Karl he would bombard her with emails, texts and phone calls, now he was invisible.

She knew she loved him, and desperately wanted him to shake out of whatever was going on and have their lives back again. But what if it wasn't something he would ever shake out of, and even worse what if his oddness developed to became even more bizarre? Pippa also feared, this was all a ploy that Karl had planned from a financial motive!

Pippa continued to see Amber for five more sessions. It was the first time in her life she had spoken about Pippa and she knew Karl would be disappointed, as apart from the first session the discussions were not all about him.

The time allowed Pippa to discuss her grief from the bereavement of Matti and the loss of a life they had planned. She realised she'd gone through everything so stoically and never allowed a moment to think about herself, and it all happened when she was such a young age. Then her health scare more recently, when she had the awful realisation that she may not see her beloved son get married and not see future grandchildren.

The sessions with Amber gave her more strength than anyone could have believed, not least Pippa.

CHAPTER 10
'Who let the Hens out.'

Pippa was invited to Sophie's hen party. She'd been looking forward to it since the very first mention of it, which was September the year before.

Sophie's sister Clare was naturally Maid of Honour and appointed Chief Hen Party Organizer. Everything Clare arranged was perfect. Pippa thought this must be a family trait as it didn't matter whatever Sophie, Clare or their mum Sally did, it was always just right. Sally's girls had a lovely confidence, appropriateness and kindness which seemed unique and so special to them.

Clare organised several 'pre-hen afternoons' for Sophie, the mums and the four bridesmaids who were Lauren, Robyn, Chloe and Millie. They would have afternoon teas at lovely tea rooms or at Churchside where the girls would always put on a wonderful tea of small sandwiches, cheese scones and cakes. Pippa would usually be picked up by Sally and they'd become very close.

Their flights to Ibiza and four hotel rooms were booked for the first week in July, for three blissful nights. Pippa did wonder if her and Sally were more excited than any of the other hen party members.

On one of the early pre-hen afternoons, Sophie outlined in her lovely manner, what the itinerary was to be. They were also told who would be sharing rooms with who. Each would have their own overhead case and it had been agreed that each of the room buddies would share a suitcase that would go in the aircraft hold. It seemed natural to Pippa when the mums were told they would be together, Sophie would be with her sister Clare, Lauren with Robyn and Chloe with Millie. They were all very happy with the organisation and looking forward to the trip.

Clare's husband Dave had been roped in big style. He would be driving the minibus with the Hens to Stansted airport early on the Friday morning and collect them late afternoon on the Monday.

Clare's hold belongings: her half of the hold case allowance shared with Sophie, was taken over to Eddie and Sophie's the night before. What with Sophie being the Bride there was no way she was going to be rushed. She needed to make sure she had everything she wanted. If Eddie was asked to weigh the case thirty times to make sure that it wasn't over the allowance, then you could double that to sixty. Eddie didn't mind in the slightest, he was happy to see his fiancé enjoying herself. His efforts had nothing to do with ensuring a good deal of brownie points built up now would come in very handy. As Eddie was going on his Stag Do the following weekend and the Stags were certainly going to enjoy themselves in Las Vegas. They were heard enthusiastically saying.

'What goes on in Vegas, stays in Vegas.'

Early on the Friday Dave picked up his mother-in-law Sally, Clare was already on board the minibus, the cool box was filled with ice, bottles of Prosecco, orange juice, fizzy waters and a very tasty breakfast for them all to munch on the journey. Dave was really into the theme wearing a grey suit and a chauffer's hat.

The next person to be picked up was Pippa. She was eagerly waiting. Karl made sure he was working from his home office as he needed to look after Billy and the chickens. He kissed Pippa on the cheek, instructing.

'Make sure those girls look after you and don't go lifting your case, get someone else to do that.'

Then she was off to Sophie and Eddie's where the rest of the Hens would be. Oh dear, thought Dave.

The journey to the airport in the safe hands of Dave was perfect. The atmosphere was lovely, with a music playlist to get them in holiday mood. There was plenty of giggling, helped by the delicious food choices and no doubt the Prosecco had some input.

Pippa and Sally hadn't been to Ibiza before. They both laughed and said they could have been going to Islington with the Hens and they would have thought it perfect but going to the holiday isle really made it a special treat.

Sophie and Clare were organised booking the hotel early, they secured a really good deal. When the party arrived, they were pleased with what they could see from where they were standing in the hotel foyer. It was a very good hotel, and they were pleasantly surprised with the top quality of everything. Lauren and Robyn in particular were suitably impressed, starting straight away taking photos to post on Instagram.

All their rooms were on the same floor, adjacent to one another and for some reason the main meeting point became Pippa and Sally's room.

Clare had organised the weekend fully, including a little black dress evening meal, a shopping trip, plenty of sunbathing and even booked a select private beach bar with sunbeds and pool. Robyn didn't stop taking photos showing they were enjoying themselves in the sun, at a select location. Secretly Pippa hoped Robyn would post loads of photos from the weekend or at least show them to her mother. She knew it would make Bella bloomin' Robertson green with envy to see Pippa joining in the fun.

Early in the organisation for the Hen weekend there was one evening which Sally and Pippa decided not to join, it was very much out of their comfort zone. The Hens were going clubbing. The mums preferred to stay at the hotel for their very own G&T club event.

On the Hens' clubbing evening the mums joined the girls for their evening meal and then saw the giggling bundles off in the taxis, hoping on their return they would be as giggly, and not the victims of any drink induced tears.

The mums took themselves back into the sanctuary of the hotel. They walked up to the first-floor bar, taking themselves to a table on the balcony. They both took a deep breath, looked at one another, grinned and Sally said.

'Thank goodness for that, peace at last, phew it's like having small children again, I'm truly exhausted.'

They sat watching the sun go down, listening to the very pleasant soft jazz music, chattering as they sipped their G&T's. The temperature in the air was wonderful, both of them comfortable in sleeveless dresses.

Sally asked.

'So how are you now Pippa after that awful health fright?'

Pippa did her usual answer of yes, very well thank you, blah, blah blah. Sally asked again.

'So how are you now Pippa after that awful health fright?'

Pippa was taken aback and thought I've just answered that and as she was looking at Sally, she realised Sally was actually asking her how she was, not just wanting to hear Pippa's normal spiel.

Pippa thought for a moment then replied.

'Truly Sally, I am very well now in myself, thank you. Yes, it was a fright. I think one of the worse things before the operation was Billy would keep coming up to sniff the swelling in my tummy, he was obsessed with it, and I'd read dogs can smell cancer. I kept hoping and praying he was wrong, which thankfully he was. It has all taken its toll. Not only is there the nerve damage caused by the huge mass what with just being free to do whatever it wanted, pushing everything out of any orifice downwards and pushed everything up into my other organs, ribs and what have you, and that will all take its time to heal. But if that isn't enough, I've got an additional problem. As the surgeon has to cut through everything so deeply in a Laparotomy, they then have to keep everything together, and they do this with what they call a cheese wire, which they thread through the abdomen and what with them having to open me up from here to here.'

Pippa pointing to her lady area up to her ribs.

'The problem is the wire has broken in several areas and is poking under and right through my skin and dictates to how I sit or move. I've got to let it disintegrate fully on its own, which will be a good while yet. The only alternative is for them to open me up again. It was bad enough to be opened up and go through once let alone twice, believe you me. Apparently its very unusual for this wire to break and I've been told to be a patient patient.'

With a big and heartfelt sigh, she continued.

'Yes, it's fair to say, so far 2014 has been the oddest year of my life, well 2013 was a bit on the odd side too if I really think about it, but it's all turning round now, I can feel it in my water.'

Whilst the weekend had gone in a flash, they all knew the wonderful memories and friendships made would stay with them forever.

CHAPTER 11

'Be careful what you wish for.'

On three occasions Bev took Pippa shopping up the City, to help her find a suitable dress for the wedding. It was the one-time Pippa was not buying an outfit off eBay. They would arrive in Norwich, park and get straight to the shops and despite Bev's efforts they could not find anything that suited Pippa's brief.

Pippa didn't know exactly what the dress she wanted was like, but it had to be appropriate for Mother of the Groom and she definitely didn't want frumpy. She wanted to look back on the photos in years to come and know it was the best choice she could have made. But it seemed no sooner than they arrived at the shops, they had given up on shopping and would be in their favorite tearoom.

It was only three weeks to the wedding, when Pippa thought at this rate she'd have to rush and buy any dress just so she had something to wear and that would never do.

She was sitting in the garden randomly looking at outfits online and saw the most perfect dress. She quickly looked at the pictures, enlarged the photos to see the fabric and looked to see if it was in her size. She was disappointed to see that the size twelve was out of stock but the size ten was available and she ordered it, hoping it would be of a generous fit.

Two days later the dress arrived, beautifully wrapped, and she laid it on the bed admiring her purchase. Oh, it's so lovely she thought. She quickly slipped out of her sundress and popped the new dress on, it was perfect. She brushed her hair and did a twirl looking in her long bedroom mirror.

It was a darkish blue colour, the material was quite heavy of a jacquard design. It was sleeveless and at the neck it was embellished so she wouldn't need any extra jewellery. It fitted her perfectly, she was pleased the twelve hadn't been in stock as it would have been far too big. The dress was tailored around the bust, with an empire line, the high waistband emphasised her slim rib cage and then under this was slight pleating leading down to an A line skirt. It met her brief, it was appropriate, certainly not frumpy and what it also did was conceal and protect any of the wire that was sticking under and through her skin in the abdomen.

When Karl came home on the Friday, within minutes of him walking through the front door, she was excitedly showing him her new dress. He acknowledged it was the most perfect dress for her. He asked how much it cost and confirmed he would go straight into the office and make a transfer from his account to hers as he wanted to pay for the dress and put something towards her shoes. He was very quiet when he was saying all this and looked very distracted. Pippa didn't enquire if anything was up, she herself was more than distracted having found a beautiful dress that was so perfect and by Karl, totally out of character, offering to pay for her outfit she saw as a bonus.

She was on the phone to Sally telling her all about the dress, describing it in full, saying as soon as she'd tried it on, she knew it was the one. She went back online and ordered two pairs of shoes to see which pair would go best with the dress. She could return one or both of them if they weren't right. Pippa was on a roll and found the most delightful little bag which looked the same dark blue colour as the dress fabric and had a little wrist strap.

Karl sat down on the sofa still very distracted, he'd normally put the TV on, but he just sat slouched while Pippa on the phone enthusiastically described her purchase and in turn listening to Sally confirming that she would pick Pippa up the following morning promptly at ten o'clock and drive them to join the girls at Select Bridal Gowns for Sophie's final wedding dress fitting. Afterward they would all go back to Churchside, while Eddie was dutifully out of the way at cricket, and Sophie and Clare would prepare a light lunch for them all.

When Pippa finished her call still excited, she looked at Karl.

'I'll get the jacket potatoes out of the oven now. I'm having mushroom with mine did you want tuna or something else with yours?'

'I'm not coming to the wedding. You can let Eddie know.'

Before she had a chance to say anything he went on.

'Tomorrow I want you to phone the holiday company and have your name taken off the holiday, I'm still going and I'm not sure if I'll be going on my own so just get a blank ticket, then if I decide to take someone with me I can.'

Pippa couldn't think what to say or where to start but asked.

'Not coming to the wedding?'

'No, I don't want to be in the photos. You can stay at The Marshman's until the wedding but then you get out and I'll give you one hundred thousand pounds, but this place goes in my name, I'm the one who's worked for it.'

The only thing Pippa could think at that moment to say was.

'You can't get a blank ticket for a holiday, you need to provide a name, they have to do passport checks.'

'I'll have what I want, thank you. All you need to do is phone the bloody holiday company, they have to speak with you, I can't do it they won't speak with me.'

Pippa thought, he's tried to phone up and do it without me knowing. Out of character, she assertively asked.

'Where will you get one hundred thousand pounds from?'

'That's none of your business, keep your nose out.'

Rather than have the effect to shut Pippa up, Karl's comment loosened her tongue.

'Oh, and by the way if you think I haven't done anything, you're having a laugh. I don't know what you're going on about, saying you're the one who's worked for it, from what I see you haven't worked for anything! You say you're on a good salary, but what money have you put in? None, and that's well documented. You're so tight we don't ever do anything. Your property in Colchester is still in your sole name, apparently with a mortgage on it. But what would I know you keep everything to yourself? I don't even know if it exists! And while we're talking about money, which if ever I raise, I'm seen as obsessed and greedy, but as the subjects in the air. You can return my forty thousand pounds that should have come to me in November from Eddie, and you demanded secretly in July to come early, then you squirreled it away. Also, what the hell happened to the rental lump sum? These are not small amounts of money. The way I see it, you have stolen that from me, it's not too late for me to go to the police! All the money to purchase the properties came from me and has nothing to do with you. You needn't think I'm giving any of my inheritance away without a fight. My parents, Matti and his parents would be turning in their graves. I bet they are looking down on me right this minute, and they can see what you're up to Karl Taylor. God rest their souls having to witness all this going on, you should be truly ashamed of yourself.'

With that Karl stood up and simply said his thoughts out loud.

'Oh, that's not going to work, is it?'

He knelt in front of Pippa, took her hands in his and looking into her face sadly said.

'I'll try, I'll really try. I will come to the wedding and go on holiday with you. I never said I wanted a divorce.'

Pippa didn't answer, she sat looking at him thinking there is something really wrong with you. She couldn't believe what she was putting up with.

She stood up and took the jacket potatoes out of the oven but didn't have the appetite to eat anything so wrapped them up to put in the fridge for when they cooled down. She went through the motions of tidying up and disposing the bag that her dress had come in, but she still could not take on board what Karl had said.

By the following day to all and sundry life at The Marshman's seemed to be at peace and playing out its normal routine. Karl was polishing his car, the chickens were free ranging and Pippa had walked Billy who was now laying in the garden. She got herself ready for Sally to pick her up.

Sally pulled up, beeped her horn and Pippa quickly got into the car, relieved to get out for the day. Sally was soon chattering away. Her conversation was about Harold it seemed even though the stag party was the week before he was still suffering the effects of the copious amounts of alcohol, having tried to keep up with the lads.

Harold was the only mature guy on the stag party, Karl said right at the outset he wouldn't be joining them as it wasn't his scene.

Pippa was belly laughing hearing Sally's detailed description of how overhung her husband was.

'Oh, poor Harold, let's hope he recovers in the next fortnight he needs to be ready to walk Sophie down the aisle, she can't be seen to be propping him up as they walk down.'

Well, that vision set them both laughing.

They had another lovely girly day. Sophie looked stunning in her bridal dress, Sally was very emotional, which in turn started Pippa and the Hens off. Even Sophie had tears running down her beautiful cheeks. They all stood in the bridal shop in a soggy huddle of joyful tears.

They went back to Churchside for the lovely lunch Sophie and Clare had organised. Everything was prepared in plastic containers in the fridge or placed on the worktop on plates wrapped under cling film. No sooner they were through the door and the table was heaving with the edible delights. Pretty tea pots and jugs of elderflower cordial which Cousin Ruth had made and gifted to nearly everyone she knew.

Two of the bridesmaids, Chloe and Millie, were watching what they were eating very carefully, conscious they needed to get into their bridesmaids' dresses, and both had put on weight since their own dress fittings.

Millie asked Pippa how she managed to stay so trim as she always seemed to be able to eat or drink whatever she wanted. Pippa saying, she was disciplined most of the time, but she did let herself have what she wanted when out at one of their special events, which was possibly a little bit misleading. Pippa didn't say that of late, there were so many occasions when she didn't have an appetite due to silly situations being brought on by Karl!

Pippa was describing the beautiful dress she'd finally found to wear to the wedding and how it was a size ten and grateful that it hadn't been available in her size, as it would have been far too big. The girls asked could it be that Pippa was used to buying clothes in one size and since her operation she had lost weight and now she was another.

Pippa agreed they were probably right. She never measured or weighed herself and goodness she wouldn't be able to go back to the Diet What Diet classes if she'd lost too much weight and be out of target, Amy wouldn't have any of that. The girls all laughed.

At the end of the afternoon, they said their goodbyes knowing the next time they would be together was the day of Sophie and Eddie's wedding, which made Sally emotional again. Oh dear, thought Pippa, what is she going to be like on the actual day.

CHAPTER 12

'The devil is in the detail.'

The day of the wedding was finally here. There was a perfect blue sky and not a cloud to be seen. The ceremony was at St John's. Eddie and his best man Shaun would go from Churchside, a two-minute walk.

Sophie stayed overnight at her parents', The Old Rectory. She would leave for the church from there, in the vintage wedding car with Harold to arrive for the service at two o'clock. The hairdresser was booked to arrive at The Old Rectory at seven thirty and start first with Sally's hair, then the bridesmaids would arrive at eight.

One of Lauren's friends, Jen, was a make-up artist, and Lauren had arranged to book Jen if the practice session was to Sophie's satisfaction. She was totally delighted, and Jen was booked as Sophie's wedding present from Lauren. The bridesmaids and the mums all had their practice session with Jen and agreed she was fantastic, with them all eagerly booking a slot with her.

Pippa arranged to do her own hair, but she would pop round to Harold's and Sally's for eleven thirty for Jen to work her wonders.

On her way Pippa dropped Billy off at Ruth's, he would stay over at hers. Ruth would be at the church, the photos and the wedding breakfast, but she would then head off.

Pippa arrived at The Old Rectory, a beautiful property in Upper Wansted, she pulled onto the long tree lined driveway. It opened up to a large expanse of lawn, the house, two barns and outbuildings housing Harold's classic car collection.

Harold had worked as an Investment Banker and retired just before the crash. 'What luck was that', he wasn't bashful to express his good fortune at getting out, cashing in his bank shares and buying several investment properties with the money before all their savings and personal investments would have gone down the drain.

Despite being very wealthy or well healed as Ruth always put it, Harold, Sally and the girls were not in the least bit snooty, quite the opposite, down to earth with nice morals. The whole family came across as not scared of putting in a day's work.

Pippa parked and went through the open front door, shouting hello and walked into a lovely hubbub of girly giggles. Sally was trying not to get emotional and Harold in a state of wishing it were half past one, when he would be in the peace of the wedding car with his beautiful youngest daughter on their way to St Johns.

Sally and Harold greeted Pippa with a good squeeze and Harold offered to take Pippa out to show her the good job the company had done with the marques and she could see how everything was set up.

As they walked across the recently mown lawn with the well tendered borders, Harold said.

'I know it sounds daft to say this out loud Pippa, but I'm going to say it anyway. Sally and I are thrilled that our

Sophie is marrying your Eddie, and this is not meant to sound condescending in any way, but goodness me Pippa you've done a jolly good job with that boy, he's an absolute treasure.'

Pippa was understandably taken aback.

'Why thank you Harold, he's always been a very well-balanced lad and not difficult. I can't take all the praise as both mine and Matti's parents put so much into his formative years. But what I'm going to say is truthful, as I have always thought how lovely Sophie and Clare are, they are a true credit to you and Sally. I feel so blessed that Eddie is marrying Sophie, she is truly beautiful in looks and personality, with such a kind heart, a true and rare quality. I think Eddie and Sophie are a perfect match.'

With that they both stood on the lawn in front of the main marque and hugged. Pippa realised being emotional wasn't something unique to Sally as Harold was now in a complete mush. Pippa gently, wiping the tears off his cheeks.

'Oh Harold, please you'll start me off, you silly sausage.'

Harold took a deep breath and said with a broken wobbly voice.

'Yes quite, anyway let's see what I've spent all my money on, thank goodness I only had two daughters, I'd be bankrupt at this rate.'

Harold had not skimped, the wedding had cost an absolute fortune. Sally said as much in Ibiza, with her comment of 'the devil is in the detail'. Everything looked beautiful, the linen, table arrangements, flowers, ribbons, lighting and the food and wine menu were all to die for. The caterers and waiting staff were all busying themselves getting everything in order so when the guests arrived it was a surreal organised and calm setting. They carried on walking through the marque and Harold stopped, smiled and pointed.

'Here it is, the Piece de Resistance.'

There set on its own table was the wedding cake.

'Oh My Goodness Harold, it is so beautiful.'

The four-tier cake was truly a special center piece.

Harold walked over to the Harpist who had just arrived, wheeling her majestic instrument into position. He was keen to ensure she was happy that everything was to her needs. What a lovely kind chap he is thought Pippa.

They went back to the house and as they walked through the French doors to the music room, he handed her a glass of Bucks Fizz. She saw Jen was all organised with everything set up to work her magic. She was finishing off the make-up of one of the bridesmaids Chloe when Pippa walked over to her.

'Oh, my sweet Chloe, you always look so pretty but you look stunning, whatever will Shaun say when he sees his fiancé.'

Chloe smiled shyly.

As Pippa sat in the skillful hands of Jen, she felt very relaxed. Jen was a true professional and recognised some clients want to talk and others want to sit quietly, Pippa was certainly a sit and savour the moment client.

Lauren walked through to greet Pippa, she gestured an air kiss as she wasn't going to get in the way of Jen's artistry.

'Hi Aunty Pips, hope all's well.'

She adored being called Aunty Pips. Jen was at a stage where Pippa could speak.

'Hello my sweet, I'm very well thank you and I feel like a bottle of pop that has been shaken up as I could burst with all the joy I've got inside me.'

All three of them giggled.

Just as Jen was working on Pippa's eyes, Robyn walked in, greeted in the same air kissed manner. Pippa thought they probably all received the same email on makeup artist protocol.

In Ibiza the hens had become very close. Pippa couldn't believe the great news Robyn was now saying that her mother, Bella bloomin' Robertson, wouldn't be at the evening reception after all as she'd had to go to France suddenly two days before to attend a funeral.

'I'm sorry to hear that Robyn, please pass on my condolences to your mum. I know Bella loves a party, not to mention a wedding so I know it would have been something major to keep her from coming.'

Pippa thought thank goodness I have to keep my face straight for the makeup or I would be grinning like a

Cheshire Cat. She still hadn't forgotten how angry Karl had been with Bella for whatever she'd said to him at Lauren's birthday party, and she'd never felt comfortable in the company of that bloomin' awful woman.

Robyn answered honestly.

'She's only showing her face at the funeral to make sure she secures her part of the Will, anyone who knows my mother knows she's not interested in the person, she's totally materially driven.'

Despite the make up being applied, Pippa's eyes widened and thankfully Jen was also taken aback by the comment and stopped for a few moments. Robyn carried on.

'Yes, she's nothing like you Pippa.'

Pippa was truly taken aback by this out of character comment, Robyn always appeared to be very superficial about possessions, brands and also in the same vein as her Goddaughter Lauren, completely preoccupied by the in place.

Thankfully Jen had moved on to Pippa's lips, so she was instructed.

'Quiet now please.'

Everyone, not only Pippa complied and held their breath.

Jen finished, took the headband carefully off of Pippa's hairline, ran her fingers through her hair and passed her the mirror.

Pippa was so pleased.

'Oh Jen, thank you so much you have done such a miraculous job, I feel a million dollars.'

'Aunty Pips, if I look as good as you when I'm forty-five I'll be well pleased. You look gorgeous.'

'Oh my woman, all these compliments, I won't be able to get through the door and put my dress on at this rate. But thank you, that's very kind of you to say such a nice thing and the age of forty-five does seem so long ago.'

Pippa got back to The Marshman's, made herself an omelet and cup of tea. She called through to Karl there was a cuppa on the side and went through to the bedroom to run the straighteners through her hair and get into her dress.

The males of the wedding party, including Karl were in black tails, white shirts, waistcoats and a cornflower blue cravat.

Pippa was completely fed up with Karl always having to spoil every special occasion and it seemed if someone was enjoying something he would try and rain on their parade or make it all about him, so she'd decided he wouldn't taint anything from this moment on.

When he walked into the room smiling at her and looking very handsome in his suit, Pippa threw him a glance, smiled saying.

'You look nice, goodness I'm looking forward to today, weddings are always such lovely happy days.'

It had been arranged for Karl to drive Pippa and himself to St John's and after the service on to the Old Rectory. He'd leave his car at Harold's and Sally's overnight, and a taxi was arranged to pick them up at midnight. They could pick the Jaguar up anytime that suited them the following day and Pippa would then go on to pick Billy up from Ruth's.

As they locked up, Karl looked at Pippa and pulled her to him.

'You look so beautiful my lovely wife, I'm so lucky to have you. Do you think it would be nice to renew our wedding vows sometime, shall we look into it?'

Pippa was taken aback, and thought here we go, let's change the focus from anyone else and put attention back on to him and she found it hard not to reply in a curt manner.

'As you know I've always thought wedding vows should only be the taken once, they're sacred and supposed to see you through, you don't renew them. Anyway, today is Eddie and Sophie's day, it's all about them.'

They arrived at St John's, already there was a glorious warm atmosphere of people arriving, with everyone looking so wonderfully turned out and happy. The organ was playing, and the Reverend Francis Trevor was at the door to greet everyone.

The Ushers, Pete and Ben gave Pippa a big hug. They had been friends of Eddie's since they were all babies and it seemed strange that within a blink of an eye, they were all big strong handsome men. It didn't seem that long ago they'd all been in the garden at Churchside as chubby little babies playing together while the mothers would all chatter, drinking tea. The bond of all Eddie's friends was so strong and genuine, they were like family.

Karl went straight to where he was directed by the ushers to the pew, one behind the front on the right. Pippa was too busy chattering to various people, when there was a gentle hand placed on her shoulder and she turned round to see Eddie with his best man Shaun standing behind her.

'Oh boys, you look so handsome.'

Eddie scooped his mother into his arms and gave her a huge hug.

'Thank you for everything, I love you so much. Oh Mum, I'm so happy I can't believe how lucky I am to be marrying Sophie, she is such a wonderful, kind, beautiful person, I love her so much.'

Pippa took a few moments before she could speak.

'I'm so very proud of you my boy, and I'm so very proud of Sophie too and I know Daddy and all the Gramps are looking down on us today joining in with this wonderful celebration. Thank you for being such a wonderful son and marrying such a wonderful person, I love you both so very much.'

'And Mum were both proud of you too. I had a few moments with Dad and the Gramps this morning, Sophie has organised flowers, matching all those in the church for their graves, they look really nice, have a look before you go over to the reception.'

Pippa nodded that she would, but unable to speak as she was overcome with the emotion of the occasion and what a lovely thoughtful girl Sophie was to arrange flowers on all the graves, ensuring they were fully involved.

More people were coming through and St John's was now filling wonderfully with the congregation to witness this glorious happy event. Pippa took her seat next to Karl, he held her hand, squeezed it firmly and looked lovingly into her face.

'I love you totals Pippa Taylor.'

She looked lovingly at him.

'I love you too Karl, this has to be the greatest day of my life.'

Reverend Francis was at the front of the church speaking with Eddie and Shaun. Also at the front was a grand piano and Cello, at the appropriate moment Reverend Francis nodded towards the organist who sat respectfully quiet, and the duo of piano and cello started playing 'A Thousand Years'. Everyone stood and there was a respectful movement of bodies turning to see the bride. And what a beautiful sight she was.

Even though Pippa had seen Sophie's dress and knew she looked beautiful, nothing could have prepared for seeing her now. It was an antique ivory of the most exquisite lace. Her natural beauty enhanced by the sophistication and cut of the dress, a delicate tiara in her beautiful fair hair.

Pippa passed Eddie a handkerchief. He and so many of the congregation were truly overwhelmed with the moment. In the opposite pew was Sally with her son-in-law Dave keeping her company. He was passing her reams of tissues to mop her cheeks as she was trying so very hard not to spoil the good job Jen had done with her make up.

When Harold and Sophie reached Eddie, Shaun and Reverend Francis, they all took a few moments to gather themselves. Harold turned to take his seat next to Sally, taking a moment to give his nose a good blow which was very loud, resulting in the whole congregation giving a warm chuckle.

Before they could all have believed, the register was being signed and the organist was playing Mendelssohn's Wedding March. The bells were ringing, and the photographer was directing the guests into their places for the photos. Everyone that was except Karl.

Before Karl drove them to the reception Pippa said she needed to see the flowers at the graves and took herself over to have a few minutes with all her special people. Sophie had organised each of the flower arrangements to be different but made up from the flowers that were both in the church and at the reception.

'Such a thoughtful girl. Our Eddie has done us proud.'

It was strange to see The Old Rectory's gardens and the marquees busy now, and the whole afternoon was wonderful. The wedding breakfast was a delight. The speeches were funny and to Sally's relief appropriate.

At the evening reception, Eddie came up to Pippa.

'Mum make sure you're at the edge of the dance floor when Sophie and I have our first dance'.

'Goodness I wouldn't miss that for the world.'

What Pippa didn't know Eddie had arranged that near the end of their first dance Harold would dance with Pippa and then Sophie would dance with her dad and Eddie with his mum, then the DJ would invite everyone to join in.

Everything had been planned so well and with such care and love, within a short time everyone was on the dance floor having a great celebration party. Before Pippa and Karl knew, the taxi had arrived to take them home.

CHAPTER 13

'Every action has a consequence.'

Pippa busied herself getting everything ready for their regular Corfu holiday. Karl was being very loving to her and it was as if the last few odd months hadn't happened. Pippa was relieved and thought if we can just move on, thank goodness. But his strange comments and behaviour had been very disturbing, and all in all, it had been a most unsettling time. She realised he could slip at any time and she would need to keep on her guard.

In fact, Karl was totally out of character, he'd been very talkative, which Pippa only saw as a positive. He enthused about their holiday routine, noting the only exception was his wonderful wife could not join any of her normal exercise classes, as she was still recovering from the damage caused by the mass and her operation.

The day before their flight Karl took himself to the shops and bought several very nice and expensive items of clothing, saying 'a shroud doesn't have pockets.' When they arrived on holiday Karl was ignoring his phone, and to Pippa's relief he was continuing to be talkative, relaxed and most of all, he appeared happy.

The second day into their holiday Karl said they really deserved an extra holiday and for Pippa to look online for somewhere hot for spring the following year. She quickly did, and as they sat on their sunbeds, she showed him a lovely hotel in Dubai and he told her to book it, which she did. He said he wanted to treat his wife and would arrange the deposit payment from his account and Karl was put down as the lead passenger. He ran up to their room, brought down his credit card to secure the deposit payment, and a five-night extra holiday was booked for the following April.

The next day was equally as lovely, Karl was really good company. He even made the effort to swim in the sea with Pippa, which she thoroughly enjoyed, previously he would always say he couldn't swim as the sea or swimming pool irritated his skin. A few times he disappeared off on his own, but Pippa wasn't concerned and not worried about anything. They returned to their room and were getting ready for their evening meal and entertainment. Pippa finished her hair and Karl was laying on the bed, looking at his mobile phone and all of a sudden, he was looking very sad. Oh no thought Pippa, I hope it's not a problem with work that's all we need we really do need this break. She didn't want to ask but felt she had to.

'Everything OK?'

Karl still looking at his phone replied sadly.

'No problem'

They got dressed and walked through the beautiful paths of the resort to the restaurant and Pippa looked at Karl and could see he was fighting back the tears, he was swallowing hard, she could see his Adam's apple, something she'd never noticed before, he was visibly upset.

'Are you sure everything's OK, you look sad?'

He nodded his head, swallowing hard, still unable to speak.

They arrived at their table in the restaurant but stayed for less than thirty minutes, which didn't go unnoticed to other guests, who asked Pippa if she was OK and she said she had a bit of a pain, pointing to her head.

'I must have had too much sun.'

They went back to their room, and Karl took off his clothes and got into bed. Pippa looked at him, she'd never seen him so upset.

It seemed far too early to go to bed, but knew she needed to join him and support him in any way she could and got in bed next to him and put her arm round him.

'Oh Karl, what's the matter, you can tell me, we've been through so much, whatever it is just tell me what the problem is we'll get through it.'

She lay still and he said quietly.

'Yes alright, I'll tell you the truth.'

He took a deep breath and then he was quiet, a few minutes later he took another deep breath, and this went on several times. Then he sat bolt upright, shouting aggressively at her.

'What have you done, what have you done, what have you been saying to Theresa?'

Pippa was totally shocked.

'I haven't done anything. Who the hell's Theresa?'

He was just shouting over and over again she knew what she'd done, she was so deceitful and manipulative, how dare she!

It turned out the Theresa that Karl was referring to was Theresa Small, their conveyance solicitor. Karl was accusing Pippa of having contacted her and Pippa knew what she'd done.

Pippa was apologising saying she was sorry that he was upset but she hadn't been in contact with Theresa.

Pippa lay in the dark, sobbing. She thought when her husband said he was going to tell the truth she thought he was going to do just that, tell her the truth, not come out with a load of rubbish to try and put any blame on her.

Karl put his arms round her and pulling her to him, said.

'I believe you it's all been a terrible mistake, you didn't mean to do anything wrong, I believe you Peppa you didn't mean to do anything wrong.'

Pippa thought the saying of the darkest hour being just before dawn had never felt truer, and the morning could not come soon enough. When they went to breakfast, she kept her sunglasses on as she felt awful and scared that others would see that she had been crying all night.

They returned to their sunbeds and as their normal routine dictated Karl at the appointed time went to the gym for his workout. As soon as he was out of eyeshot, Pippa picked up her iPad and sent Theresa Small a message:

…. Hi Theresa, I hope you are well. Strange question but I'm wondering if you have had any contact with Karl lately. We are currently on holiday and your name came up. Kind regards, Pippa ….

Theresa came back straight away:

…. Hi Pippa, yes, I am well, I hope you are too. Karl has been in contact with me, but under solicitor code of conduct I am bound by confidentiality and not able to say in what context. I hope your holiday goes well. Take care, Theresa…

Pippa was even more confused. Whatever is wrong with him, yesterday we booked an extra holiday and then in the evening he was accusing her of, well she didn't know what he was accusing her of, but it was certainly one of the most awful evenings anyone could imagine.

By the time Karl returned from the gym, Pippa was in the sea having a swim. It seemed surreal, as Karl was in a pleasant, happy, relaxed mood and seemed oblivious to anything bad occurring the night before.

Strangely they went on to have a pleasant remainder of their holiday. There was a déjà vu moment with Erik and the chin-chin ritual of the glasses, with Karl refusing to make eye contact with Pippa, but Erik dismissed this with the realisation this was Karl's new routine.

When they returned to The Marshman's all was calm. Karl was working from home for the next two days and Pippa had an appointment with Amber. She was looking forward to the appointment as Amber had also been away on holiday and so much had happened in the space of five weeks since they last met. But despite being keen for the appointment Pippa had decided this would be her final counselling session.

When Pippa settled in front of Amber, she said she felt she was on an out-of-control roller coaster. There were the good moments, her husband was speaking nicely and lovingly to her, an additional spring holiday was booked for Dubai. But then, there were the major dips of the roller coaster when it was in free fall, with all the very bizarre comments and behaviour. Karl saying that he wasn't going to the wedding, the blank holiday ticket and she wouldn't be going on holiday, that he'd give her money to clear off, but he didn't want a divorce, and the very strange outburst when they were on holiday about their conveyance solicitor.

Pippa opened up her thoughts of when she'd been laying in the dark and Karl said he would tell her the truth, she had expected him to say that he had another woman. Now she wished he had said that because that would be more normal than all this obscure weird oddness and uncertainty.

She asked Amber if she could recall from one of their earlier sessions when she'd said that Karl would relay stories and she was never sure if these things had happened or rather what he wanted to happen. In particular could Amber remember the story about his colleagues Steve and Nina who had an affair?

Pippa was now convinced that never actually happened, it was all in his mind. There were so many similarities of what was meant to have happened to his colleagues back then, to what was going on now. It was all very disturbing so much so; she had twice asked if he needed an appointment at the doctors. Despite her concerns being raised when he was on one of his 'balanced moments', which were very rare, with her gently saying she thought he looked tired, perhaps a medical checkup may help? He aggressively rebuffed the suggestion telling her to mind her own business.

Amber shook her head with a worried expression on her face.

'Pippa you really need to find out what's going on, I have such fears for you. You've said yourself you know nothing about this man. He goes away all week, you don't know his history and you've never met any of his family. The one person you've met knew him as a colleague only for a few months and hasn't been a colleague for a long time. Karl could be spinning you any story, you have no way of verifying anything. Yet, you are financially fully tied up with him. Did you never think that was all very odd? He could be trying to take the houses from under your nose for all you know. Why would he contact your conveyancing solicitor when you are on holiday? I just sense you are wishing everything will be OK and that's not going to happen. Please be honest, it isn't is it?'

Pippa didn't answer and Amber continued.

'Karl simply doesn't understand the rules of life. You ask how he can hold down a good job when he displays such bizarre, odd behaviour on a personal level. My answer is quite blunt, it's because he knows what he needs to do in the role of his job, but on a personal level he doesn't know how to behave. I've never met Karl and I will be honest and say I'm grateful I haven't. I'm not sure if he has a personality disorder with tendencies to fantasy and a fragile ego, or as you yourself have intimated, that you may have been the target of someone with mercenary intentions? All I will add is whilst you haven't said or even possibly thought this, it may be Karl is pretending to have a problem to confuse you and create pity, which becomes the role of his 'job'. You really need to protect yourself Pippa. Please take care.'

Pippa thanked Amber for the clarity and support she had provided, as this offered her more strength than she could ever possibly have imagined. But she really felt now was the right time to call an end to their sessions. In particular, she wondered if over thinking and talking about everything could actually make things more negative?

They said their goodbyes, but Amber was very concerned for Pippa, asking she keep in touch by email. She wouldn't expect payment, she just needed to know she was safe. Pippa confirmed she would keep in touch.

She got home and Karl had gone out. She went into the kitchen popped the kettle on and said to Billy.

'We'll go out in a little while old chum and have ourselves a nice little walk.'

She heard Karl come through the front door.

He came into the kitchen and kissed his wife.

'How did it go with Amber, I hope she didn't upset you, was it OK?'

'Yes, very well thank you and she has never upset me, she's a nice lady. I told her that will be the last one for now but if I change my mind, I can always contact her. I'm now making a cuppa, do you want one?'

'Yes please. I've got to get to the loo, I've been dying for a poo all morning.'

This made Pippa laugh, she knew her husband was precious where he went to the toilet. He rushed through to the bathroom leaving his Blackberry mobile phone on the kitchen table.

Amber's words were still fresh in her thoughts and she picked up the phone and was surprised to see it wasn't locked. She looked through the unread texts for the time they were on holiday and there were several along the lines of 'Call me', 'We need to talk'. But she wasn't really interested in them, she went straight to the emails.

Sure enough, there was an email thread to Theresa Small. She clicked on them and sent them to her own email address. She was then about to delete what she'd done and thought, no I'm not worried, every action has a consequence. So be it.

She finished making the cups of tea. Took hers with her to the orangery and started looking at the email that she'd just received. Karl came from the bathroom and she called through.

'Your teas on the side.'

She was taken aback by the stupidity of Karl's email to Theresa, it read:

... Hi Theresa, I hope you are well. I need to instruct you to do the following. Transfer The Marshman's property in to my sole name. Deal with the sale of the Bagby property. Oh, and by the way, don't tell Pippa. Kind regards, Karl ...

Theresa wrote straight back in reply:

... Sorry, there would be a conflict of interest as I work for both you and Pippa. I suggest you get yourself another solicitor. Theresa ...

Pippa knew straight away what Karl thought she had done wrong. He'd taken Theresa's reply to mean that Pippa had similar plans to what Karl was intending and he assumed Pippa got to Theresa first.

At that moment Karl came shouting through to the orangery at the top of his voice.

'What have you done, how dare you, what have you done now?'

She looked at him.

'Don't you dare, I can see what you're up to.'

Within minutes he apologised. He'd become worried whilst they were on holiday that she was planning on leaving him and the insecurity made him contact Theresa. It hadn't helped when Pippa went to the shops the day before their holiday. He thought she must be seeing another man and he just couldn't cope with that.

'Karl, I went to the pet shop to buy Billy's food, so Eddie and Sophie had it while we were away. Apart from anything else I am still recovering from my whole body being, as you yourself so delicately put it, being split open like a suckling pig. I probably will never get the opportunity to say this again, so I'll say it now.'

Pippa took a deep breath and her voice raised, with an unusual spiteful tone.

'What kind of cruel person says that to anyone, let alone to his wife the week before she's due to go under major surgery. Well, I can tell you, no one in their right mind would, that's who! So, with that delightful vision in your mind, why the hell would I want any bloke apart from my husband looking at my body and since you can't even look at me without an expression like you're going to be sick, I have to say you've not done an awful lot for my self-esteem. I shouldn't have to remind you, but our marriage vows were meant to be in sickness and in health. Give me strength, I cannot believe I'm putting up with all this, how the hell I haven't cracked under the strain. I've been unwell, had a horrendous cancer scare, been through a major operation and I've had to be supporting you. By any stretch of the imagination that isn't right and whilst we're on the subject you take all the credit for looking after me. How dare you!'

She didn't say anything more, she knew there was no point, in Karl's mind there was only one sort of truth and it didn't matter if it was in written form, or if there was an audit trail. If it wasn't the truth according to Karl it was a lie. In his view he was the one that had been hurt by everyone's actions, in particular Pippa's and anyone associated with her.

Karl went out of his way to try and make it up to his wife, he was kindly and contacted her whilst he was away, but as always Karl had an alternative plan.

CHAPTER 14

'If it's meant to be, it will be.'

It was late September and Pippa loved this time of year, the Norfolk countryside always looked so wonderful with its wide skyline and the autumn light casting its golden glow. She wished she could paint, she had so much material on her doorstep. Perhaps she would ask Ruth if she would add her to the waiting list for the Wednesday Art Classes, she ran.

She was now out for little walks every day, much to Billy's delight. Walking had always offered Pippa clarity of thinking, but at the moment everything seemed a real mess and she knew even if she was able to walk all day, she wouldn't be able to sort this tangled web out.

Ruth came round for Pip's homemade cheese scones and they sat in the kitchen, drinking tea and Ruth emphasising the importance of butter, not only for taste, but it was also far less fattening than people thought. She seemed on a campaign to promote its use against 'margarine or spread as the current fashion calls.' Pippa smiled and agreed the virtues of butter were indeed plenty and in total agreement with her cousin. Pippa then asked.

'Ru, do you get lonely?'

Ruth could see there was more to this question.

'Sometimes dear.'

Ruth's wonderful husband Geoff had passed away shortly after Pippa lost Matti.

'It's just I feel I need a break from here and everything. I wondered if I could stay over at yours?'

Ruth was looking at her cousin who was just staring at the contents of her teacup.

'Of course you can dear. You are welcome anytime. I won't ask you if anything is wrong, I can tell if you need a break then things are not right, but Pip if you do need to talk, I will always be there for you. Does Karl know you are thinking this way?'

Pippa, still looking at her cup, answered sadly.

'Well, he doesn't know I'm thinking of a break. He knows things aren't right, haven't been for some time. I'm not sure if I'm hoping that if he thinks he's going to lose me he'll come to his senses or the alternative, that he might be relieved that I'm out of the way and things take their natural course.'

'That does sound a huge risk. I've never seen you as a gambler but certainly I'd be happy for you to stay over. The annex is yours for as long as you want. Obviously, Billy and the hens too. I was planning on getting some more chickens, so the coup is available.'

That evening Pippa went round to Churchside and told Eddie and Sophie she, Billy and the girls were having a break at Ruth's.

They had been concerned for some time with Karl's odd behaviour and when the money was transferred over and

Eddie checked if it had been received, Pippa out of character said in a sharp tone.

'Yes, thank you it was received, it went in and then it was spirited away to Karl's sole account, never to be seen again.'

Eddie knew the money were his mother's, from his father's and grandparents' inheritances, but he also knew she did not want to discuss it.

Hearing the announcement that Pippa was taking a break, Eddie and Sophie offered a hand moving the chickens, or anything over to Ruth's. They then gave her a hug.

When Pippa left, Sophie started crying. She had managed to keep everything together while Pippa was there but once the door was shut, she was beside herself. She wished Pippa would tell them exactly what was going on. It was as if she were scared to say the problem out loud. She really shouldn't bottle everything up, they were family, and she should tell them. Eddie consoled Sophie and agreed with everything she said, adding it were as if his Mum were still trying to protect her little boy from anything bad.

They had noticed Karl acting very strange for a good while now. Eddie reminded Sophie they had been very unnerved by the secretive manner of Karl's demand for the money by July. This could have put them in a very difficult position, since the money was not due to be repaid to Pippa until November. What would have happened if they hadn't said anything and come the due date his Mum handed them her bank details for the transfer to be made. The monies would have been paid over and as it transpired, according to Pippa, spirited away, never to be seen again!

Eddie had been very selective what he told his mother with regards Karl's demand for the money. He only said they were concerned by Karl's need for secrecy and wanted to check as the funds came from Pippa, should they be paid to her sole account or the joint account being specified in Karl's emails.

Eddie and Sophie had decided they wouldn't mention to Pippa the details of the messages. Karl had sent numerous emails and text messages daily for a week, getting more and more desperate that he needed the money. The same demand running through all the messages, don't delay, just get on with the transfer and why was Eddie being so awkward. Each and every message emphasised not to tell Pippa, they didn't want to worry her.

Their decision to tell Pippa was prompted when Karl turned up at Churchside late June. Eddie had just left for cricket practice, as Karl would have known. Sophie passed the window on the landing to see her soon to be father-in-law sitting in his car outside.

She ran downstairs and opened the front door calling to him, but Karl just sat in the car looking straight ahead with a blank expression. She immediately became concerned that something had happened to Pippa and ran to the driver's side window.

'Hi Karl, nothing wrong is there, are you coming in?'

Karl just sat staring ahead and then eventually said.

'No, it's OK I've got to get home.'

Sophie was now really concerned.

'You're welcome to a cup of tea, I was about to have one myself. Are Pippa and Billy well?'

Still looking straight ahead with a blank expression he said

'Yes, a cup of tea would be nice thank you. I'll be able to see what changes you've made to Churchside since me and Pippa used to live here.'

Even that seemed strange as whilst Karl was never a frequent visitor, mainly only ever coming to their pre-Christmas family get together he would have known they hadn't made any changes since his visit last December and he'd certainly been in Churchside since he and Pippa had moved five years before.

Karl came in and sat nervously in the lounge and Sophie went through to the kitchen to pop the kettle on, then went back through to join him. She sat down and all of a sudden Karl jumped up.

'I can't stop for tea, just tell Eddie he needs to get on with transferring the money and don't go worrying Pippa about this.'

And with that he was gone.

But while they certainly did have cause for concern, it was a blessing Pippa was moving in with Ruth. Eddie wanted to reassure Sophie that his mother was strong. She'd always had an inner sweet gentle strength that saw her through previously and would get her through again. The only difference was this time Eddie was a grown man with the loving support of his wife and they would be there to help, if she needed.

Eddie also knew that Billy would be at his Mum's side and there was no way Billy would allow anything to happen to Pippa. He would lay his life on the line for her, she was his love.

The following day Pippa sent Karl an email saying she was going to have a break away. She ended writing that Billy, the Girls [the chickens] and she would go to Ruth's on the Friday.

The next evening Karl came home late, Pippa was watching TV in bed. They didn't say anything apart from hello, he got ready for bed, she turned off the TV and they went to sleep. In the morning looking straight ahead he said.

'You'd better get your things packed and get going, I've got a friend coming over at the weekend to watch the football, best you stay away. I'm away with work from Monday until Wednesday. When are you coming back, what about the fish?'

Pippa said Eddie was coming about five to help move the Girls, she would pop back on Tuesday to check all was OK and feed the fish. She wouldn't disturb his weekend with his friend. She didn't ask but thought, what friend, you haven't got any!

Ruth's farmhouse had land attached with stables, livery, miniature goats and although it was always calm, there were always plenty of people and a quiet hustle and bustle of things going on. Ruth simply said to them all that Pippa was still struggling from her operation and would be staying for a while to convalesce. All of which was true.

Ruth had everything in place for her guests. She put a notice on the chicken house with a list of the five hens' names, a description and cartoon drawing of each. Chickens being given names was a novelty for Ruth. She had been the owner of chickens for more years than she cared to remember, they were just chickens. Pippa's hens laid a daily egg, but were pets, each had their own name and came enthusiastically when she called them.

The Girls arrived first, transported in a motley array of boxes in Eddie's Range Rover with Pippa and Billy following behind. They all eagerly waded in to get things sorted then Eddie left them to it.

When Pippa walked into the annex, Eddie had already put Billy's bed in the bedroom with her case and a pretty plant in the lounge, with a 'Welcome to Your New Home' label. That made it all feel suddenly very real.

Ruth was busying in through the door behind Pippa, with all three dogs in tow. She did seem happy with the company that had suddenly landed on her, to Pippa's great relief.

The cousins nattered all evening about everything and anything, and certainly nothing about Karl.

Ruth saw her brother-in-law George every Sunday and they would go out for a roast lunch. He also was in his eighties and widowed. A lovely jolly, kindhearted chap. Pippa suspected Ruth had confided in George about her situation. But Ruth didn't know much more than what Pippa had said of things would go one way or the other due to her time away. Interference would be against Ruth's principles of letting nature take its course and never to force a situation.

George had booked for the three of them to have Sunday lunch out, the table originally booked for one o'clock for two people and the number was increased with Pippa's arrival. George also had a dog, a lovely young female black Lab, Tilly. Ruth's farmhouse easily accommodated the four dogs. George walked through the door and cheekily commented how pleased and relieved he was not to be embarrassed because the girls scrubbed up well. They all laughed and left for their pub lunch. The three of them just nattered, and George had them all laughing. What a nice treat, such a very pleasant change, Pippa thought.

After lunch they took the four dogs for a walk, then settled back in Ruth's lounge for convivial companionship and copious cups of tea before George went home in the evening. Pippa retreated to the annex, getting herself ready for bed. Ruth followed through in her cotton nightie covered by her long candlewick gown and sat on the bedroom chair whilst Pippa was lying on the bed and again, they just chattered.

It was a nice girly time and Pippa knew whatever the future would bring she was fortunate to be surrounded by such kind and lovely people.

CHAPTER 15
'Out of sight, out of mind'

Pippa was up early most mornings, but today she had slept soundly and was up a little bit later than usual. She quickly slipped into her jeans and top, threw on her jacket and wellington boots and with Billy at her heels went down to open the chickens.

She met Ruth on the way.

'No problems dear I've sorted the Girls. They will stay in their run for a couple of days until they've got their bearings. Hate to say it but they seem to be really picking on the little grey one, Daisy. Once they're all out and about hopefully they will be occupied and not venting their frustration on that poor little thing.'

'Ahh thank you Ruth.'

They hugged. Billy was having a good sniff near the paddock but not so pre-occupied that he wasn't keeping an eye on Pippa and as soon as they turned to walk back, he did an about turn.

Ruth had organised breakfast in her kitchen, the porridge was already on the stove and she had recently got into smoothies. There was a green concoction on the side with Ruth's latest mixture of vegetables, nuts and fruits. As they ate breakfast Ruth asked.

'Are you taking Billy with you when you pop back to The Marshman's or did you want him to stay here?'

'He may as well come back with me, I'll pop over there once I'm showered. Did you want me to get anything from the shops on the way back?'

Ruth thought for a few moments.

'No, I'm fine thank you dear. I thought we'd have leek and potato soup for lunch and then I'll do a vegetable lasagna for tea, how does that sound?'

Pippa smiled at her lovely cousin.

'Sounds perfect, thank you, but let me help out won't you. By the sounds of it Ru you're becoming a veggie.'

They both laughed.

Pippa was surprised to receive two emails from Karl, the first asking where was his dressing gown and the second, where had she put his jeans?

She exclaimed out loud.

'Good grief!'

When Pippa pulled onto the drive at The Marshman's the place appeared different, it had a cold look about it. She collected the post from the box and went round the back. Billy was outside having a good sniff and Pippa went over to the pond to feed the fish.

She picked up the key from under the boot scraper at the back door and let herself in and the place was tidy but again had an empty feel about it and smelt different. Pippa's normal large photo collection had gone, she wondered where they were. There was no evidence that she'd ever existed.

She was surprised to see their bedroom door now had a lock on it, and she went into the dressing room where the main wardrobes and drawers were. She was relieved to see all the photos in their frames had been put in two carrier bags and were safely there. She thought she'd take them back with her she didn't like the thought of them hidden away and when all said and done, her special people should be with her on show around the annex.

She went to use the toilet in the bathroom and was taken aback for there was someone else's shampoo and shower gel on the side of the bath. She picked them up and looked closely at them, she knew they were definitely not Karl's he was far too macho to use strawberry and avocado. She put them back on the side and saw hairs in the bath. She surprised herself by picking them off the side and looking at them. They were a dyed dark colour with grey roots and she stretched one out and looking in the mirror held it to her head it came to Pippa's chin.

She collected the bags of photos, locked up and called Billy.

Over lunch Ruth asked how she got on, was everything in order?

Pippa said she'd brought the photos back with her as they had been bundled up into bags. She was pleased to have all her precious people with her, and she didn't know why she hadn't brought them with her originally. She went on to say there was now a lock on their bedroom door and relayed what she'd found in the bathroom, which had taken her aback.

Ruth wasn't taken aback she was completely and utterly shocked. It was the timing of it, the very first weekend Pippa was away. She was upset for Pippa and wondered how on earth she was coping so well with the knowledge that a woman had moved straight in, to Pippa's home!

For once Ruth couldn't answer, she really didn't know what to say. While Pippa was clearing the dishes away, she went upstairs and was on the phone to George. He let her finish without interruption and then said.

'So much for you always saying let nature take its natural course or an unnatural situation would be forced. Well, it sounds to me as if the course has not only been set but already taken.'

Even though it had only been a few days the cousins had settled into a daily routine. Pippa was setting the table in the kitchen ready for their evening meal, with Ruth in charge of the cooking. Pippa's mobile rang and she picked it up.

'Oh my goodness its Bev, I haven't told her yet.'

Pippa answered the phone and Bev started speaking straight away.

'Goodness me Pip I thought you'd dropped off the planet, I've been calling you at home all afternoon. I'm now on my way round to see you and tell you about my holiday to Croatia, Oh My God Pip, I've met a bloke he's gorgeous, anyway I'll tell you about that in a mo, I'll bring your present with me. You're very lucky as I had decided if you didn't answer this time then I would keep the scarf myself. Oh I can't believe I've gone and told you what it is.

Anyway, you can let me know all about your holiday too, goodness me I haven't seen you for ages. Have you had your tea?'

Finally, she came up for air and Pippa could get a word in.

'Ooohhh a new scarf! Glad I answered, I wouldn't have wanted to miss out on that. You cheeky monkey trying to put a timeframe for me accepting my gift.'

Then taking a deep breath she continued.

'Yes, it will be lovely to see you and I'll have finished my tea in about half an hour, but I'm not at home tonight I'm at Ruth's. I'm staying here for a little while for a break.'

For once there was silence, eventually Bev said.

'I'll be over at seven, see you then.'

As they sat and ate their meal. Ruth suggested.

'What might be nice dear, is if you take Bev into the annex to talk and I'll pop through after about half an hour, that way you can have a little natter and then with me coming through we can move the conversation on to something else, well, hopefully. I hate to ask Pip but have you thought what you might say.'

'Well, I've thought roughly what I'd say. The truth is I don't know exactly what is going on at the moment myself, so I don't want to say anything other than I'm taking a break.'

So that's what happened. Bev arrived earlier than she'd planned, they greeted at Ruth's back door.

'Tell you what Bev, shall we go through and sit in the annex. Ruth can join us shortly, she's got some phone calls to make, we don't want to disturb her.'

As soon as they walked through to the annex, Bev saw Pippa's photos in their frames neatly distributed around the lounge.

'Pip, what the hell is going on, please don't tell me you've moved out of The Marshman's.'

'I don't know what's going on Bev, and no I haven't moved out, I've just come to Ruth's for a break. I've just had enough. Everything has got too much of late and I really don't know what to say other than that, it all seems a bit complicated at the moment, well apart from to say Billy and the Girls are here too.'

For Bev that said it all. Yes, she would expect Billy to be glued to her hip but for the chickens to be there too was a real need for concern. She knew Pippa would need them all to be together.

Pippa walked into the kitchen and was nattering away of how lovely the annex was, that she went for a meal on Sunday at the Wild Pheasant with Ruth and George, which was so lovely and made such a nice change. Bev knew she was just chattering to avoid the actual conversation that was needed.

Pippa made the tea as Ruth joined them. The conversation moved on as planned to Bev's holiday. Pippa and Ruth enjoyed hearing about it all, not least as it sounded quite fruity. It was a single's holiday and she had met a chap called Desmond, and much to Bev's joy they would be keeping in touch. Both Pippa and Ruth were genuinely pleased for Bev and wished her all the best.

Karl sent Pippa a polite but official email, which he asked her to get hold of Adam Jenner of Wilkinsons to ask for an agent's valuation of how much The Marshman's was worth. Pippa could then choose. Either she could get further valuations, or they could go with Adam's figure less 15%. This would be used as the figure for him to buy her half share out of The Marshman's. He seemed to have selectively forgotten that Pippa's share was 70%!

He also said that he needed the valuation to take place Monday the following week and while she could come to The Marshman's for the valuation, he was working from home all week so there was no need for her to come to feed the fish. He would see her with the agent just for the valuation but other than that he didn't want to see her, he was worried he may get upset if he saw her.

Pippa called Wilkinsons and booked the appointment with a story they were looking to downsize. Adam was very keen to have The Marshman's on his books. It was a prestigious property in a wonderful location, and he was confident he could turn it around quickly at a very high price. Yes, Yes, Yes thought Adam and arranged for his assistant Michael to accompany him.

With her only chore for the day of booking the estate agent out of the way, Pippa got on with her break, or was it new life, at Ruth's.

Ruth had a busy social calendar, she was very popular due to being a genuinely nice and interesting person. She had her holistic healing center, was an artist, ran an art group and if that wasn't enough, she sang in a rock choir. Ruth was a generous soul and keen for Pippa to join in everything. She thought the distraction would do her good and it certainly could do no harm. Pippa did just that, she enthusiastically joined Ruth in everything.

Pippa would be the first to say she had a fair, but certainly not good singing voice and was relieved to be told there was no voice test required to join the choir. Much to her delight and even greater surprise she was now a full member of Sing, Sing, Sing. She went along with the words and music sheet with the view she would just have a jolly good time, and as the name of the choir said, she would enjoy herself and sing, sing, sing.

Pippa was driving and Ruth was playing a CD of the music they would be singing that afternoon. Pippa was chuckling away as her cousin was totally in her own very special zone. Ru would sing, then correct herself and join into the song but there were times when the song was further along than where Ruth had joined in.

They pulled into the Wherryfields Village Hall, Pippa parked, and they went in. Within minutes or possibly seconds, Ruth had people running up shouting her name and hugging her. Pippa was so pleased to see her cousin so happy and Pippa was proud to see how popular she was.

Debbie, the Choir Director, set up her music system to play the backing music. She gave the brief for the session and all the members enthusiastically sang their part. Halfway through the afternoon they stopped for coffee and cakes. It was all so very gentle, and Pippa wondered why she had not been privy to this side of life before?

On the Sunday Ruth and Pippa drove over to George's house. It was beautiful, a 1940's property with a lovely garden and it was evident that George was a dedicated gardener. They arrived and the four dogs all played in the garden.

Ruth had come down with the most awful cold and Pippa was concerned this was a result of her stay and hoped she wasn't creating extra work or stress for her cousin.

Pippa had been told that the table was booked for two o'clock at a lovely country pub about a mile from George's. They planned to walk the dogs before their lunch and Ruth insisted that the four dogs were still exercised by George and Pippa, but she really didn't feel up to joining them for the walk, she'd stay behind and have a ginger tea.

Off they went along the footpath from George's house with the dogs all excited and happily darting in different directions.

The area was only about thirty miles up the coast from Hepton-on-the-Marshes but the landscape was totally different. It put Pippa in mind of an area of Kent where her and Eddie would holiday each year with Matti's parents in their caravan. She had such lovely memories of those holidays.

While they walked, they talked about the countryside, the problems George was having to deal with on the parish council, what had been a success in his garden this year. Then quite out of the blue he said.

'You do know don't you Pippa, we all have moments in our lives when things seem to go wrong. It doesn't have anything to do with the stupid situation we find ourselves, it's how we deal with it that gets the result and that's all down to the type of person we are. I know you're feeling confused and delicate at the moment, but it will work itself out, you just need to ride the storm. You have good morals and principles. The one thing you NEVER allow yourself to do is to lower your standards, because whatever happens you want to be able to walk anywhere and hold your head high. Do you understand what I'm saying?'

Pippa did understand what George was saying.

They were on their way back, when all of a sudden George excitedly said.

'Hey up, there's Dean down there, he's not caught sight of us yet, play along with this Pippa.'

He looped his arm through hers and they walked towards Dean, smiling sweetly at one another.

As they got to Dean, he said hello to the couple arm in arm and George replied with great surprise in his voice.

'Oh, hello Dean I didn't see you there. How are you, is Stephanie well, how are the horses?'

Dean wasn't interested in any of that he was just staring at Pippa.

'Yes fine, very well in fact, thank you for asking George. Is all good with you and I take it this is your friend?'

George replied, looking at Pippa.

'Most certainly a friend. Got to rush, we need to get the dogs back, we've got a meal booked can't be late for that, we've worked up an appetite. One has to keep ones' sustenance up, don't want my energy levels dropping if you know what I mean.'

Throwing Dean, a wink and a nod as they walked by.

They carried on arm in arm right back to George's where they quickly told Ruth of the trick they had played on Dean. That made her feel better more than the ginger tea. They had another lovely Sunday lunch and more laughter.

Pippa and Ruth had only been back at the farmhouse about twenty minutes and the phone rang, it was a very excited George. He relayed first to Ruth and then Pippa that his phone was a hotline with people from the parish council and the bowls club all asking who the blonde was and was George dating her! George proudly relayed that he answered in his typical Norfolk way.

'I think that's my business, don't you?'

He announced to the cousins that from this moment forward his name would be 'Clooney, George Clooney.' The name stuck.

As arranged on the Monday morning Pippa went over to The Marshman's to show the estate agent Adam and his assistant round. Karl was there and very keen to point out any negatives of the property. Adam simply saying, such a sought-after property such as The Marshman's any negatives were insignificant. Pippa could see Karl was trying to put the price down.

As soon as she saw the agents out and their car pulled off the drive, she went to leave herself and went via Karl's office to say she was now off. He sat at his desk looking very sad and asked.

'When are you coming home?'

This did surprise and throw her, and she tentatively asked.

'Would you like me to come home?'

With his swift reply, in a curt fashion.

'It's up to you not me. You do what you want!'

Not knowing how to reply, she didn't.

Adam sent his quote through that very afternoon and she thanked him saying they would look at his figures and would let him know if they wanted to downsize at this time.

Eddie and Sophie were pleased to see Pippa looking brighter and felt the break had indeed resulted in a positive effect on her wellbeing. She agreed she was feeling stronger in herself and hoped this would help with the recovery from the operation.

A couple of weeks passed in the same lovely calm but busy manner and one morning Ruth was coming back from the chickens.

'Oh goodness me, we are going to have to do something. That little grey one Daisy is being picked on terribly. They have been pecking at her and she is bleeding.'

Ruth and Pippa quickly went straight back to the coup, just as they got near, they could hear poor little Daisy screaming in fear as two of the other hens were pecking at her. As quickly and as safely as she could Pippa entered the coup bending carefully not to aggravate her tummy area and scooped Daisy up. The cousins brought her back down to Ruth's pretty garden area near the farmhouse. Daisy now had her own coup, which was a cat basket filled with straw, this by day was placed with the door open inside the dogs' kennel.

Daisy would walk around the garden and sit on the kitchen windowsill where she would preen herself in the autumn sun, keeping an eye on Pippa and Ruth through the window. At dusk she would take herself to the cat basket and Pippa would pop the door down and wrap a big blanket right round it, to stop any passing rodent chancing its luck when Daisy was placed in the summer house overnight. Without fail, every night and morning Pippa would remind Daisy that she was a lucky and very spoilt chicken, but she was worth every ounce of spoiling.

CHAPTER 16

'A good heart and humble spirit.'

Pippa's oldest friend was Stella. They met when they were five years old and remained firm friends. They could go a year or two without seeing one another with the only contact by email and cards at birthdays and Christmas. But within seconds of meeting again, it was as if they had not been apart. A sign of true friendship they'd say.

Pippa left school at sixteen, but Stella had gone on to take her A Levels, then to University to earn a First Degree in Pure Mathematics.

Unsurprisingly she was accepted as a graduate by a top accountancy firm in London. Within a short period of time, she was in a senior position and despite it being demanding with high expectations and even the hours were 'as much as is required for the job', which translated in reality to sixty hours plus per week, she never stopped studying. Pippa was in awe of her school chum as not only was she the cleverest person she'd ever had the pleasure of meeting she was the sweetest too.

Early that year Pippa dropped Stella an email letting her know she was waiting for an operation and they were then in full and constant communication with Stella giving her friend full support from afar. Arrangements were put in place for Pippa to visit Stella in London late October. The friends planned to see the Memorial Poppy display in the gardens at the Tower of London. Pippa would stay overnight at the home of Stella and her husband Maxwell in the very well healed area of South Kensington. The following day they would go to the Victoria and Albert Museum, have lunch and then Pippa would return on the train. Well, she wouldn't be staying actually at theirs but with their neighbour. Pippa was intrigued to hear that Stella would fully explain when they were together, but she was not to worry as her accommodation was all sorted.

Stella had lived in central London since the age of twenty-seven. She loved the multicultural society and the vibe of the big City. She knew Pippa rarely got out of Norfolk and if it wasn't for a couple of breaks a year, she would never get out of the county so it was important to reassure her she would have a lovely time but ultimately, she would be safe and sound during her break in the Capital.

The week before the visit Pippa emailed Stella to say she was about to book her ticket; was it still OK for her to come? Stella replied straight away saying most definitely, she was so looking forward to having the time together.

Pippa let Stella know when the train ticket was booked, and she would arrive at Liverpool Street at five minutes past ten. Oh, and by the way I'm staying at Ruth's at the moment, been here for the past four weeks. Likewise, I'm so looking forward to having the time together.

Ruth took Pippa to the station and she settled quickly on the train. She was surprised by paying just an extra one pound her seat could be in first class. Strangely this was the first time Pippa had been in first class. Not that surprising possibly as it was over fifteen years since she had been on a train. She chuckled to herself she was a true tourist. It was not long before the trolly dolly came down with a complimentary hot drink and biscuits. Pippa settled back, enjoyed her journey and sat comfortably with her reminiscing.

Before starting up his Expedition Services business, Maxwell had been a lecturer at Cambridge at the same time Stella was taking her mathematics degree and they became close friends, and it was simply and nothing more than that.

For anyone looking at Maxwell they would say he was a solicitor, consultant, or accountant. No one would look at him and say with any stretch of imagination or enthusiasm that he was an explorer as he just did not look the part. He had a squat, stocky frame, no more than five foot five inches tall, receding hair and wore thick rimmed glasses. He had a warm personality which made anyone who met him comfortable in his presence within a short space of time.

Stella and Maxwell continued to be the best and dearest of friends and after eleven years Maxwell awkwardly asked.

'Stella, I know this is an odd thing, well not odd it is possibly the most bizarre thing to say, but you mean so much to me and I hope you will not be offended as I would hate to jeopardize the friendship we have. But do you think. Oh dear, Stella I will start again, I would be honoured, if you could join me, just the two of us, for a meal, on a date.'

Stella was completely shocked. She had always seen Maxwell as a dear friend. She knew she had the greatest affection for him and often thought, if only I could meet someone like Maxwell. But within seconds of these thoughts, they would be dismissed as she assumed his feelings towards her were very much those of a friend no more than that and she would never damage their friendship. She finally found her voice.

'Maxwell, thank you that would be wonderful. I am completely shocked so please forgive me for the lack of words. Shocked in a good way I should add. But all I will say is, the honour would be mine.'

They then both took a deep breath, smiled warmly to each other and inwardly to themselves, as they realised from now their lives would be united and from that moment their bond was the strongest, their love was true and solid.

They married two years later. Even though neither had married before it was held in a registry office. Maxwell was a Jew and Stella would say she was 'spiritual but with no faith' but neither would ever profess their beliefs on anyone, especially not someone they loved.

Stella's brother Kevin and Pippa were witnesses. It was a lovely ceremony and after a meal with Stella's elderly parents and the whole of Maxwell's family it was a wonderful day, oozing love and affection.

Stella had run Maxwell's Expedition Services business with four staff until six years earlier. With the growth and the company becoming global, they now had fully staffed offices in various countries to ensure all was running smoothly. This allowed Stella to carry on with her studies which at that time concentrated on counselling and she worked as a volunteer with the Samaritans. Sadly, what she heard was far too grueling and she had to concede that she was far too sensitive to support others in this way, she was a delicate soul, with a good heart and humble spirit.

When Pippa's train pulled in at Liverpool Street station her friend was waiting for her. Stella was tall and slim; she always had been. She had a sweetheart face with the darkest eyes and curly-bubbly hair, natural dark brown, now with a few streaks of white at the fringe and was currently in a stylish mid bob cut. They greeted with the biggest squeeze. Pippa hadn't realised how relieved she was to be away from her normal environment and knew full well she was safe in the hands of her lovely friend Stella. In turn Stella was so pleased to see her friend and relieved to see she was looking so well, but she sensed all was not right.

Stella had the Oyster cards ready, and they quickly got to Tower Hill on the tube.

Stella was desperate to catch up on all the news of Eddie and Sophie's wedding as she and Maxwell had been away on a work commitment to New Zealand and could not join them. When Pippa sent through the photos, she yearned for missing both the wedding and being back in Upper Hepton, as since her parents moved to a retirement flat in Fulham, the only time Stella went to the area was to visit Pippa.

This was the first time since their wedding that Pippa had visited them. As any visits were made by Stella and Maxwell to Norfolk, staying at Churchside and then The Marshman's. Pippa always enjoyed being a good hostess, but she was now thinking she should have made the effort to visit her friends.

Pippa was keen to hear how Stella and Maxwell were keeping, she always felt comforted in the knowledge that their life and their love was such a wonderful success story. She was always amazed to hear about the Expedition Services, it was so interesting and unique. Pippa loved anything to do with the countryside, sea, wildlife and in particular the descriptions of the landscapes enthralled her.

Stella wasted no time in explaining where Pippa's accommodation for the night would be. Up to six years earlier their home in South Kensington had been their main office. They had adapted two of the upstairs bedrooms knocking them through to one large room. This office room was still used and had PC's running twenty-four hours of the day to keep track of the global business. This was the reason why they didn't have guests stay at theirs as all the flashing and beeping would wake even the deepest sleeper.

Stella was saying their neighbour, Nancy, had been looking to move as she wanted, or should she say needed, to release some capital. Stella moved swiftly into action and suggested to Maxwell she had a plan to avoid Nancy having to sell. If they rented a room for a year, paying the money up front, Nancy would not need to move, and they could keep their neighbour. After all, they often said how awful it would it be if ever they had to put up with different neighbours as Nancy was so quiet. Renting a room would also mean when friends or family stayed, they would not need to sleep on the sofa bed in the lounge, it seemed a great solution.

The arrangement was put in place, Nancy was paid the money, and it was agreed that she would be told the dates and details of guests to prepare the room ready for their stay. All Stella needed to do was to provide two lots of bedding, so Nancy had a change in place ready to launder in between any guests. Perfect!

Stella went on to say, Nancy was an interesting person; Blue blood, but sadly due to addictions she had blown most of her money. Thankfully she had turned her life around. Stella was very fond of her and would join her and her little dog Jessie for walks to the park and they had become very close. Oh, and by the way Nancy was a Shaman, a witch, but a good one! To which they both laughed.

When they arrived at The Tower of London the number of tourists was overwhelming, yet despite the numbers everyone was in a respectful, thoughtful and generous spirit. The friends took photos of themselves, the Tower and in particular they took numerous photos of the Poppies, they were moved by the sight.

They walked over to a little restaurant for lunch and were lucky as a table for two just became available, with the most perfect view of The Tower. They both ordered marinated Tofu in a pot of noodles and Stella suggested a bottle of Gavi, which Pippa eagerly went along with, not that she'd had it before, but it was a white wine, she didn't drink red, but most importantly she was now keen to try different experiences.

They had both been vegetarians since the age of thirteen having seen a news article on Japanese whale hunting and they both decided, whilst to the best of their knowledge they'd never eaten whale, they would become vegetarians. Both sets of parents thought it was a phase they would grow out of, but no, the resolve to not eat meat had been set.

The wine was brought to the table and Stella poured a glass for each of them.

'Right, so what's going on, why are you staying at Ruth's?'

Pippa started along her normal line of she didn't know what was going on, so she didn't really know what to say. Before she knew it that barrier had been removed and by the time their noodles were eaten, and they were on their second glass of wine she started to confide in Stella. Pippa told of the changes in her husband's behavior. Some of the bizarre things that he'd done; him not wanting to go to the wedding, the letter he handed her after taking the money and then clearing off, him not wanting her to go on holiday and the blank ticket and the stupid email he sent to the solicitor. After she had been away from The Marshman's for one weekend all sign of her ever having lived there had been removed and then as if that wasn't bad enough, she knew she had been replaced by the evidence she had found in the bathroom. Pippa finished saying she'd been to a solicitor and started divorce proceedings as it was obvious Karl's heart was elsewhere and she needed to accept their marriage was over.

Stella let her friend speak without interruption and was grateful for her training in counselling, for nothing could have prepared her for hearing her dear friend's horrendous time.

'Oh Pippa, you have been through the mill and I'm not talking about the disturbing things you have just told me. You have had a horrible year with your health, and

I cannot even start to understand how you have dealt with all this on top of that. I cannot believe life could get any harder than what you've been through so take time to recharge, take control of your life and enjoy it to the full.'

Pippa took a deep breath grateful for her friend's words.

'Right, that's enough of this maudlin talk, I haven't cried since that bloomin' awful night in Corfu and I'm not starting now. I've been looking forward to this trip so much, as you say let's enjoy life to the full.'

Looking into her lovely friend's face she smiled to try and reassure her.

They went for a walk, taking in more sights before arriving at Stella and Maxwell's house. Pippa knew it was beautiful from the photos she had been sent over the years and she had also looked at the property on Streetview, but to see it in real life was a delight. It was an Edwardian mid terraced property in a quiet tree lined road. When they walked through the gate into the small pretty front garden Pippa felt a wonderful sense of serenity.

Stella was chattering away as she opened the unusually wide front door, painted in the shiniest white gloss Pippa had ever seen. The mahogany staircase was impressive, but it was the original parquet flooring which went through the hall and open plan lounge that stole the show, it was stunning. In the lounge the front windows had wooden shutters and there was a gorgeous fireplace. French doors to the rear led out to the wonderful garden full of trees, shrubbery, flowers and the birds were bobbing about singing.

Stella told the story of how they found the property. They visited this house after looking at so many before, but none had the right feel. As soon as they walked in, she knew this was the one for them and Maxwell happily agreed.

The house had suffered a direct hit in the back garden during the second world war in the blitz and as a result the rear of the property had been damaged, and an extension was added in the repairs. So it was even more surprising that the parquet flooring, staircase, wooden shutters and fireplace had survived.

They sat and chattered about happy things, there was plenty of laughter and Stella ordered a Thai meal to be delivered at seven. All this seemed a million miles away from the life Pippa had grown accustomed, and she realised in the last few weeks she had become used to not only being spoilt with nice meals and company but had got back to feeling relaxed when she was talking, she was no longer walking on eggshells, she could talk and not justify why she had said something.

The evening sped by and when Maxwell came through the door at nine, he was so pleased to see Pippa and the hug was solid and heartfelt. Stella had confided to him of her fears that all was not well. Pippa was staying at Ruth's which confirmed what she thought when Karl was in none of Eddie and Sophie's wedding photos.

Pippa was pleased to see Stella and Maxwell's attitude to one another, it was as if they had fallen in love only the day before. Their love was genuine, fresh and on show for all to see. They spoke to each other with true respect and were interested to hear what the other was saying, it was so wonderful to see.

The three of them were all chattering and catching up with life and before they knew it, the time was eleven. Stella said with a fright.

'Oh my goodness, we have been talking so much I forgot to take you round to Nancy to introduce you, best I get you to your room.'

Pippa said goodbye to Maxwell, picked up her haversack and Stella led the way next door with the keys in her hand. Stella was whispering as they walked round. As soon as they got through Nancy's gate Pippa felt an awful foreboding, a feeling she had never felt before, it was so oppressive she nearly turned round to return to Stella's, but her friend was whispering away with the keys in her hands.

'These locks are a bit fickle and need to be done in a certain way.'

Stella was turning the numerous locks and had all but given up, saying with a sigh.

'Right if they don't work this time, don't worry you will be at ours, sorry but it will need to be on the sofa bed in the lounge, no one could put up with the flashing and incessant humming of the PC's.'

Pippa was thinking please, please don't open, and the door opened!

The foreboding she felt at the gate was nothing compared to the feeling she felt when she looked in through the hall. There could not be two properties next door to one another so different as Nancy's and Stella's. This difference wasn't just from the ambience but the appearance too, even the stair carpet at Nancy's was threadbare. Just at that moment Stella looked up the stairs saying with surprise.

'Oh, hello Nancy, I'm really sorry if we disturbed you, please go back to bed, I'll see Pippa in.'

Pippa looked up the dark stairs and there was a painfully thin woman standing at the top with a strange looking creature by her side. Pippa strained her eyes and worked out it was a tiny whippet dog. Nancy's appearance wasn't helped at all by the white calf length nightie and straggly white hair. Pippa was terrified. Nancy didn't speak, and Stella's voice was still whispering but now in a worried tone.

'Come on Pippa, up we go.'

They walked up the stairs, Stella going first. Pippa almost being dragged behind her. The only light came from the streetlight through the window next to the front door and as they were going up the stairs Pippa caught sight of a large painting. She could see it was the inside of a church and she thought straight away it was in the style of an old Methodist church with the wooden balcony and at the center of the picture was a man, in modern day clothing, on a crucifix and either side of him was a dark ghostly type being.

Stella was at the top of the stairs and walked into the bedroom straight ahead at the top of the landing. She put on the light and went to the window to close the venetian blind, but she struggled, it was clearly broken and the best she managed was half open and half shut with some of the broken slats hanging. Stella did her hostess with the mostess best, whispering.

'Here's the kettle, tea, milk, water, cups, the bathroom is the first door on your right, and I'll see you in the morning, just come back round when you're ready, no rush. Nighty-Night.'

Then she gave Pippa a hug and kiss goodnight, and as an afterthought quietly said.

'Oh, best you have the front door key, goodness me, the key rings got a big letter P on it, it's meant for you.'

With that she was down the stairs on the way back to her house.

Pippa stood in fear, she had never been so scared in all her life. She had always lived in the middle of the country, she could walk out in the pitch dark and not be scared and here she was trembling with fear.

Stella's words of come round when you're ready echoed in her mind, blinken' heck she wanted to be there now, never mind in the morning for breakfast! The coincidence of the key ring having the initial of her name on it, far from reassured her filled her with trepidation.

At that moment her phone rang and made her jump, she answered it and it was Stella, asking if she could go downstairs and lock the door as the key had been left with Pippa, she couldn't lock up. Pippa ran like the wind down the stairs, locked the door and on the way back up caught sight of the painting of the crucifix again.

She ran straight to the bathroom for a pee, thinking sod a wash and brush my teeth, I'll forgo them tonight.

She returned quickly to her bedroom and didn't take her clothes off, she just got straight in bed and lay with the cover up to her neck nervously looking around the room, scared to turn the bedside light off.

The walls were painted white, with three large, framed pictures of charcoal drawings. The one to Pippa's right was of a church and churchyard and there were spirit figures coming from the graves. The second was the outline of a person with a cross going through the body with spirits around it. The third she couldn't work out at first what it was and as she stared, she could see it was witches on broom sticks.

She took a deep breath thinking, it will be a miracle if I get a wink of sleep tonight and thank goodness I'm not a virgin as I dread to think what on earth would happen to me. She told herself to pull herself together, just have happy thoughts and she thought of Eddie, Sophie, Ruth and of course her wonderful Billy.

Pippa fell straight to sleep and didn't stir until just after seven o'clock. She couldn't believe she'd slept through, she started to look around the room. Yes, without a doubt it was as she had seen it the night before, the scary pictures and the broken blind at the window. When fully awake she retrieved her phone from under her pillow where it had been strategically placed should she need it in the night.

She checked the phone and she'd received two texts. One from Eddie and Sophie saying they hoped she was having a lovely time away, give their love to Stella and Maxwell and the second text from Ruth with virtually the same words with the addition that Billy was fine but missing his mum. Ruth attached a photo she'd taken in the afternoon of the three dogs in the garden, center of attention sitting proudly between the dogs was Daisy the chicken.

Pippa went to the bathroom and showered, totally embarrassed that the night before she couldn't even bring herself to brush her teeth. She went back into the bedroom, stripped the duvet and covers off the bed and folded them in a neat pile ready for washing and started to creep down the stairs, as she didn't want to disturb Nancy.

She was halfway down the stairs and in line with the dark painting of the man on the crucifix in the church hall and she heard Nancy call from the kitchen.

'Hi Pippa, will you be back later on tonight, how long are you staying dear.'

Pippa went through to the kitchen and there was Jessie, the whippet dog, laying in a bed full of cushions looking like the princess and the pea. Nancy was at the worktop wearing an old bottle green dressing gown, still looking awful and painfully thin.

Nancy came and hugged her guest and Pippa confirmed her stay was just for last night, thanked her for everything and hoped her late arrival hadn't disturbed her too much. Nancy said that she was welcome as often as she wanted or possibly needed as she'd got the impression from Stella that Pippa's stay was open ended and for her to keep the door key in case she was ever in the area and needed somewhere to stay. If she turned up and Stella's room already had a guest Nancy would make sure Pippa had somewhere to stay for the night.

As she was talking Pippa glanced round the kitchen and was very surprised as it was modern and of good quality. Again, it was the framed pictures on the walls that caught her eye. These had all been drawn by Nancy of when she was in Africa, they were very good and colourful. It was as if the kitchen were light and happy, and the rest of what Pippa had seen was dark and sad.

Nancy spoke for quite a while. She was a nice, kind, very interesting person and Pippa could see why Stella and Maxwell were keen to keep her as a neighbour and a friend. Pippa said goodbye and returned to Stella's.

Again, as she went through Stella's gate, she felt the peace and serenity. The kitchen table was laden with wonderful healthy food choices, Radio Three was quietly on in the background playing choral music. Stella greeted her and was chattering away, saying they could take their time over breakfast, but after she would pop upstairs to place her online food shop on one of the office computers, with that out of the way they would be free for their visit to the Victoria and Albert Museum.

They sat and certainly did take their time over breakfast. When they finished Stella went upstairs to place the online grocery order. Pippa took herself into the back lounge and sat down on the sofa by the large stylish coffee table and flicked through the books of art, mindfulness, cookery and yoga. Yes, if you could sum Stella up in a collection of books, these would be exactly what she would have chosen. Stella wasn't long on her grocery order and when she walked in said.

'Right, that's the shopping done, have you managed to entertain yourself?'

Before long they were happily chattering and on their way to the tube station and the museum for the next part of their day, which sped by in a flash.

Stella reluctantly saw Pippa off at Liverpool Street station and they hugged long and hard. Stella didn't want to let her friend go as she knew she still had a hard slog on her hands. Pippa was also reluctant, she really didn't want to have to deal with the challenge which she knew she had to face.

Stella insisted that Pippa keep the Oyster card and the key to Nancy's house and if ever Pippa needed or wanted a change of scenery she should just turn up. Billy was also welcome, but he would stay with her and Maxwell because Jessie may just be a little jealous of the big black and tan bundle of love.

Pippa comfortably settled into her reserved seat. She chose a cup of tea from the trolly dolly and sat deep in her thoughts of the wonderful trip, the conversations she'd had and grateful in the knowledge of how lucky she was to have such wonderful family and friends.

She thought how Stella and Maxwell looked and spoke to each other with such love and respect with Stella's words ringing in her ears 'We were friends for years so knew each other fully before we became lovers.'

Pippa didn't know anything about Karl with the exception that as a child he had an orange chopper bike and his father was a strong Labour supporter, hence his son's name being Karl Mark [Marx] Taylor. On a Sunday evening his mum would go in the tin bath in the kitchen, then his dad, followed by all the kids and Karl being the youngest was last.

Pippa had been brought up in the country, she never thought they were classed as posh, but they had a proper bathroom, so it seemed strange that anyone a couple of years older than her had to go in a tin bath in the kitchen with water eighth hand!

Perhaps that was part of the problem, she had fallen in love with someone she didn't know. She had friends who said that they thought they knew their husbands until something had gone wrong and then, they realised they didn't know them at all.

For Pippa her husband had never let her know anything about him, he could have said anything about his past she wouldn't have been the wiser as he made sure she didn't have any contact with anyone or anything from his previous life to contradict his version of events.

Karl's only friend Hew, admittedly a contact she'd always been precious to protect and encourage. When they stayed over in Thetford Karl was always keen to hear Hew speak about his work in reproduction furniture, making Pippa wonder if he was thinking about changing from his work in modular buildings to a completely different area. Karl's conversation was only about the two-month period he and Hew worked together and never about anything personal. The only personal things discussed were what Pippa, Hew and Jeanette spoke of. Karl would always appear to agree, and look interested at what they were saying but he never made any contribution.

Possibly it wasn't just Pippa who didn't know Karl, she wondered if he even knew himself.

CHAPTER 17

'What doesn't kill you makes you stronger'

Pippa walked out of Norwich station, looked across to the car park and saw Ruth waiting ready to take her home.

Pippa quickly got to the car, opened the passenger door, smiled at her cousin who smiled back saying.

'Taxi'

They both laughed. Ruth drove them home and quickly ran through what she'd been up to, how good Billy had been, that Daisy the chicken was now completely in charge of the garden and the dogs knew it, well come to think of it, Ruth did too!

As soon as they got through the farmhouse back door, they were greeted with a full-on fluffy cuddle of dogs excited to see them. Billy made sure he was at the front of the pack to welcome the love of his life back into the fold.

Ruth put the kettle on, and they sat in the kitchen catching up on how Stella and Maxwell were and Pippa's wonderful trip away. It was quite late when Pippa said she'd go into the annex and unpack her things. Billy took himself through with his mistress.

It was lovely to walk into the annex lounge, the lamps had all been popped on ready to welcome her home and she noticed Ruth had been in and changed some of her paintings around, with one she had not seen before on the wall above the sideboard where most of Pippa's photos of her special people were. She went to take a closer look at the painting.

It was of a Norfolk Broads landscape, the skyline was beautiful, she could see it was at dawn with a lovely warmth of the sun coming through from the east. To her amazement it was of all the places Pippa had a special connection with.

It was as if she were looking out from her kitchen at The Marshman's. To the left was the hedging and tree line, some of Pippa's garden, then the fields of Upper Hepton leading into the reed beds and the river at Bagby in the distance. To the right of the painting was a church and she could see the distinct tower of St John's where her special people were resting. There was one solitary swan flying in from the east, its wings wide and it was so graceful. She wondered if the swan was supposed to be her.

Pippa was still looking when Ruth came through to the annex with another cup of tea for each of them.

'I hope you like it, it's for you.'

'Ruth its beautiful, thank you. You've managed to get everywhere I hold dear in one picture yet in life they're miles apart, you're so clever, when did you paint it?'

Ruth had been painting it since Pippa's arrival. Her art studio was actually the entrance hall, but the front door was hardly used, and the light was perfect from early morning to late afternoon with natural light from the dual aspect windows it was the perfect place to paint. Each time she went off to the studio she would say she was working on a very special commissioned painting.

Pippa carefully hugged Ruth as she juggled their mugs of tea and nodded her head in the direction of the sideboard.

'There's post on the side for you.'

Pippa tore herself away from the beautiful painting, picked up the post and sat down. She sighed when she started to look at the envelopes and thumbed through them, there was a large official looking envelope.

'Oh no, this isn't for me, it's been redirected here by mistake, it's addressed to Karl, it's obviously the divorce papers as it's from the Courts.'

They decided they would finish their tea and deliver it to The Marshman's, hopefully Karl would be away. Ruth insisted on going with Pippa. So off they went.

Pippa slowly pulled on the drive to The Marshman's, and Karl's Jaguar was sitting on the driveway, so she tried to reverse as quietly as she could back down the drive and pulled up further along the road. She got out of the car and as she did Ruth said in her normal strong voice.

'Thankfully you're under the cover of darkness dear you shouldn't be seen. Keep quiet, covert operation under way.'

With that they both burst out into laughter which they fought hard to suppress. Pippa still finding it difficult not to laugh put her finger to her mouth saying.

'Ssshhhh.'

Pippa quickly put the letter in the post box and returned to the car. As she drove them back, they couldn't stop laughing and they were saying they really shouldn't be finding it so funny, but Ruth kept repeating.

'Thankfully, cover of darkness, keep quiet, covert operation under way'

Which they found hysterical.

The following day Ruth phoned George first thing as she was keen to tell him all about last night's manoeuvres.

Pippa was still on sick leave, Dr Newcome had signed her off for two more months and reiterated she needed to be a 'patient patient' as it was something only time could heal.

It seemed strange that she was still on sick leave as she was busy and enjoying life, she was joining Ruth at various activities, going over for meals at Eddie's and Sophies and meeting Bev. The only physical problem she had was that she couldn't sit upright for very long without this causing her great discomfort. She would sit in a slightly reclined position. A sitting position she knew she couldn't adopt whilst at work in the branch and most definitely not at the counter!

When Pippa went to Ruth's for her break, she hadn't brought too much with her as she hadn't wanted to tempt fate. She'd returned to get some more clothes, but the back door key had been removed from under the boot scrapper. This must have been the door Karl was going in and out from as all the other doors had been fully secured and bolted from the inside and the only key Pippa didn't have was the one for the back door.

She'd contacted Karl asking if she could pop round for some things, but when he replied he didn't answer the question, instead he would write long and lengthy of how she hadn't realised how lucky she'd been to have the life he gave her, and she was obviously regretting her selfish action in moving out.

One morning at breakfast Pippa asked Ruth if she wanted to join her on a shopping trip. What with the change in the season she needed a few things to see her through until she could get her own clothes, so planned on going to some charity shops. Off they went and were delighted with their purchases. Pippa had a couple of warmer outfits appropriate for the late autumn season.

At the next choir practice both cousins were proudly wearing a new outfit, well it was a new outfit to them. Ruth bubbly told everyone of their successful charity shop trip.

The choir practices were twice a week and there was one song that was always rehearsed. Each time Pippa would get to a certain part in the song she would have a big lump in her throat, and had to stay quiet, she hoped no one noticed. It was a song by Keane 'Somewhere Only We Know'. The words felt so personal to Pippa, she knew all she'd wanted for over a year was for her husband to look, talk, touch and above all be kindly and loving to her.

She just wanted him to scoop her up and take her to their special place and for them to talk and everything to be as it was before he shut her out of his life.

But today, the intro of the music started, and Pippa was looking at the song sheet and she couldn't even mouth the words, she was overwhelmed. The choir sung it so beautifully and all she could do was to stand and listen to the words.

The part where Pippa always struggled came and she hoped she wouldn't start crying. She just listened as the choir sang.

'... Is this the place we used to love, is this the place I've been dreaming of. Oh simple thing where have you gone? I'm getting old and I need something to rely on. So tell me when you're gonna let me in, I'm getting tired and I need somewhere to begin ....'

By the time the song had come to an end, still nothing came out for she had no voice and was looking down to her left hand and the third finger where her wedding ring used to be.

Whilst she drove them home Pippa opened up to Ruth that she was struggling singing 'Somewhere Only We Know', as she always lost her voice due to the overwhelming emotion that she felt. She'd hoped the more she read the words she'd become less sensitive but quite the contrary and today she was totally overwhelmed and didn't know how she fought back the tears. Ruth quietly listened and after a respectful moment or two asked.

'Do you think it would help to have a cry, you've been bottling it all up for so long and my dear little Pip it may help.'

Ruth herself was crying as she could feel the hurt her cousin was going through.

Pippa quietly drove them home, swallowing hard, but she couldn't allow herself to cry. The truth was she was scared that once the floodgates were opened, they would never stop.

When Matti died, she felt her heart had broken and was numb but knew she couldn't crumble, she had to carry on for Eddie. Now she felt her heart had broken again, she even had a physical pain in her chest in the area of her heart. But this was different, as unlike the awful sudden closure from a bereavement there was a horrible on-going torment. A pang of hope that Karl would realise he loved his wife and say he was sorry for everything that had happened, and they would have their lives back. But she feared that wasn't going to happen.

The following Sunday they were over at George's, they took the dogs for a walk and then on for dinner at a restaurant just down the way from George's house. It had been booked for over two weeks and the cousins could see he was looking forward to it, very much. He told Pippa that both he and Ruth had been there many times and never had a bad meal. He went on to describe the set up. They would be served at their table with their drinks and be given a ticket to take to the carvery area to collect their meal. He'd forewarned the restaurant that Pippa was a veggie, so she needn't worry she wasn't going to be causing any mischief. To which they all laughed.

The Hackfield Cock like so many, had been a pub that completely turned into a restaurant, and while dated in style, it was very popular. When they arrived, the car park was heaving so it wasn't only George that rated their Sunday roasts. They ordered their drinks, were given their tickets and asked if they wouldn't mind waiting about twenty minutes as the chef needed to get Pippa's meal sorted.

'Well, there was me thinking you wouldn't cause mischief and you have. I'll use my time wisely and go to the gents. Excuse me ladies.'

As soon as George was out of the way, Ruth lent towards Pippa across the table saying.

'You do know we are soon to be joined at the table by George Clooney. I've just spotted a few of the people over there who are on the Hackfield Parish Council. Fair to say our George is going to be in his element.'

They both chuckled.

Sure enough when George returned he was smiling broadly, shoulders back with a spring in his step ready to further enhance his reputation as the Stud of Hackfield out at lunch with the mystery blonde. He moved his chair just a tad closer to Pippa's, lined his cutlery into position and they all giggled.

The meal was certainly delicious. They had just ordered their puddings when all of a sudden Pippa had a thought, she didn't know from where it came but it was there in a flash.

There was a spare back door key in the summer house. She'd hidden it there years earlier and completely forgot about it. She told Ruth and George what she had just remembered and that she would pop over the following evening and if Karl was away, she would get the key and let herself in to take more of her clothes.

Ruth excitedly asked.

'Do you want me to come with you dear? Oh, you could wear your nice mac the one we got at the charity shop, it's so lovely.'

As she threw the brown mac on the back of Pippa's chair an admiring glance.

George couldn't believe his ears saying straight away in disbelief.

'Good grief, you come out with some rubbish, here she is going on another covert operation as if she wants you to join her. You nearly broke her cover last time and as if it matters what's she wearing to go into the summer house.'

They all burst into hysterics of laughter and the conversation then took the direction of Pippa in true James Bond style, making her clandestine entry to get more of her clothes.

Ruth was very pleased, finally her cousin was getting a backbone. Pippa was told by her solicitor that she should have access to The Marshman's, and he really couldn't deny her access let alone prevent her from popping in to get a few belongings.

The following evening meal was planned to be early so Pippa could get to The Marshman's for six. George phoned to wish her luck with the operation, and she laughed when he asked her to synchronize watches.

When she pulled up onto The Marshman's drive she was shocked to see Karl's Jaguar parked in its normal place and an additional small old car parked in Pippa's usual spot on the drive. She stopped the car and took stock of the situation. She knew she couldn't sneak around the back to retrieve the key, should she leave and go back to Ruth's, or should she just go up to the front door and as he had company surely, he would be on his best behaviour and let her get a few things?

She made her decision; she was going to ring the doorbell. She had come prepared with a holdall with some carrier bags tucked inside and picked them up with her mobile phone and walked up the drive.

She was in line with their bedroom window, and as The Marshman's was a single storey cottage this was on the ground floor. She stopped in horror as she could hear a woman's voice loudly moaning 'More, more, that's it, aaaggghhh, aaaaggghhh, that's it, that's it, keep going. Yeesss!'

Pippa froze, she couldn't believe it. She quietly walked back down to the car where she sat and stayed for about half an hour. She finally came to her senses as she realised she was very cold. To her surprise she picked up her car keys and phone, marching up to the big oak front door and rang the doorbell.

To her greater surprise Karl rushed to open the door, he seemed keen that someone had visited him. He was standing there in a tee-shirt and pyjama bottoms!

She assertively said,

'Hi, I'm glad you're in, I need some things.'

She walked straight past him into the hall. He answered bewildered.

'But what sort of things do you need?'

She didn't answer and carried on walking through the hall and went straight to their bedroom with Karl quickly following behind. There was lady's jewellery on her bedside table, ladies' clothes on her stool and next to it an overnight case on the floor.

Pippa looked him straight in the face and asked.

'May I know your friends name?'

He didn't hesitate in his reply.

'She's called Tracy.'

Pippa refrained from asking if this was his friend that liked watching football the first weekend his wife was away. She carried on through to the lounge. There was a woman sitting on the sofa in a dressing gown, holding a mug of tea to her lips. She was shocked when Pippa walked in and even more so when she confidently walked forward to the opposite sofa, sitting down and simply said.

'Hi Tracy I'm Pippa, no doubt my husband hasn't told you much about me.'

Tracy said sheepishly in a deep raspy smoker's voice.

'Hello Pippa, no he hasn't said about you.'

Putting the mug back to her mouth. Karl came in and sat next to Tracy and furiously spat,

'What do you want Pippa?'

'I need some of my clothes and as you haven't replied to any of my polite requests, I thought I'd come when you were here. Apologies I didn't realise you had company.'

Karl used the opportunity to have a whinge saying Pippa hadn't realised how good she'd had it with him, blah, blah, blah and went on and on like a broken record.

Pippa sat and looked at Tracy who in turn was looking up at her beau, still with the mug close to her mouth. Pippa was interested to see Tracy's body language change. First Tracy was looking at Karl, and as he was mid-rant, she turned towards Pippa and pulled a face of what is he going on about, shrugged her shoulders and moved a little away from him and crossed her bare legs turning them away from Karl towards Pippa.

Karl was still harping on how wonderful he'd been and how badly she'd treated him. Pippa wasn't even listening she was more interested in this woman who'd replaced her. She was a totally different look than what she'd imaged. She'd correctly guessed the hair length from the hairs she'd found in the bath, it was very thin and chin length. She was free of make-up, plain and quite common looking. She was probably a similar age to Pippa but had the appearance of someone who'd had a hard life. On her right leg which was now turning towards Pippa there was a large angry varicose vein.

Strangely she felt sorry for her, until she realised the dressing gown Tracy was wearing was Pippa's! She had spilt a blob of nail varnish on the front which she couldn't get out. This now served as a signature to identify it as Pippa's.

Finally, Pippa had seen enough of Tracy, and certainly had more than enough of listening to Karl ranting rubbish. He stopped when she interrupted him, assertively saying.

'As you have company shall we organise a time that would be suitable for you so I can collect some of my clothes?'

'What? OK Thursday at eleven you have two hours, no more. I don't trust that you won't clear the house. I know what you're like!'

Pippa selected the camera setting on her mobile phone, looked at them both, saying.

'Let's get a photo of you two Love Birds. Smile.'

She took the picture, stood up and turning to Tracy said.

'Strange to say, but I am pleased to have met you.'

With that she left. As soon as she was in her car, she sent Ruth a text simply saying ... Blank Ticket has a name, its Tracy ... and attached the photo of the shocked couple.

Ruth could not believe her eyes seeing the photo nor her ears when she heard the story. She hugged her cousin and praised her for the bravery she showed. George phoned and heard the story from Ruth and asked to speak to Pippa.

'Well done young lady, you held your head high, you kept your respect and you've now got a proper time to go to the house and collect what you want, get organised and make a list.'

The following morning when Pippa woke, she checked her emails and there was one from Karl. He was furious that she had embarrassed herself, she should be ashamed and how dare she humiliate him in such a way in front of his friends, she was a disgrace!

That was it, the barrier was lifted and the floodgates opened. When Ruth called her through for breakfast she didn't come. It was brought to her and Ruth left her to her privacy but checked on her a few times with mugs of tea in hand. Pippa was slumped on the sofa with a blanket over her and was completely beside herself.

Ruth insisted that she joined her at the kitchen table for their evening meal and when Pippa came through Ruth was relieved to see she'd made an effort, in fact she looked wonderful. Pippa was wearing a nice dress, black opaque tights, she had put on her make up and her hair had been straightened.

'Are you going out dear?'

'No, I thought that's it, enough of this crying. I've got a wonderful life, great family and friends and I'm not going to allow this to spoil me. Apart from anything else I need my strength to recover from that bloomin operation. I've known so many people when they've gone through a divorce, they've become bitter and I will not allow that to happen to me.'

'Good, well done it's in our family never to let things get us down. As the saying goes, what doesn't kill you makes you stronger.'

Pippa was looking forward to her appointment at eleven on Thursday, she had her bags ready and a list of things she wanted to take back with her. She didn't want to overload the wardrobe in the annex, but she knew she needed to be sensible just in case time dragged on to the spring and summer.

When she arrived at The Marshman's she went straight round the back and the key was under the boot scrapper. She opened the door and then quickly rushed over to the summerhouse and located the spare back door key. She tested to see if it worked and was relieved it did, popping it in her purse for safe keeping.

Pippa went to the dressing room, going through the list of clothes she wanted to take. She neatly put them in a pile ready to bag up. There were some of her work trousers she couldn't find so went into the guest room to look in the wardrobes there and found them.

On the outside of the wardrobe was a pair of Karl's going out trousers and a shirt. On another hanger was a lady's party dress, it must be Tracy's! Pippa picked it up and looked at it. She took it back to the dressing room. Held it up against her looking in the mirror and before she knew it, she had put it on! She was pleased with the result as it was snug on her bust and loose on the hips, so obviously Tracy was not as girly as she was. She quickly put on a pair of her heels, ran her fingers through her hair, looked into the long mirror, smiled and took photos of herself. Then quickly slipped it off.

She was about to pop her clothes back on and a wicked thought crossed her mind.

She chuckled to herself as she gently took the lining of the dress, dropped her knickers and wiped her fanny with the dress lining, twice for good measure. She popped it

191

back thinking none will be the wiser, only me. She was going to always hold her head high but if she could do it with a wicked smile all the better.

She finished collecting her things and couldn't be bothered to look round her home as it certainly didn't feel as if she'd ever had any association with it. She locked up, returned the key under the boot scrapper and drove back to the annex still wearing the wicked smile on her face.

She showed Ruth the photos she had taken of her in Tracy's dress and sent one to George who replied straight back.

'Not you at all Pippa, it looks far too tarty. You're more Mary Hopkins.'

Pippa read the text out loud and looking at Ruth.

'Blinken Mary Hopkins, I want to be someone sexy!'

To which they both laughed.

Ruth went onto the iPad and brought up photos of Mary Hopkins. Pippa looked at them.

'On second thoughts I'm very happy to be likened to her. Well done George good suggestion.'

Ruth quickly went on You Tube and played Mary Hopkins signing the song 'Goodbye'.

They both pranced around, arms waving in time with the music, singing at the top of their voices with the dogs all laying in their beds sighing at the thought of their afternoon sleep being majorly disturbed.

The following week Karl contacted Pippa and asked if they could meet for a coffee and she agreed.

When she arrived at the Willow Café, Karl was already waiting. He'd ordered his coffee and her tea which were put on the table together with some fruit scones, butter and jam within minutes of Pippa sitting down. She thought either he wants to get the meeting out of the way quickly or he's trying to make a good impression. It turned out to be the latter.

He thanked her for agreeing to meet him and said when he saw her on Monday evening, she looked gorgeous, and he couldn't understand why he'd acted towards her as he had. He loved her so much, she was his world and could she stop the divorce and please come home.

Pippa was taken aback. She had to stop herself from saying yes, I'll go and get Billy. But she knew she would never get this opportunity again, she needed to have a few questions answered. Trying to look in control she took her time, finally saying.

'Karl that's good to hear, but I have to say you look absolutely awful.'

He went on to say he'd had the most awful bout of food poisoning. He'd bought a filled chicken baguette from the deli counter at a butcher's shop, and it must have been contaminated with raw meat. He'd lost so much weight, if Pippa thought he looked bad now, good job she hadn't seen him two weeks before he was like the walking dead.

Pippa felt justified hearing this, hoping it caused a problem for him trying to have sex with Tracy and needing to keep stopping to run to the loo!

'Karl, I don't think you will ever know how much you hurt me. I could never have imagined anyone being so horrible to someone let alone someone they loved and when that someone is ill, it beggar's belief. I need to know how long this has been going on with Tracy, do you have feelings for her, and can I trust you to be honest with me in the future?'

Karl put his head in his hands, took a deep breath pulled himself together and explained that he had only started with Tracy the day after Pippa had moved out. The Thursday when she'd said she needed the break he paid to go on a dating site. He'd had loads of women to choose from, he had online conversations with several and decided to meet Tracy and a woman called Arlene. He was actually seeing them both and no he didn't have feelings for either of them he just wanted the company as he was desperately lonely.

Arlene hadn't been to The Marshman's, but he had been to hers which was an impressive property in Cromer. She was a widow, had her own recruiting business and was more in Karl's league, presented herself well but she was bossy.

The reason Tracy had been to The Marshman's was her two daughters and their boyfriends were still at home and anyway, from what she said of the area it sounded a grotty house not somewhere he would want to visit. She worked as a cleaner in a hotel. She was divorced and was well experienced in the bedroom department as she'd had several short and long-term partners since her divorce, all the guys sounded control freaks.

Karl was feeling very sorry for himself. All the time Pippa was away no one had contacted him, it was the most

194

horrible time. He wanted to reassure her she could trust him to be honest with her in the future. He would never want to lose her again and that is why he'd come clean about Arlene so that she knew everything of what had happened as he didn't want any skeletons in the cupboard.

'Me and Billy will move back tomorrow.'

Ruth helped Pippa pack her things to take back. But when Ruth went to take the painting off the wall to wrap it in bubble wrap Pippa stopped her and asked if she could leave it there, together with some things in the wardrobe, just for a while.

'Of course dear, that's no problem at all.'

But she thought that didn't sound as if Pippa was confident that she was returning to The Marshman's for good.

Whilst Pippa had been relieved to hear what Karl had said in the coffee shop, Ruth felt all his answers were about him and he hadn't said sorry for anything. She thought the reason he hadn't gone to Tracy's had nothing to do with the daughters, but because as he himself said it was a grotty house, in a lesser thought of area than what he had become accustomed to since living with Pippa.

Pippa and Billy returned to The Marshman's and that evening Karl took her for a meal and was again open in his conversation, in fact he didn't even need to be prompted, he just spilled things out.

When he was out with the two women, he called them Babe as he was easily confused which one he was with. Pippa tried to make light of it saying he must have a thing for comical pigs as he had been calling her Peppa. She laughed and he tried to join in, but it was more trying to please her than laughing. As she looked at him, she remembered he wasn't a person that laughed and while away she was used to laughing again and she certainly wasn't going to fall back into bad habits.

He wanted to put Pippa's mind at rest that he used condoms. He could tell these women had been about and he wasn't going to catch anything from them!

Pippa said she would be in the guest room to start with to ease herself back to being back home, plus she didn't like the idea of sleeping in their bed until she had washed and cleaned everything in there and Karl agreed that was probably for the best as the bedding hadn't been laundered since she'd left six weeks before!

Pippa suggested they take up a hobby together and they decided on Ballroom dancing. Karl seemed very keen to please his wife, he would make sure he was home the night of the classes.

Two nights later they went for their first lesson. Karl was a very good dancer and took the instructions quicker than Pippa. He made her smile when he said it suited his OCD down to a tee as it was so repetitive. What she didn't know, he previously had lessons when he was with Kelly!

Kelly became suspicious of him being away so much, which indeed he was, as he had just started seeing Pippa and staying over at hers a few times a week. The lessons allowed Karl to buy himself time until he had everything in place to finish with Kelly.

He certainly didn't need to bring that little nugget up, he had enough on his plate at the moment with Tracy and Arlene being on Pippa's radar. He didn't need to drag Kelly or anyone else into the mix.

Two evenings later they were sitting on the sofa watching TV and all of a sudden Karl changed. He started accusing her of being deceitful, she was masterful in ganging people up against him, that was why no one contacted him whilst she was away. She was manipulative, she had been lying to people about him and she should be ashamed of herself. She better make sure she changed her attitude and behave, or she'd be out.

That was it, Pippa stood up, walked to the hall and he followed thinking she was about to leave. She opened the door, looked him squarely in the eyes saying.

'Get out. You've always had an overactive fight or flight response to anything. But do you know what Karl Taylor, you're never going to fight this girl again. I'll call the police if you start on me. So that leaves you the flight option. You can just bugger off. Yes, I have changed, big style. My eyes have been opened and I will not be bullied by you or anyone. GET OUT.'

Billy put himself in front of Pippa and adopted a low deep growl. Karl looked at Billy and knew this mountain of a dog would not hesitate to protect Pippa. He picked his car keys off the hall table and left.

Pippa was straight on the phone to Ruth, who was furious.

'Lock the gates and doors he can get a dose of his own medicine, you gave him a chance and he's thrown it in your face!'

Pippa did just that locked everything up, tidied around and let Billy out for the night. While she waited for him to come back in, she thought poor Billy, he was so confused, he'd never seen his mummy angry or shouting. He took his time patrolling the perimeter. When he came in, she gave him a cuddle and thanked him for being such a loyal boy. She moved his bed into the bedroom as a reward and they slept through till quite late.

On waking, Pippa realised that she'd had the dream with her in the container. But where it usually stopped with her lying on the bed, with the artificial light dimming and the air getting less and less, the dream carried on.

She was laying on the bed and all of a sudden, she could feel a stream of fresh air coming from the other side of the container. The light was getting brighter, but it wasn't the bulb it was natural light.

Pippa was now sitting on the bed looking towards where the air was coming through and on the wall was the picture that Ruth had painted for her. Normally Pippa would have been scared to move for fear of the air disappearing completely, but she knew there was enough air for her to breath and she got off the bed and went up to the painting.

The light now was bright like early dawn and as she was looking at her painting, the four walls of the container slowly dropped down, and she was in her garden at The Marshman's.

Pippa knew exactly what the dream meant, she had been controlled which was suffocating her and taking all the light out of her life, finally she'd made it clear that she would never be controlled again.

She went and opened the gates at the bottom of the drive, vowing from now they would never be closed.

Pippa never had the container dream again.

CHAPTER 18

'No Leopard ever changed its spots.'

Pippa didn't contact Karl, she was fed up placating his every whim and as Ruth quite rightly said give him a dose of his own medicine.

He sent her an email Monday morning saying he would be away all week at the modular buildings' annual exhibition in London, which he couldn't get out of attending. He really didn't feel up to going he didn't feel at all well. He couldn't believe it, but the company's stand was the biggest it had ever been, and he was going to be so busy.

He wanted to reassure her he had been on his own over the weekend and he didn't want her mind going overtime thinking he was with someone. He knew he needed to keep himself occupied and what with having to be in London for the exhibition the following week, it seemed natural for him to spend the weekend there.

Since he didn't have anything with him as she'd locked him out, on Saturday he had spent his time buying new clothes. He had to buy a new suit for the exhibition he couldn't be on the stand in the tracksuit bottoms and tee shirt he'd been wearing when he left the house Friday evening.

On the Sunday he went to see the Memorial Poppy's at The Tower of London. He agreed with the description that Pippa had relayed of when she went with Stella, it was so moving and he was pleased he had seen it, just a shame they hadn't seen it together.

He couldn't understand why he'd acted like he had. He was due to be back home late Friday morning and he would book an appointment to go to the doctors the following week.

He loved Pippa so much and he hoped she could forgive and forget the recent incident.

Pippa read the email, thinking he does need help from a doctor! He'd been over tired for some time and he had such a demanding job, no doubt made harder because of the extra pressure he placed on himself.

She sent an email by reply that she would certainly try to forgive, and she'd book the appointment for him with the doctor, what were his movements the following week?

They were now in full and loving communication. The emails were flowing, the texts were saucy, loving and fun but there were no phone conversations, his phone only kicked into voice mail.

Pippa was looking forward to her husband's return. She wondered if he'd just got a bit bored with her and what with the huge cyst being in the way and her operation their sex life had vanished and it had always been so important to both of them. She took herself into Norwich to a sexy underwear shop to buy some things to add a bit of spice to their lives.

Zoe the young assistant helped Pippa with her choice, and they looked together at the different outfits with

Zoe pointing out the plus and minus of each garment and what would suit Pippa's shape. She corrected Pippa that the size she was choosing wasn't right for her as she needed to go down a size or possibly two. Pippa agreed, she had lost weight and kept forgetting the size she was now. Zoe informed with a saucy grin.

'With glamour wear, it's not for comfort, you need it tight.'

Then with various outfits in hand, Pippa took herself to the changing room. After a little while Zoe came along to check she was OK and if she needed any help with anything. Pippa answered that she was thrilled with the choices and she thought she was going to buy the red chemise she had on. Zoe asked?

'Are you sure it's the right size, did you want me to check?'

Before Pippa knew what she was doing she'd moved the curtain to let Zoe in.

She didn't feel self-conscious, she was pleased to show off the outfit and Zoe was suitably impressed. This reassured Pippa as Zoe was certainly knowledgeable of the items she sold. Pippa also bought some lube and other things to spice up their bedroom antics.

In the email that evening she told Karl all about her shopping trip and he sounded very pleased with what was on offer.

The Friday was here before she knew it. Karl emailed first thing that he'd probably be back by two. At three she called him and no reply it went to voice mail and she left a nice upbeat message. She was getting concerned when it got to four o'clock, she was about to call again when an email came through from Karl. She read it over and over again and couldn't digest what it was saying.

Then as she was reading it yet again, she felt afraid that Karl was going to end his life.

In the email he wrote, he'd resigned. He'd put too much into his job and was now wondering if it was all worth it. Doug had been very understanding and let him go straight away without having to work any notice. She needn't worry, he was driving West, and he'd be off radar for a while so she wouldn't be able to reach him.

She tried his number several times and each time left a message saying she just needed to hear he wasn't going to do anything silly, and could he call her please or she'd need to call his work.

Her phone rang and it was Karl. He exploded telling her to leave him alone and under no circumstances to call his work. What was wrong with her did she have no shame, was she now trying to embarrass him at his place of work. She'd done enough damage to his reputation in his personal life he didn't need her to start with her malicious talk to his colleagues and with that he slammed the phone down.

Pippa phoned Bev and asked if she was busy as she was hoping for some company, could she stay overnight? She was round in an instant.

Bev hadn't been impressed when Pippa said she'd given Karl a chance, so for him to throw this second chance back in her face didn't go down well. How dare he treat her this way. She was incandescent but tried really hard for that not to show.

'Pip are you sure you hadn't misunderstood the email?'

Pippa passed the iPad to Bev for her to read the message for herself. She too had to read it a few times.

'That's beyond cruel, who does that, it sounds as if he's about to commit suicide. So much for being honest he's lying through his teeth, he hasn't resigned why would he be so concerned about being embarrassed with his colleagues. I bet he's not driving west, he's more than likely at Tracy's grotty house or even started back with that bossy Arlene so at least he can have a decent bed to sleep in. Truly Pip you're better off without him.'

Pippa had a nice meal ready for her and Karl to have that night, a nice bottle of red for Karl was on the side and a bottle of white chilling in the fridge. None of that would go to waste. Pippa and Bev would have the meal and Bev would stay the night so they could both have a drink.

'I don't know about you Pip but I certainly need a couple of glasses of wine after all this nonsense!'

Pippa thought, tell me about it!

Just before they sat down to eat Eddie and Sophie came through the door to check she was all right after the most recent knock back and ask her to come and stay at theirs. They were reassured to hear Bev would be staying overnight to keep her company.

They were surprised to see Pippa looking and sounding incredibly balanced and not upset.

'It is what it is, I can't dictate what he does. All I need to concentrate on is making sure that the consequences of his actions do not affect me. They are of his making, so it only seems right he's the one they affect. You know me I'm a great believer in karma. Strange really because one of his sayings is what goes round comes round.'

Once Eddie and Sophie had gone the friends sat down to their meal and girly sleepover.

There was plenty of saucy talk about Bev's new chap. Most of the time she called him Des but sometimes she would call him Desmond. He phoned during the evening. He was away with work, currently in India, training staff for his software security firm. By all accounts it sounded he was very successful and much sought after with many contracts abroad including the Middle East.

Pippa told Bev about the sexy outfit, and that apparently you wear glamour wear tight, she wondered if she could take it back as it wouldn't be seeing any action now. Bev asked if she could see it, perhaps she could buy it rather than the fuss of Pip having to return it. Pippa got it out of the beautiful carrier bag, it was all wrapped up in pink tissue paper. She held it up and Bev just glared at the red chemise.

'I think it's fair to say there's tight and then there's impossible to get in and out of, best you return it to the shop.'

They both laughed.

Then Bev sat bolt upright, acting as if she were quite solemn and gave a dramatic sigh and started to speak emphasizing her normal hoity toity manner acting as if she were a barrister in court.

'In all the years I have known you Phillipa Taylor, you have always come out with a saying for a situation, which I have to say has driven me more than a little round the twist. Anyway, enough about me. Where you, or should I say we find ourselves is every negative has a positive. Now before I continue may I ask you Phillipa Taylor, is that a saying you have said to me over the years and just to clarify for the court, is that a saying you've said once or possibly three hundred times over the years? Please speak up the court cannot hear your reply.'

Pippa was smiling and chuckling inwardly and nodded in agreement as she knew exactly where her friend was coming from and she was very much looking forward to hearing where it was going. With a big beaming smile Bev announced.

'The positive dear friend is that I will take it upon myself, without payment it has to be said. As from this moment forward, I will be your Social Secretary and I will not shirk in my responsibilities or from the energies I put towards my role. Because my dear friend we are going to let our hair down and enjoy ourselves. What do you say? Speak up please, the court cannot hear you.'

Pippa stood up and said in true accepting an Oscar award manner, holding a pretend microphone to her mouth.

'Well firstly I would like to thank my family for all their love and support but mostly for making me the person I am. It needs to be said without my parent's enthusiasm and perseverance I would not be here today.

I wish to thank my friends who I know are plenty, especially since I have received this nomination and I know it has nothing to do with the fact that they are all hoping to receive payment from articles they want to sell to the tabloids.

Finally, I need to thank my Social Secretary Beverly Constance who has been my friend and greatest supporter since we first met in the banking hall of The Eastern England Bank when I was sixteen and she was eighteen years old.

I feel or should I say need to mention that Beverly Constance works in her capacity of the said Phillipa Taylor as her Social Secretary with the expectation nor the actual receipt of any financial reward for her services. In closing I'd like to say. I wish each and every one of you the following.'

Pippa standing very straight, she took a deep breath and still holding the pretend microphone in her hands which were now in prayer position, she closed her eyes and lowered her head saying respectfully.

'May you be granted the senility to forget the people you never liked. The good fortune to be able to run into the ones you do like and great eyesight, so you know the difference. Because the last thing you blinken well need is to mistake the two.'

With that Pippa fell on top of Bev where they dissolved into uncontrollable laughter. Until Bev pushed Pippa off as she needed to rush to the bathroom from all the laughing.

When she came back from the loo, still straightening her knickers through her skirt, Bev excitedly shouted through.

'So here we go, a date in the social diary is Jasmine Spalding's Ladies Evening and Christmas Fair, where's your calendar as I'm going to write it on straight away.'

Taking herself in the kitchen Bev was calling.

'I've got the calendar, where do you keep a pen in this kitchen, ah here it is. There you go, that's on the calendar, 8th December, I've put the time on half an hour earlier than when it starts because you can pick me up, that's what friends are for.'

'Huh, I think that's what's known as services in kind. So much for not wanting payment.'

Pippa thought, that's a couple of weeks away, I haven't been to the last two what with the spiritualist being there, I'm sure something will come up to allow me to wriggle out of it by then.

CHAPTER 19

'A change is as good as a rest, especially in the sun.'

After a very nice, relaxed breakfast Bev left for home. She was reassured that Pip was happy, chattering away and had plans to take Billy for a walk and probably go round to Eddie and Sophie's that evening. Bev saying in her normal assertive but caring manner, that she needed to keep occupied, suggesting in a kindly tone.

'Sometimes it's about doing new things and to break old routines, you have to admit Pip you are very much a creature of habit.'

Pippa couldn't deny her comfort zone could be stretched, possibly just a little bit, as she waved Bev off the drive.

She went to empty the post box, and apart from the usual leaflets for mobility scooters and having insulation fitted for free there was a handwritten envelope with a Spanish postmark. She thought it was a bit early for a Christmas card, plus she didn't know anyone in Spain, she didn't even wait to get indoors before she'd eagerly opened it.

It was a card with a photo of The Marshman's and inside the writing said.

'To Pippa and Karl, found this and thought you'd like it, from Felicity.' She and Jack were the previous owners of the property.

There was a handwritten letter inside, addressed to Pippa saying that her and Jack were divorced as he'd cleared off with his cousin's wife a year after they moved to Spain. Felicity was tidying through some boxes of things which she'd never got round to unpack and found the cards. She'd looked on Facebook, but Pippa wasn't there. She hoped they could keep in touch and gave her email address.

Pippa looked at the card it was really lovely, what a nice gesture, I'll get a frame and hang it on the wall. Felicity always seemed such a nice lady. She would ask Eddie and Sophie if they could get her on Facebook and in the meantime, she would drop Felicity an email.

The email was brief, saying thanks for the lovely card and I can fully empathize with you on how horrible divorce is as I'm currently going through a divorce myself.

Within minutes an email pinged back and by the time Pippa made herself a cup of tea a further message came through in which Felicity had outpoured the whole story of what she had been through. Goodness me thought Pippa, my situation seemed odd what with not knowing anything, but she wondered if that was better than being dragged through the dirt like poor Felicity. Pippa was honest in her reply saying she assumed Karl was living with another woman, but she didn't know what was happening, all she knew he was living elsewhere.

To Pippa's surprise Felicity invited her to fly over to Spain for some fun in the sun. She attached photos of her home in Marbella and even gave the days of flights from Norwich airport.

Pippa replied straight away. How about if I fly out on next Tuesday's flight and return on the Friday?

To which Felicity came back that she would pick her up from the airport and for Pippa to make sure she brought some dresses to party, a wonderful time would be organised.

'Good grief Billy, your mummy is going on a holiday and you will be having fun with Eddie and Sophie at Churchside.'

Pippa excitedly phoned Bev and said she would pick her up in two hours. They were going shopping as she needed some new clothes to take with her on a trip to Marbella.

Bev was in total shock and had mixed reactions to the news, she was pleased that Pip was occupied and getting out, but deary me to Spain, and staying with someone she didn't really know. The only things she had in common with Felicity were The Marshman's and divorce. Pip had really taken her words of doing new things and breaking old routines possibly a bit too literally.

Pippa went online and booked her flights. She got herself ready to go shopping. On the way to pick Bev up she stopped off at the bank in Bagby and withdrew some cash from her savings account.

They had a lovely shopping experience. Bev couldn't believe the change in her dear friend. Whenever they'd been shopping before it felt more like dragging her to the shops. Pippa had been such hard work, especially when they were looking for the dress for Eddie's wedding. Back then it didn't matter what they looked at Pippa was hesitant. Now she knew exactly the look she was hoping to achieve.

They put all the shopping bags into the car and went to have a bite to eat. Pippa excitedly saying she thought going to London had been an experience but to go to Spain, stay and be entertained in a lovely house in Marbella. She really couldn't believe it.

She reassured Bev, then later on Ruth, Eddie and Sophie, if for any reason she didn't feel comfortable or if Felicity wasn't even at the airport to meet her, Pippa would book herself into a nice hotel and enjoy her own company.

Pippa booked a taxi to Norwich airport. She made an effort with her clothes and make up for the journey, as she knew the few occasions she'd seen Felicity she was always well turned out.

On the short flight to Malaga, she felt like a jet setter and couldn't stop smiling. She knew she was in for a wonderful time and thought, this is the new Pippa.

She'd always made sure her savings were used for sensible things, like the house and big purchases for the home, but now she was going to have a bit of fun and the occasional frivolity wouldn't do her any harm. She knew all her special people who made sure she was financially secure were looking down on her saying enjoy yourself. She didn't want to have any thoughts on what their views would be that she had tied a huge chunk of their money up with Karl, she knew it should be Eddie who rightfully inherited it.

She'd bought herself several magazines to read on the flight, even this was out of character as she always thought they were such an expense, but she had made her own sandwiches to eat on the plane. When the flight attendants came with the drinks, she bought a bottle of water, a gin and tonic and a cup of tea, then tried to look sophisticated while juggling them all and eating her sandwiches.

She spoilt herself when the crew came along with the duty free, she bought herself some make up and perfume. She splurged on another bottle of perfume for Felicity as a thank you for her stay.

When she walked out of the gates, she wasn't at all worried about being on her own in a foreign country. She knew Felicity would be there to meet her, they had been in constant contact all weekend. There was the usual throng of bodies waiting and taxi drivers holding up pieces of paper with names of their fares. In front of them was Felicity, waving and calling her.

The ladies greeted enthusiastically as they walked out of the airport. Felicity introduced a man who was standing next to an expensive looking black car with tinted windows. He was very handsome, mid-thirties, dark almost black hair, with a lovely warm smile, wearing a crisp white shirt open at the neck and black trousers. He was introduced as Marce, who worked for Felicity as chauffer, general assistant, oh and occasionally bodyguard!

In true chauffer style Marce opened the rear car door and as Pippa bent to get in, she saw two Boston Terrier dogs sitting on the back seat. She got in and gave them both a pat. Felicity introduced them as Bruce and Sheila and they listened intently to what Felicity was saying, snorting in agreement on her every word, which was quite often as she didn't stop talking. She had a nice jokey manner, very attractive and looked in very good shape for fifty-two, just a little bit more nipped and tucked than when Pippa had seen her five years before.

Thankfully Felicity didn't raise anything more about Jack. She'd obviously got all that out of her system in the emails over the weekend. She was now keen to explain that she didn't usually invite random people to her house for a holiday. 'I do have friends, honestly.' But how strange it all was, she found the card and here Pippa was sitting in front of her. She was so looking forward to their few days together as she had plenty of things planned, but she was conscious Pippa was on sick leave so they wouldn't overdo the partying.

They both laughed and Pippa said, if she was surprised by having her in the car it was nothing to the shock or possibly horror of her friends and family that on a whim she'd flown to Spain. Yes, she was on sick leave and not used to partying, but she was keen to experience different things and it could only do her good. Adding, a change is as good as a rest.

While it had only been a matter of minutes since their reunion, they were both very comfortable in each other's company laughing and enjoying the banter. In no time at all they were pulling up to the villa, 'Vista Maritima'. Pippa looked up the name earlier and it translated to 'Sea View'. The property looked very impressive. It had the trademark sign of a property owned by the Phillips', with high security gates, and Marce was steering the car up the steep driveway through lush and exotic trees which opened up to a large parking area in front of the beautiful villa.

Marce opened the car doors and took Pippa's case in for her. Bruce and Sheila were out and racing to see who could be the first to be greeted by the two women at the front door, Maria and Amaya, who did everything to keep the house clean and in order. They would also make sure Felicity and any guests were fed and watered.

Pippa was lost for words; she just could not believe how wonderful everything and indeed everyone was. She was pleased to see they all had a respectful affection for Felicity.

Pippa was led through the hallway into the lounge, with its huge windows looking out to a beautifully landscaped garden, pool area and uninterrupted views of the sea beyond.

Felicity affectionately said.

'I love seeing people's reaction when they see for the first time this view, isn't it spectacular, I never tire of looking at it.'

They walked outside to a patio area, where there was a table and chairs with beautiful white tablecloths. A parasol was open ready for their arrival. They sat down and soon Amaya was serving them drinks and a salad for lunch.

Pippa took a photo and attached it to a text to Bev, Ruth, Eddie and Sophie saying 'All wonderful, Felicity's very nice and I'm being spoilt, love X.' Within seconds texts were pinging back saying they wished they were there.

As they lunched, they spoke about their families, pets, likes, dislikes, looked at each other's photos and realised they had so much in common. Well apart from Felicity living the life of a WAG and she never had children. Jack hadn't wanted them and of everything that happened in her life, that was Felicity's only regret.

They decided they would change to have a swim, then do some sunbathing and rest on the sunbeds, because at eight thirty Marce was taking them to a very nice restaurant with a roof top bar. They could meet up with some people Felicity knew would be there. Pippa asked what sort of thing Felicity was going to wear to the restaurant as she wasn't used to going out like this and Felicity said she'd show Pippa her outfit.

Felicity led the way and Pippa was shown to her room and her case was already on a stool waiting for her. It was a suite, with a huge bed, dressing room to the side leading to the ensuite with large freestanding Jacuzzi bath. The balcony was fabulous, and the view was not obscured by any railings as it had a large glass screen. There were two loungers and a little table and chairs.

If Pippa was amazed by the guest suite nothing could have prepared her for the extravagance of Felicity's suite. Again, the balcony overlooked the garden with the sea views. Felicity walked into her dressing room and Pippa followed to be shown the outfit she was planning on wearing that evening. Pippa was very grateful that she'd treated herself to her new clothes, but she had also brought the dress she'd worn to Lauren's birthday party and went on to describe this to Felicity who thought it sounded perfect.

Pippa loved swimming, and to be in such a beautiful infinity pool was wonderful. She positioned herself with her elbows resting on the side looking out at the view completely lost in her thoughts. When she got out, she took herself to the lounger. Bruce and Sheila were both sitting with Felicity on the one next to Pippa's and again the ladies just chattered.

Despite being under the umbrellas they had to make sure they put on plenty of sun cream. Pippa couldn't get her head round that she'd only come on such a short flight to be in such wonderful high temperatures. Here they were in late November and back home in Norfolk they would have been very happy to have had this amount of sun and heat in July.

Later that evening they were dropped off at the restaurant Lugar Para Estar, Pippa asked what it meant and Marce said in his glorious deep voice.

'Place to be. This is where all the beautiful people come when they are in Marbella.'

As they walked into the restaurant it was obvious that Felicity was very well known to the staff and they were escorted in a friendly, happy, respectful way to their table.

The wine and sparkling water were brought without being ordered and Hugo, the manager, came up to Felicity, gave her a hug and they were talking freely. It was obvious from the conversation that Felicity was the owner of Lugar Para Estar. Pippa made her food choices, ably assisted by Felicity and Hugo, and sat back to savour the delicacies. As she looked around to the other guests, she thought Marce's description was spot on. They were certainly the beautiful people.

During the meal Felicity relayed that when The Marshman's was sold and her and Jack moved to Spain, all the money from the sale of the property was put into Felicity's name, for obvious reasons due to Jack's sensitive position. He had plenty of funds here and there, but these were used for different projects. Felicity had bought the restaurant in her sole name and while it had a good reputation, that was nothing to what it was now. She had worked front of house to ensure it met the standard she was trying to achieve. The villa too was bought in her sole name. She had bought it for its location but knew it would require total renovation.

She was upset at first when Jack left, then furious, but within a short space of time was grateful that he was out of her life. She described this as a natural course of events and no doubt Pippa would go through these stages in time, and for each person the time to realise life can be better is different, but she would get there.

Pippa said, she must be at the very early stages as she felt upset and hugely confused, she was hoping upon hope it would all work out and wondered if she hadn't got to the furious stage because she felt her husband was either unwell or had a personality disorder. Adding.

'As who would lead such a secretive life with no history, family or friends, just an elusive existence?'

'Errr, Jack!'

Felicity said, as they both laughed. But Pippa thought to herself, I don't think Karl is a crook though.

Pippa offered to pay for the meal and Felicity said that if the staff handed either of them the bill, she'd set Marce on them.

They went upstairs to the roof bar and sure enough there was a group of people all seated on the crisp white sofas with the most splendid views out to the sea. There was a lovely hubbub of mixed accents and Pippa was introduced to the group as Felicity's friend from Norfolk. She certainly was now, but this time last week she would have had to think twice who Felicity Philips was.

The evening flew by and Marce took them back to Vista Maritima. In no time at all Pippa was peacefully sleeping in the biggest bed she'd ever seen let alone lay in.

She woke early, stretched, happily looked out at the view and took herself out onto the balcony and tried to take it all in. She took some photos on her phone to send texts back home and as she checked on emails, there was one from Karl. Ugh! She sighed and felt a pang in her chest.

He wrote he would be up in Norfolk on Friday as he needed to go to the dentist, could she put the following things in a case and pop it in the summer house, so that he could swing by and pick them up. Oh, and could she make sure she put his new jeans in the case, the ones with the label still on. He wouldn't be able to see her as he may get upset, he was so emotional at the moment.

Pippa thought she couldn't be bothered to reply and then she smiled, took a photo of the view, making sure she got her toes in the shot lying on the sunbed as evidence that yes, she was actually there, and sent it with the reply.

'Sorry abroad at the mo, let me know when you're back up in Norfolk and I'll put the things in a case for you. I didn't see your new jeans about the place before I came away, best you buy another pair.'

She chuckled to herself, thinking that will eat him up. She was being truthful when she said she hadn't seen his jeans before coming away, but she knew exactly where they were.

When her and Bev went up the City to shop for her Marbella trip, Pippa took the jeans back to the shop, saying she didn't have the receipt, could she exchange them for something else. Looking at the label they said, 'no problem'. She went on to choose a little denim jacket. When they left the shop, they had to find a toilet as Bev couldn't stop laughing, resulting in her normal problem.

Pippa brought herself back to the now, she tore herself away from the balcony, and went back to her suite to get ready for the wonderful day ahead.

They went to the beauty salon. Pippa was told to choose whatever she wanted for her treatments and they would be there for three hours. It was all complimentary. The owner of the salon was keen to keep Felicity sweet so when he needed to entertain a friend or two, he could get a sought-after table at the Lugar Para Estar. Everyone knew they were like hens' teeth and he hoped his generosity would create the desired reciprocation.

In the evening, Felicity had arranged a soiree of friends to come over to Vista Maritima. Pippa met several of the people the night before and again a wonderful ambience was created by the hubbub of friends talking and laughing with music playing in the background.

One of the guests, Brendon had spoken with Pippa the night before, she felt comfortable in his presence, she particularly enjoyed listening to him. He was from

Edinburgh, very softly spoken and laughed a lot. As soon as she saw him, she could tell he was a very happy person because his face showed the tell-tale sign of plenty of laughter lines. Like everyone there Brendon had a very healthy relaxed look, it must be all the sun and the lifestyle Pippa thought.

There were also the familiar faces of Maria, Amaya and Marce topping up the glasses and making sure everyone had all they needed.

Pippa was standing in the garden looking out at the view, catching her breath with the sheer wonderment of it all when Brendon came up saying softly.

'Penny for them, your thoughts that is.'

Pippa was honest in her reply.

'This is all a million miles away from my lifestyle in Norfolk. Don't get me wrong I have a wonderful life, I'm surrounded by caring family, genuine friends, live in the most beautiful spot and I wouldn't want to change a thing or live anywhere else. But all this is so surreal. That's the great thing of holidays I suppose it gives an insight to different cultures and time to experience new things.'

They sat down and Brendon spoke more privately than he had the night before of what brought him to Spain. He had been in the oil industry on a good salary and all the trappings that brought, then three years ago he suffered a major heart attack.

That was the wakeup call, he decided he had worked hard enough and needed to relax and have some fun in the sun.

He didn't sell his house in Edinburgh in case he wanted to return, but he moved lock stock and barrel over to the house he bought here in Marbella which was just a few streets away from Felicity. He saw Marbella now as home and the Edinburgh house was very much an investment which would be sold when the time was right. He'd only been back once in the three years and that was to his niece's wedding. His parents, sister and all her family came out to visit him.

He added.

'The only problem is, I can't get rid of them as they're out here all the time, so much for my bachelor lifestyle.'

To which they both laughed.

Again, the evening went by in a flash. Time was certainly flying as Pippa was enjoying herself so much. As the days went by, she realised there was a great ex-pat community. Felicity really did welcome the company of the friends she had made there, which seemed strange because when she was at Hepton-on-the-Marshes she kept herself very much to herself. Pippa wondered if that was because of Jack and his requirement for the high security and secrecy.

Brendon popped in on Thursday afternoon to say goodbye to Pippa. He brought his lovely parents Phyllis and Bert with him. They all sat in Felicity's beautiful, well tendered garden, drinking tea and it was all so very quintessentially British.

As they were about to leave Felicity was showing Phyllis and Bert some flowers and Brendon used the time to speak privately to Pippa, he passed her a note with his contact details and asked her to stay in touch.

'No pressure. I know you haven't said much about your situation so I'm not wanting to add any confusion, but I would welcome you staying in contact even as friends, because sometimes friends go on to be something much more and I would very much welcome that.'

With that he kissed her very gently on the cheek and turned to his parents.

'Come on you two, best get you back to the old folks home. Time for your nap.'

They all roared with laughter, all apart from Phyllis who made a token gesture of clipping him round the ear.

Before Pippa knew it, she was back on the plane with lovely thoughts going through her head. Her and Felicity knew their friendship would continue, both saying the other must visit. Felicity was having a New Year's Eve party and despite Pippa saying she'd already committed to go to Bev's, Felicity was hoping she would turn up.

Pippa also knew she would keep in contact with Brendon and his words of friends sometimes going on to be something much more put her in mind of Stella and Maxwell. They had been firm friends before starting their relationship and they would always love one another completely and truly.

CHAPTER 20

'No pillow so soft as a clear conscience.'

The Thursday of Jasmine's Ladies Evening arrived, and Pippa surprised herself as she was actually looking forward to going. The trip to Spain gave her a real boost. She knew it wouldn't be long before she would be returning to work and rather than badgering Dr Newcome to sign off her return, she was actually thinking that work may even get in the way of her new lifestyle.

Early afternoon Ruth phoned. She knew Pippa was far from keen on going to the Ladies Evening, what with the spiritualist there. A note was put on her own diary to call and encourage her cousin to go along. As soon as Pippa answered Ruth knew all would be well and she would be attending the evening after all.

Pippa saying, she was pleased to be going now as she had heard from so many friends who had tickets, several saying they were disappointed they couldn't get a slot with the spiritualist because he was fully booked. This reassured Pippa that no one would think it a good idea to drag her along to see him.

At five minutes to seven she pulled onto Bev's drive, very pleased with herself as recently her reputation for never being late had suffered a terrible hit, and for some unknown reason she was struggling at getting anywhere in the evenings. Day time she was alright but anything past six was doomed.

Pippa parked, got out of the car, went to the door and rang the bell. She waited and pressed the bell again. She peered through the glass panels in the side of the door, no response. She tried again. Then she heard Bev shouting from a window above her.

'Pip, thank God, I'm stuck in my ensuite go through the back, that door's unlocked and come upstairs and get me out.'

Pippa stood back from the door and looking up shouted.

'Ok, but how did you get stuck in the loo?'

Bev couldn't believe the indignation of it all!

'I'm not in the loo, I'm in my ensuite, go round the back and let me out.'

Pippa started to run round and thought, sod it, she can wait a few minutes, I'm not rushing if she's going to be grumpy. She walked slowly round to the backdoor. Henry the cat greeted her, and she stopped to speak to him. He followed Pippa in through the door where he received a nice long and slow stroke.

Pippa went upstairs to Bev's bedroom, walked over to the ensuite door.

'So how do I get you out?'

Bev replied sternly and even more grumpy.

'Well as if I know, I'm the other side of the door, I walked in and I can't turn the handle, it's just jammed shut.'

Pippa tried the handle.

'Yes, you're right it's jammed shut.'

She couldn't help but smile as she could hear Bev on the other side of the door shouting in frustration, the confirmation that she was well and truly stuck in the loo wasn't something she wanted to hear.

Pippa stood, thought and finally suggested.

'I know I'll call the Fire brigade. Not really, I'll call Hayley Spelman, she's going tonight, and no doubt Dave will be dropping her to the Ladies Evening. He always has a power drill about his person.'

She phoned Hayley who confirmed they weren't far away, and Dave would certainly rescue Bev from the loo, which tickled them both. Bev was cringing hearing Pippa's laughter as she knew she was probably the butt of the joke.

Only a few minutes passed, and Pippa could hear a car on the drive, she let Bev know and ran down the stairs. She opened the door, it wasn't Dave and Hayley but Amy Dickens, the Diet What Diet Consultant. Pippa ran up to the driver's door explained the situation.

Amy sat and listened to the predicament.

'I've got a tool kit in the boot I'll bring it up, do you want to show me the way?'

Pippa duly led the way, leaving the front door on the latch and when they got to Bev's bedroom and the offending door, Amy put down her toolbox and looked at the door handle and started to unscrew the handle and remove the mechanisms.

Pippa cheekily said.

'Hi Bev, how are you doing, I thought you might need some entertainment while you're in there so I've arranged for Amy Dickens to come and explain the Diet What Diet plan as she thought going over it again couldn't do you any harm, plus it would be a good way for you to pass the time.'

Bev couldn't believe what she was hearing and shouted.

'Pip the last person anyone needs when they are stuck in their ensuite is Amy Dickens, so I suggest you stop messing about and…'

Amy opened the door and Bev was looking straight into Amy's chubby face.

'Oh hello Amy, how very nice to see you, to what do I owe the pleasure?

Said Bev, squirming in her slippers. Amy just stood and looked at Bev, handing her the door handle and replaced the screwdriver back into her toolbox just as Dave and Hayley ran into the bedroom. Dave in his big booming voice jokingly saying.

'I hear you got stuck in the loo Bev, I've come to rescue you, but it looks like you've made your great escape.'

They all laughed, even Bev who graciously thanked them and reminded they needed to be at Jasmine Spalding's Ladies Evening.

Finally, they got to Bagby Village Hall and the car park was full, Pippa dropped Bev at the door and said she'd park and meet her inside. When Pippa opened the hall door the noise of high-pitched women's voices and laughter was deafening. She walked in and saw Bev gesturing to her to a long buffet table which had the complementary drinks that were part of the entrance fee.

Pippa went over, and Bev had already picked up two glasses, handed one to Pippa with strict instructions not to drink any of it as that one was Bev's, then took a large swig from the other glass saying.

'This one yours, I'll go over there and have lemonade added so it's a spritzer.'

Pippa smiled and could not believe her friend. As she was standing waiting for Bev's return a man, noticeable by being the only man in the hall, walked up to Pippa.

'Hello, I'm Stewart Hethal, I'm the spiritualist here this evening and you are?'

'Pippa.'

He strained his ears against the noise in the hall and twice she said her name, emphasising her mouth and he replied.

'Tracy, did you say your name was Tracy.'

Pippa felt winded as if she had been punched in the stomach. For him to say that name of all names to her.

'NO, it's, Pippa!'

'I'm so sorry. How strange I heard the name Tracy, and that is nothing like Pippa.'

'Yes, that is very strange as my husband has a woman called Tracy, I'm not sure if the terminology is lover. I'll be completely honest with you Stewart I didn't want to come here this evening, I don't like mediums, spiritualists or anything like that. I think I've always been scared of them. It is strange of all the people here, you speak to me, possibly the one person who has a fear of you.'

'I'm sorry to hear of your fear, and possibly that stems from you having your own gift which you are fighting. For a gift it is. As for coming up to you it was not of my choosing, I was drawn to you and knew I had to make contact. The name I said out loud was a name YOU were projecting and for me the only name I can remember or associate with you now is Pippa, but please do not say or even think at this moment of that other woman's name as she and her name have no meaning to our conversation. Please believe me when I say she is definitely not relevant to you, and despite your fear of the spiritual world please believe that.'

Pippa stood and tried to understand all what she'd just heard and instinctively she took his right hand in hers as if to shake it and he in turn gently held it. She said.

'I hope I didn't appear rude. I'm so glad I came this evening and thank you for coming up to me. I do believe what you have said because I feel and know myself that woman is nothing to do with me, so she is not relevant. I think that's where my strength comes from. I'm sure most people would have gone totally mad by now if they'd put up with half I've had to.'

Stewart smiled reassuringly at her and put his spare hand over hers saying.

'I'm glad you came too, and you didn't come across rude at all. I have to say Pippa fear takes many forms, but the strength you have comes from your own gift which is strengthened by a good heart and clear conscience. I wish you well. Take care.'

Pippa was still digesting Stewart's words, when Bev came rushing up to her.

'Oh, look at you, a private audience with Stewart Hethal, spill the beans what did he say.'

Pippa took her spritzer, passed the wine to Bev.

'I'll tell you later, but it was very interesting. Shall we go over to the candle and incense stall first, I'd like to get some for Ruth and Sophie.'

Bev agreed, asking Pippa.

'Just out of interest do you know why Amy Dickens was at mine tonight, did she say?'

'Goodness me what about her having that fully kitted out toolbox, the most useful thing I've ever got with me is a nail file. No, she didn't say why she was there, are you up to date on your Diet What Diet subs?'

Both of them burst into laughter and Bev passed her glass to Pippa as she had to rush off to the Ladies. Pippa thought, really Bev, you need to get that sorted.

CHAPTER 21
'Everything happens for a reason.'

Pippa received a calm and nice email from Karl saying he was staying down south, if she needed anything just let him know. She thought she'd take that with a pinch of salt.

Later in the week the doorbell rang, and Pippa was pleased to see it was Amy Dickens from the Diet What Diet classes.

Pippa welcomed her in for a cup of tea and Amy handed over a lovely bunch of flowers. They walked through to the kitchen and whilst the kettle was boiling Pippa arranged the flowers in a vase, setting it on the dining room table.

Amy said with a laugh.

'Bev phoned, thanked me and my toolbox for saving her, and invited me to her New Year's Eve party. I asked if I could bring a plus one and she said of course, so I said lovely thank you Tanya and I would love to come. You should have heard her spluttering.'

Pippa updated Amy that she'd joined a rock choir and was really enjoying it. She was still signed off from work but hopefully early in the New Year she would be fit to return and her normality. Oh, and by the way, Karl had moved out.

Amy was shocked and asked where was he living, was he with another woman or man?

Pippa said she didn't know where he was. He'd been in touch to say he was staying down south as he needed to be there for his work.

Amy asked if Pippa could come back to the Scales of Shame or Fame on a Friday morning as everyone missed her so much. Pippa said she was way out of target now as she must be at least ten pounds under her target weight. Amy reassured her not to worry about that, she wanted her there as a friend she needn't be a member and she certainly wouldn't ask anyone to gain weight!

Pippa was genuinely touched and said she'd be there Friday morning. She'd missed the banter and again, it was another normality, it would be lovely to see everyone.

As Amy drove away, she felt very sad for Pippa. She thought she'd been through a lot and was pleased she'd popped round with flowers. She was happy that Pippa would be returning to the classes as she was a true tonic to the group.

Pippa's social life was fantastic, she'd never been so busy, ever. She joked saying.

'I can see what people mean when they say they're so busy when they retire.'

With Christmas looming the choir was busy with their practices and lots of lovely events. She was back on a Friday morning managing the Scales of Shame or Fame. Billy's walks were always an important part of their day.

She carried on with her general chores, including looking after Daisy the chicken who had come home to her coup at The Marshman's, and Pippa bought a dear little ginger bantam called Gertie to keep Daisy company.

Eddie and Sophie brought round a real Christmas tree for the orangery and he also fetched the large artificial tree down from the loft to put in the lounge. She played Christmas music and put the decorations up. When she was at the Ladies Evening, she bought some winter smelling essential oils for her burner. The place looked, smelt and felt beautiful.

The following day she received another nice email from Karl asking if she had the decorations up as he would love to see a photo and he missed everything so much, but in particular he missed her, he hoped she was well. She weighed up if she wanted to send a photo, and decided No.

Pippa wrote and sent all the Christmas cards from 'Pippa and Billy', including one to Hew and Jeanette, but as they were associates of Karl's she added a notelet saying she hoped they were well, but just to say Karl was living elsewhere, she didn't know where, but she knew Karl welcomed Hew's friendship and hoped that would continue.

She didn't expect to hear back, but by what must have been return of post she received a lovely individual Christmas card. On the front was a picture of a Scottie dog under a Christmas tree with the words 'To Our Very Dear Friend at Christmastime' and Jeanette enclosed a handwritten letter:

Our Dearest Pippa, we are sorry to hear you and Billy are home alone. Sadly, this news hasn't come to us as a surprise. Last year Hew received an email from Karl just before the Christmas markets saying you were giving them a miss and wouldn't be coming because your marriage was going through a rough patch and you found it impossible to spend any time with Karl and he suspected you were having an affair. We thought it strange at the time as it seemed totally out of character for you. That was the last Hew heard from Karl and insists he won't get in touch with him. Both Hew and I have always seen you as our friend and not wishing to take sides but have always thought you deserve better than Karl. We know you have the most fabulous family and friends, which can only help at a time like this, but please, please keep in touch and should you need anything at all just call… Jeanette popped her mobile number at the end. The letter went on describing their plans for Christmas and the coming year with an extension on their home and several lovely holidays.

She popped the Christmas card in prime position on the mantelpiece. Sat on the sofa, looking up at it, totally lost in her thoughts. Over the years she gave so much credit to her rose tinted glasses, always saying, 'whatever happens, my wonderful rose tinted specs will see me through.' She would say this especially when she knew she was completely crumbling inside, for she knew these words always gave her support.

But as she was looking at the letter, she realised her rose tinted glasses were off, she read the letter again and again. There was things Jeanette wrote that were so far from the truth. Karl had used a totally different excuse to Hew and lied saying they hadn't attended the Christmas markets, when they had. As far as Pippa had been told, Karl was totally pressurised with work and that was the reason they couldn't go to Hew and Jeanette's before the markets.

The fear and anguish Pippa felt was totally engulfing, she was quite overwhelmed and forced herself to collect her thoughts, bring herself back to the here and now. Resolving karma will rule. I'm not the one who's lied. I've seen so many people have their lives ruined with the awful pain of a divorce which is often aggravated with the dividing up of possessions and money. I will not allow this situation to make me bitter.

She reached for her mobile phone and added Jeanette to her list of contacts, sending a text saying 'Hi, its Pippa, hope all's well. Thank you so much for the lovely card and kind note, it would be lovely to keep in touch. Hugs and love to you both and wishing you a fab Christmas and great New Year xx'

Pippa previously asked Karl if she could give Jeanette her mobile number, but he became precious and huffy saying 'stop poking your nose into my friendship with Hew how dare you try and spoil that, you know Hew is my only real friend.' She apologised and backed down.

Pippa was very pleased to know the friendship with Jeanette hadn't been lost, quite the opposite as the girls could now message freely.

CHAPTER 22

'If you're willing to play the game.'

A couple of evenings later the doorbell rang, and it was Bella 'bloomin' Robertson, with a bunch of flowers, chocolates and a bottle of wine. Pippa knew Bella was away on a cruise and hadn't realised she was back. She gave this as the reason for her surprise, not that Bella was the last person she ever expected to see standing on her doorstep bearing gifts!

Pippa naturally invited her in and as the wine was chilled asked if she would prefer a cup of tea or a glass of wine. Bella in no uncertain terms went for the wine. They sat in the lounge and Pippa offered to open the chocolates, Bella refrained saying she needed to get back to the Diet What Diet classes and was dreading jumping on the scales after such a wonderful break away as she enthusiastically ran through all the Caribbean countries she visited on the cruise. She loved it so much next February's cruise had already been booked.

Then Bella went quiet, looked at Pippa and burst into tears asking for Pippa to forgive her as she felt awful when her daughter Robyn messaged that Karl had left her, with at least one other woman not only in Pippa's home but wearing her dressing gown.

Pippa's stomach sank and she suddenly thought, here we go, the joy of living in a small village and all the tittle tattles. But then realised it must have been Bev, who told her daughter Lauren, who was friends with Robyn, who in turn would have spilled the beans to her mum, Bella.

Pippa took a deep intake of breath. She knew Bella's own husband cheated on her, she took him back and then he left her again. Bella was obviously sensitive to another woman's plight of a wayward husband. In an attempt to try and comfort her, she moved to the sofa where Bella was sitting and put her arm round her.

Bella was beside herself, absolutely sobbing and then said.

'Pippa I feel such a bitch, I've been so horrible to you. The truth is I've always been jealous of you.'

'What, jealous of me? Honestly Bella there's no need.' said Pippa in amazement.

'Of course I know that. I even knew it while I was being bitchy, I just couldn't help myself. I'm so sorry and I would fully understand if you never wanted to speak to me again, especially how I was at Lauren's thirtieth birthday party.'

Pippa thought back, Bella hadn't been horrible to her, what on earth was she going on about.

Bella carried on.

'You know I go on dating sites. Well, when I saw Karl come across the dance floor, I took a second glance, he looked the spitting image of a chap I'd seen on one of the sites. I waved to him and he came over and I told him that I'd seen him on at least one of the dating sites and I was going to tell you he was playing away. He was furious and asked what the hell I was going on about, telling me I was drunk. It annoyed me so much for him to say I was drunk, so I just repeated that I knew he was on dating sites and I wasn't going to let him get away with it. Yes, I'd had too much to drink but it wasn't that. Oh Pippa, I knew how awful I looked, mutton dressed as lamb. Robyn tried to steer me away from wearing that dress, but I wouldn't listen and just before we were about to leave, I looked in the mirror, but the taxi was there, and we came to the party. Then when we walked in and I saw you. You don't seem to realise Pippa, but you always look nice and appropriate. Anyway, when I saw you looking so lovely that was the last straw, and I was determined to hurt you. I'm really sorry. Then you and Karl were dancing to that Carly Simon song, Coming Around Again and I came up to you after and made those horrible jibes with words from the song, 'if you're willing to play the game' and 'more room in a broken heart.' I'm really sorry Pippa, when I think back to how badly I behaved it makes me feel sick.'

Pippa just sat trying to take on board what she'd heard. There she was thinking Bella had offended Karl about his Geordie accent, and it was on a totally different level to that.

Finally, she said.

'Oh Bella, I know it must have been hard for you coming here tonight and telling me this. Thing is for Karl he was doomed if he repeated to me what you said as it would have cast a suspicion, especially with his behaviour and attitude to me having changed. You are right that was a weird thing to accuse someone of, but let's put that in the past and move on.'

Pippa passed the box of tissues.

'Tea or more wine?'

Bella mopped her cheeks, her mascara fully running now.

'Definitely more wine please. Oh, Pippa, I've never seen anyone look as furious as Karl did when I shouted across the dance floor, Hello Mark, fancy seeing you here.'

That stopped Pippa in her tracks, she thought Mark, that's Karl's middle name. She passed Bella her wine and asked.

'Bella I've never been on a dating site, could you show me this chap that looks like Karl. I'll get my iPad.'

She handed Bella the iPad who went onto the site straight away, she stopped crying and seemed pleased to be able to redeem herself by showing Pippa the process.

'Pippa its natural for people on these sites to come and go, Mark might not be on there now, we're talking a good eighteen months since I saw him, but everyone has their own profile and filters for what they're looking for which makes it quicker.'

She went on to explain what Pippa would need to do, you just do this, that and the other. This site is free, and it will only take you a few minutes to join. Pippa wasn't interested in joining the site, and thought, free, Bella must be wrong it couldn't be Karl as she could remember him saying he paid for the dating site he joined in October, less than two months before.

'Bella, what area did this chap Mark, Karl's double live, was it Norfolk?'

Bella said no Mark was further afield as she continued with her search and within minutes Mark was there in front of them.

Pippa was shocked, it was Karl!

'Bella you are right that is my husband, I took that photo of him seven years ago in Corfu. He told me he joined a dating site in October the day I went to Ruth's for a break. Is that the same photo you saw in May last year?'

Bella confirmed it was.

It was quite late when she left and Pippa was surprised that now Bella wasn't trying to do her usual one up man ship, quite the reverse, she was very good company.

Pippa went to the bathroom, ran a deep bubble bath.

The bathroom was set with candles, her music was playing, and she lay back and soaked. As she lay, she tried to think of Karl that night on the dance floor but realised she couldn't bring his face clearly to view. The old photo she'd just seen of him on Bella's dating site was clear in her mind. She smiled to herself that it was certainly a complimentary photo and he'd aged quite considerably since. She wondered what people thought when they met the person in the flesh for the first time, especially from a photo seven years before in a very kind light!

The vision of Matti's face was clear, it was as if he was standing in front of her, but she wondered if that was because Eddie was so like his father, perhaps that was why. She considered if before she went to bed, she should look at some photos of Karl to jog her memory but decided no, she knew her mind was protecting her.

She lay soaking and thinking, what a strange year she'd had and thank goodness it wasn't long before the New Year would be here, bring it on. She got out of the bath, wrapping a big fluffy towel around her, brushed her teeth, popped on her creams and got into bed thinking tomorrows another day.

Pippa was up her usual early self, she had a busy but nice day planned. It would start with walking Billy. She was getting stronger, and this was reflected in the length and pace of the walks. She had choir that afternoon which she was really enjoying, not just the singing but also the banter with the other members, they were all so sweet.

Before choir practice she needed to do the household banking, work out how much to take from her savings as her salary had stopped five months before and she was only receiving statutory sick pay. The rental monies from the Bagby property would easily have covered the bills, but as soon as the payment hit the joint account Karl was removing half and wasn't putting any money in.

She knew she could do nothing to stop him taking money out, as foolishly she'd put the rental agreement in their joint names. All the utility bills were in her sole name so she was covering it all, the last thing she needed was any payments to bounce which would affect her credit score and could jeopardise her position at the bank. She drew up a list of all the payments and about to draft an email to Karl asking if he would contribute to the bills and the phone rang.

It was Karen, one of the admin team from the Field View Sports Club. Karen asked how Pippa was, she hoped it wouldn't be too long before she could return to the gym. Karen updated on how well her job was going and she was very pleased that Janet had entrusted her with extra responsibilities, she was now helping with the accounts of the monthly membership subscriptions, and the reason for her call was Karl's standing order.

Pippa jumped in straight away.

'Well how spooky is that I've just been sitting working out the finances, I have the bank statement in front of me, the standing order for FVSC was definitely paid, and as Karl doesn't use the gym anymore I was about to cancel the mandate.'

'Oh yes you're right, Karl's membership payment has gone through. He still uses the gym, admittedly not as much as he used to, but he's supposed to be paying Tracy West-Green's membership too and that hasn't arrived. I was just wondering if he's going to change the standing order. Tell you what Pippa I'll send the letter for fees to you by email perhaps you could sort it.'

She could not have been more taken aback!

'Karen, I don't think that would be appropriate. The thing is Karl doesn't live here anymore it's absolutely nothing to do with me.'

'Oh, I'm really sorry to hear that but as we only have your details could you forward the email to Karl. What with Janet being away on holiday I've got so much to do.'

Pippa couldn't believe what was being asked of her.

'Karen, I'm not promising anything, but send it through to me and I'll give it some thought.'

Within a few minutes the email came through. Pippa read it, thinking out loud, he's obviously staying at Tracy's, why else would he offer to pay her gym membership. What a cheek taking another woman to the gym that I introduced him to. He has no shame!

She looked at the name Tracy West-Green and thought back to when she received the cruel email indicating he were to do something as awful as commit suicide, saying he was going off radar, had resigned, driving West. The only thing he actually did was drive to Tracy West-Green's in the east of Norfolk, no doubt he found that very funny! Well as far as Pippa was concerned if he's going to send her such a warped email, she would not be forwarding the sports club email onto him. It was nothing to do with her, it was between Karl, Tracy and the sports club, her conscience was clear.

She went straight back to the banking, cancelled the standing order for his gym and transferred all the utility direct debits into her sole account. She contacted the rental agent Adam Wilkinson asking for her half of the payment for future months to go to her sole account and prepared Adam that Karl would probably be on the phone reading the riot act that the payment had been changed and it was up to Karl if he arranged for his half to be credited somewhere else.

She knew she was in a temper and tried to calm down as she got herself ready to go off to choir practice. During the break she took Ruth to one side and told her of that morning's escapade! Ruth listened in disbelief, this man was a monster it gets worse and worse. She praised Pippa for taking control with the finances.

When Pippa got home, she sat at the kitchen table eating her tea and a thought came to her. I'll look in the telephone directory to see if this woman's local. Sure enough the name she was looking for was there: West-Green, T. 22 Primrose Close, Sumson. Oh, at least I know where she lives, and Karl was right about one thing, Sumson is well and truly a grotty area.

Pippa decided she would make Mr Elusive aware she knew where he was living. She wouldn't send an email, she would personally drop a Christmas card round to him at Tracy's house in Primrose Close. Saying to herself.

'That will spook him.'

She found one from an old box of cards, she didn't want to go to any expense. The envelope didn't match but none the less it was quite a sweet card, it had a little girl putting her stocking up on the fireplace. She wrote inside, To Tracy and Karl, From Pippa.

Within an hour of her dropping the card through Tracy's letter box, Karl sent a vicious email telling her to stop stalking him, did she not know stalking was a criminal offence he was calling the police. The threat didn't bother Pippa, she felt vindicated and quite smug by delivering the card. The main thing, Karl was aware she knew where he was living, he had confirmed it by sending the email.

Mr Elusive had been found.

CHAPTER 23

'Acquaintances become friends.'

The following morning Pippa phoned Brendon. As always, they had a lovely banter and she asked if his parents were spending New Year's Eve with him in Marbella or in Scotland and was told Phyllis and Bert would never miss being in Scotland for Hogmanay and they would be staying at his sister's home in Edinburgh.

This was music to Pippa's ears, and the smile she was wearing came across in her voice, as she asked.

'I know you've asked several times if I could come to Marbella and join you at Felicity's New Year's Eve party, but I was wondering if you would like to fly to Norwich and come with me to Bev's party. As you know Billy and I are staying overnight at her garden lodge and there's a lovely little B&B within walking distance of hers so there wouldn't be the normal problem with taxis on New Year's Eve, did you want to give it some thought?'

Within a heartbeat Brendon said.

'Yup, I've given it thought, I'd love to come with you, I'll be there.'

Pippa was more than a little taken aback by the speed of his reply but feeling very happy and pleased she said.

'Brilliant, I'll call the B&B straight away, I've heard it's really nice there. How many nights shall I book? New Year's Eve falls on a Wednesday?'

Brendon excitedly replied.

'Well, if the flights are the same as when you came earlier this month, Tuesdays and Fridays, best book me three nights. Pippa you've made my day, I'll go online now and book my flight.'

They quickly finished the call, as both were excited to get on with their arrangements. Pippa called the Old Railway Station B&B and was surprised they still had availability. With it being so close to Bev's she had been worried that other guests would have totally booked it out. She messaged Brendon confirming his accommodation was sorted and received a text back … 'Flight arrives Tuesday 30th, at 2:30 XX'

Pippa couldn't stop smiling as she took Billy for his walk and thought, goodness what a difference a day makes. I'd better let family know Brendon's coming over and also tell Bev that I'm bringing a guest.

Bev was thrilled with the news that Brendon was coming.

'Oh Pip you have a plus one, that's so wonderful and he sounds such a lovely chap, I can't wait to meet him. Finally, you have worked out everyone's entitled to a relationship.'

Pippa wasn't sure if she had worked this out or not, but either way she felt the happiest she'd been in years. She also knew only the day before she wouldn't have thought it appropriate to go to a party or anywhere with a man, she was by all accounts still a married woman!

Pippa's solicitor sent the divorce papers out to Karl at Tracy's address as he still hadn't acknowledged the original ones sent to him two months earlier and unless he did Pippa could not move on with divorcing him. Her solicitor said it was unusual for someone not to acknowledge the papers and if he continued to put his head in the sand, they would need to formally serve the divorce papers. That would involve paying a Process Server to personally hand the papers to her estranged husband. Pippa was happy to pay for this service but was told they needed to know where to serve them and when Karl would be there. Pippa knew his work's address and she now knew an address where Karl was staying, but she would never know in advance when he was at either of these addresses. She phoned the Head Office number shown on his business cards but only got through to a list of options which in turn led to an answer machine.

It was arranged that Pippa and Billy would go over to Churchside from Christmas Eve through to Boxing Day. Then Boxing Day Pippa would join Eddie and Sophie at The Old Rectory, her parent's house, for Harold's and Sally's Boxing Day feast.

Pippa loved Christmas and was always organised buying the presents but even more so this year, as the gifts were already in the house. Karl had a fine wine collection and she decided she would purchase a batch of bottle bags, then carefully choose a wine appropriate for the person she was giving it as a gift. Write the name on the label. Wonderful all sorted.

Every year she gave a little something to the postman, refuse collectors, window cleaner and gardener. But fair to say they were all very surprised when they opened the wine bags to see a very nice bottle of Chateauneuf du Pape!

Billy was excited when he saw his bed and food, together with Pippa's case and all the Christmas presents being loaded into the car. He didn't care where he was as long as he was with Pippa.

As soon as they pulled up outside Churchside, with the icicle lights making it look like a gingerbread house, she knew it was all familiar but different and that difference was going to be in a good way. Eddie and Sophie were there to greet them at the door and Eddie helped Pippa get the things in to her room. Sophie joined them upstairs and Eddie said.

'Oh yes Mum, we've got something to show you, we've been decorating.'

They walked through to the next bedroom; it was now a nursery. Pippa just stood in an emotional, happy trance. She turned to Eddie and Sophie who were cuddling each other, and they all hugged. She said how wonderful, this had to be the best Christmas present ever, and was told Baby Jackson was due in early July.

This Christmas Eve lived up to being Pippa's favourite night of the year. Eddie and Sophie said they would be showing the nursery and announcing the pregnancy to Harold and Sally when they arrived the next day late morning, but they were keen for Pippa to be the first to know.

It was the same room Eddie had as a baby and the look of the nursery was perfect. The carpet was a light lemon, the cot, changing table, wardrobe and nursing chair were all in white wood. The walls were painted a soft lemon and above the cot there was a wall freeze which matched the curtains and covers in the cot with a fabric mobile over it.

As they stood in total joy and wonderment the proud soon-to-be parents offered for Nanny Pip to try out the nursing chair. She didn't need to hear the offer twice and quickly sat in joyful anticipation of holding her grandchild. The rest of Christmas Eve evening was spent in happy baby chatter.

They really couldn't wait for Harold and Sally to arrive and when they did, Pippa stayed downstairs to allow them to savour the happy moment without interruption. When they came downstairs, true to form, Harold and Sally were both an emotional wreck.

Sophie was pleased the one time she was cooking Christmas Dinner was also the time no one was letting her lift a finger, so all in all, that worked out very well.

Eddie had to stop Sally notifying the whole world, with the reminder they needed to wait until Clare and Dave were told on Boxing Day and then the news could be spread wide and far.

Pippa received many messages on Christmas Day, including one from Brendon. The whole Christmas period was wonderful with everyone so happy.

CHAPTER 24

'A First Footer never tempts fate.'

The day after Boxing Day, Pippa and Bev hit the shops, both girls wanted a new dress for the party. Pippa found her outfit quickly; she now knew what suited her and the look she wanted to achieve. Bev was not far behind her and they finished their trip with lunch at Ellie's, their favorite tearoom just off Elm Hill.

Both girls were feeling very happy. Bev went through the guest list; most were known to Pippa and she was thrilled to hear that Desmond would be arriving in time for the New Year countdown and should be at Bev's by nine from his current business trip to the United Arab Emirates. From what Bev said he was a man on a mission to ensure he was at hers in good time.

Pippa was genuinely looking forward to meeting Desmond and likewise Bev couldn't wait to meet Brendon. Pippa tried not to dampen her dear friend's enthusiasm by gently reminding her that Brendon was only a friend, and her situation was very confusing. She was a married woman and while she had been truthful to Brendon of her situation, she hadn't gone into detail about Karl, mainly as some of the things that had happened beggared belief, even to Pippa and she'd gone through them!

The arrangements for New Year's Eve were sorted nicely. Brendon would be at the B&B, a short walk from Bev's, with Pippa and Billy staying the three nights at Bev's beautiful house, well not the house as such, 'the garden lodge' as Bev called it, but most people would call it a detached log cabin.

Before Bev and Ashley divorced, they spent a fortune making their home and gardens beautiful. Bev didn't seem to recognise how guilty Ashley felt with his affair and he gave her much more than half of everything. She came out very well with her settlement, but at the earliest opportunity she would speak badly of him. Pippa knew it was because Bev loved Ashley so much and was devastated that he could look at anyone else let alone love another. She was truly hurt.

When the day arrived to pick Brendon from the airport, Pippa was feeling very content, her and Billy went over to Bev's and arrived at the garden lodge. Billy's bed and water bowl were put in place and he was happy. They went for a short walk round the garden, but it was more like a park with a lake and woodland area which they both loved. She then made herself presentable to meet Brendon.

As she was driving to the airport, she was understandably nervous. They met very briefly in Marbella, became acquaintances and were now friends, she wondered if anything could develop and if it did was it the right time or, even right?

Pippa waited at arrivals and wondered how she should greet Brendon, should it be with a little hug or a kiss on the cheek, she really didn't know. Before she could think any longer of what would be right, Brendon walked through and she caught sight of him, she thought how handsome he looked. Then he was standing in front of her, neither spoke just smiled and Brendon gently wrapped his arms around her, and she instinctively hugged him back. He kissed her softly on the lips and she found her lips slowly moving over his. Her heart literally missed a beat, and it was as if time stood still.

Eventually Brendon said.

'Thank you Pippa for inviting me.'

All Pippa could do was smile and say.

'Thank you so much for coming.'

By the time they got to the car park, they were both chattering away with ease as if they had been friends for years. There was so much laughter on the way to drop Brendon and his case to the B&B.

They were invited to Bev's for their evening meal at six o'clock. Brendon arrived just after Pippa with a chilled bottle of Pol Roger champagne, which impressed Bev no end.

They were all having a lovely evening, apart from Henry the cat. He was not at all impressed with Billy, the huge ginger and black giant. He'd put up with him before stealing the attention, he didn't like it then and certainly didn't like it now, especially when the giant went and drank out of Henry's water bowl, emptying the contents in one slurp. That was the final straw and with an almighty hiss he took a swipe at Billy's face, drawing blood. The chaos that followed was one of the stories that would be relayed for years to come.

Billy in shock of the assault howled. Henry was hissing and spitting. Bev was screaming at Henry and in the process of grabbing a tea towel to throw at him knocked over the unopened bottle of Pol Roger, which exploded when it hit the floor, spraying Pippa who was moving to comfort Billy and soaking her blouse.

Brendon who has a knack of finding humour and making people smile in the direst of circumstances, blurted out.

'If I'd known we were going to have a wet tee-shirt competition I'd have brought a magnum of Prosecco. Good grief did I just say that out loud?'

Pippa proudly thrust out her breasts, then disintegrated into embarrassment at what she'd done. Bev and Brendon followed suit with the laughter, which echoed through the house for a long time before anyone could catch their breath.

Pippa went upstairs with Bev to her bedroom, took off her soaked top and bra and Bev gave her a dry top to wear. Bev was grateful for the opportunity to have a private word.

'Oh Pip, he is absolutely wonderful, a dream, such a nice guy, I don't think you realise he's totally besotted with you.'

Pippa took the top Bev had passed her and pulled it on.

'Do you really think so?'

Bev looked totally astonished.

'Pip, there are times I just want to give you a slap, a blind person could see it!'

And then standing back said.

'How the hell do you look lovely in that top. I've tried it on so many times and I look awful in it, Pip that top is yours.'

At the end of the evening Brendon suggested he should walk Pippa and Billy home, adding tongue in cheek he was concerned after the awful assault from Henry the cat if Billy would be up for it. Both Bev and Pippa found this hilarious and confirmed it was a fabulous idea.

They arrived at the garden lodge and Brendon thanked Pippa for inviting him to join her for Bev's New Year's bash and she replied.

'I'm so very glad you've come, I don't think you realise how much you make people smile, and I'm talking smile inside and out, thank you for coming into my life.'

With that Brendon put his hands on her shoulders and bringing her into him, they kissed slowly and passionately, Pippa found her body simply mirrored Brendon's. Every breath and movement he took she responded. When eventually they broke away, Pippa said.

'Night, night, Brendon, I'm looking forward to seeing you tomorrow.'

'I'm looking forward to tomorrow and seeing you too, Nighty night Pippa. I'm grateful too that you came into my life.'

With that he pecked her on the cheek, turned and walked back to the B&B feeling quite lightheaded.

It was arranged for Brendon to have breakfast at the B&B and then join Pippa at the garden lodge and they could go for a walk with Billy around the lovely grounds. They stopped off at the marquee on their way back to check how everything was going for the party later on. Both saying how fabulous the marquee looked. Bev was so excited that everything was going so well, she had organised hired help and she felt the party was going to be the best she'd ever had, especially as Desmond was going to be there.

They returned to the lodge for Pippa to prepare baguettes for their lunch. Brendon lit the wood burner, then sat at the breakfast bar chatting to Pippa as Billy laid contently dozing in his bed knowing his mistress was feeling very happy.

After lunch they sat on the sofa both surprised how at ease they were in each other's company. Brendon was telling funny stories of parties he'd been to and Pippa realised she had only ever been to half a dozen and they had all been held by Bev or at Harold and Sally's, but she wouldn't raise that as it made her sound boring. Instead, she said.

'I always feel a little bit emotional with the words Auld Lang Syne, should old acquaintance be forgot, as I'd never ever forget my loved ones.'

'Oh Pippa, nor should you and it doesn't actually mean that, even being a Scot, the words are confusing as they're from old Scottish folk custom so no wonder they're often misinterpreted. What the words mean are reunion and remembering not parting or forgetting. That's why when it asks should old times be forgotten, it answers, we'll take a cup of kindness, meaning we'll have a drink together and look back on the past.'

He gently pulled her towards him and cuddled her, stroking the top of her arm and they sat for a good while savouring the moment.

After a while Brendon suggested they got on with calling their folks to wish them a happy new year. Pippa made a video call to Eddie and Sophie and they had the opportunity to see and say hello to Brendon and then he made a similar call to his sister Fiona where his parents were staying, with Pippa also wishing them all a Happy 2015.

Brendon knew Pippa needed enough time to do her hair and makeup for the party as she had said earlier, twice, he thought this was to ensure he got the message. He suggested he walked back to the B&B to get himself ready and swing back down to call for her at seven thirty, but Pippa said.

'I'll be ready by six thirty, how about you pop down any time after that and we can have a drink before walking up to the marquee.'

Brendon eagerly confirmed he would be at the garden lodge for a pre-party drink.

'Shall we say six thirty-one?'

She was so looking forward to wearing her new outfit. The midi length halter neck dress was a stunning cobalt blue, cut out lace, with the lining a few inches above the knee to discreetly show some flesh beneath through the lace. The sandals were in nude with a kitten heel, she'd even bought a new pair of earrings and matching bracelet. She would wear Matti's grandmother's sapphire and diamond engagement ring; she loved any occasion when she could wear this as it was truly beautiful, and she knew it was very expensive.

She was ready only just in time. When she opened the door to Brendon, she was thrilled to see him holding a beautiful bunch of peach roses which the B&B had arranged to be delivered. He looked so wonderfully smart in his natural casual way and she jokingly said.

'What, no kilt?'

'Pippa you look so beautiful, you've taken my breath away.'

As he stepped in, they greeted with a kiss on the lips. She put the flowers in a jug, as the one thing the garden lodge didn't have was a vase. She poured them both a glass of chardonnay and they sat down on the sofa.

For the walk up to the marquee Pippa wore her wellington boots and coat and took her new shoes in a carrier bag. She was surprised when they walked in that the party was already fully underway and thankfully Bev had forewarned all that knew Pippa of her situation.

Desmond arrived earlier than Bev expected, and both Pippa and Brendon hit it off with him straight away. He was such a nice chap and Pippa thought what a wonderful couple he and Bev made.

Bev took Pippa to one side and nervously but excitedly asked.

'Pip what do you think of Desmond?'

Pippa could honestly say what a wonderful chap she thought he was, which made Bev's broad smile even broader, then Bev lowered her voice even more asking.

'Surely you're not going to make Brendon go back to the B&B tonight?'

This genuinely shocked Pippa.

'Oh Bev, you're so naughty, of course he's going back to the B&B tonight, it's far too early.'

Bev just shook her head in disbelief!

Just before midnight the DJ announced there would be a countdown to tie in with the radio to Big Ben striking midnight. Which didn't go exactly to plan, as they counted down three times before they were in time with the gongs, but it joined everyone together even more in spirit. Brendon kissed Pippa at the final gong, and they wished each other and everyone around them a happy New Year. Then the music was back on and everyone joined hands, gathered in a circle to sing Auld Lang Syne. For the first time in her life Pippa felt happy to sing the words and thought of all her special people.

As the party was coming to a close, they said their goodbyes and Brendon offered to walk Pippa back. When they were at the garden lodge doorstep both had the same nervousness with their kiss before they said their goodnights.

As Pippa closed the door behind her, she couldn't help but feel a twang of disappointment that the kiss didn't go further but amongst the butterflies fluttering in her stomach she told herself it was far too early. Pippa made herself a cup of tea, hoping that would help settle her unfulfilled desires and she was saying to Billy how happy she felt. She was totally lost in the most pleasant thoughts, sipping her tea and there was a knock at the door, she knew instinctively who it was, and she thought she would burst with the intensity of the butterflies.

She answered the door and Brendon was standing in front of her, smiling broadly and in one hand he was holding a hip flask and in the other hand a carrier bag.

Pippa started to speak and before she could say anything, he interrupted her.

'I'm your First Footer, may I step in?'

Pippa didn't speak, she just opened the door fully and simply with her hands gestured, enter. Brendon walked in, turned to her and started emptying the carrier bag saying.

'I'm hoping you know what a First Footer is?'

She nodded in agreement and he went on.

'I'm sure no one has been here since we said goodnight.'

She shook her head, no. They both had broad smiles on their faces.

'Thank goodness for that. I've come bearing gifts to ensure 2015 will be a year of good fortune, for Pippa you really deserve it and I have to confess if your good fortune is what I intend it to be it will be my good fortune too.'

Out of the carrier bag he took a little jute bag and other things.

'Here is a silver coin which my Dad Bert sent you, a box of shortbread from my Mum and we need to seal your good fortune with a toast to the New Year.'

Without saying a word Pippa reached into the kitchen dresser and took out two small shot glasses placing them on the breakfast bar, Brendon poured a measure in each, and put his hand back into the jute bag saying.

'Not sure if you know, but tradition says any First Footer that enters empty handed is bad luck so that's why I've been so careful I've come prepared. Coal has always been important but it's the blackness that is significant, I've something special from me to you."

He put his hand in the jute bag and brought out a platinum necklace with an infinity locket made up of black diamonds and passed it to Pippa.

She held it, looking at it in awe, it was truly beautiful. Brendon gently took it out of her hands and put it round her neck, slowly moving her hair off her shoulders and fastened the clasp, bringing her hair back over her shoulders. He turned her to him.

'Oh Pippa, I hope you like it'

Instinctively she kissed him on the lips and turned back to the mirror, looking not only at the necklace but at herself. She couldn't believe how lovely she looked. She knew it wasn't just the necklace, the joy she was feeling was glowing through her body.

Pippa turned and looked at Brendon, she put her hands on his shoulders and quietly said.

'This is the most beautiful gift anyone has ever given me, thank you.'

Brendon smiled took the shot glasses, passing Pippa hers and raised his to offer a toast.

'Without a doubt 2015 will be our year.'

They chinked the glasses and Brendon raised the glass to his mouth knocked it back in one. It took Pippa a few swigs to get the strong spirit down, which they both found very funny.

Brendon put his empty glass down on the side, he went towards the door and as he was about to leave, he turned and again they kissed good night.

He put his hand back in the carrier bag.

'I know the diamonds in the locket are black, but I didn't want to tempt fate so here's something extra for you and also something for Billy.'

He handed her a lump of coal and a black onyx locket in the shape of a bone for Billy's collar.

Jokingly saying.

'Apparently the B&B only use smokeless fuel, but it should be alright.'

Smiling he lent forward and kissed her on the cheek, turned and walked back to the B&B feeling the happiest he'd felt in years.

On New Year's Day, Brendon arrived as arranged and they sat down on the sofa with a cup of tea and recapped the wonderful night before. Pippa said.

'Without a doubt that is the best party I've ever been to, but I think a lot of it was to do with the company, thank you for coming.'

'I had the most wonderful time too and I'm loving every minute of our time together.'

Pippa gave an embarrassed laugh saying.

'Bev is so naughty you know last night when she took me to one side and I told you she wanted to know what I thought of Desmond, well she also suggested I let you stay here the night, but I thought it was too early.'

Brendon laughed and clapped his hands.

'Well done Bev. Too early so that was last year, what about this year?'

They both laughed and Pippa looked even more embarrassed.

'Thing is, yes I do think it seems a little early. As you know my situation is very strange, technically I'm still a married woman and I don't think it would be appropriate for you to come to The Marshman's.'

Brendon took her hand in his.

'Pippa, I respect your privacy and you have said the barest of things about what happened, but our friendship is moving on, and you will have to trust to tell me things. Even the nasty horrible things. I will be here for you.'

She took a few moments before speaking.

'What are your plans for us seeing each other again?'

'Well, I need to be back in Marbella on tomorrow's flight to make sure I'm home in time when my parents return on Monday from Edinburgh, but then my sister will fly over late the following week and she can ensure they're not getting up to mischief. I could be back in two weeks' time if that suits you, and I'll be free for just over a week until I'm needed for parent sitting again?'

'That suits me very nicely. I'll ask Bev if you can stay here. You are right I have to be honest with you and I do need to tell you certain things. The truth is I'm scared if I tell you some of what happened, you're go running for the airport and I'll never see or hear from you again.'

Brendon was shaking his head from side to side. She carried on not daring to stop now she had started.

'Why I don't want you at The Marshman's, I don't want to be seen as the same as Karl. What happened, things hadn't been going well and I stayed at my cousin Ruth's. I'd only been gone a few days he locked me out and wouldn't let me have access. I kept asking in emails as I needed more of my things, so after six weeks I returned one evening to ask for some of my clothes and as the cottage is on one storey when I got in line with the bedroom, I could hear a woman's voice and it was obvious from the noises having sex. I waited in the car, then after a while I rang the doorbell, and he opened the door and I just walked in and when I got to the lounge this woman Tracy was sitting on my sofa in my dressing gown. If I let you come to The Marshman's I feel I would be no better than him. I need to divorce him, so I can move on and have a life. But he won't acknowledge the divorce. A few days before Christmas I found out where he is living at Tracy's and my solicitor sent the divorce papers out again to him. Well, that's it in a nutshell. At least you're not running for the airport.'

Brendon tried not to show on his face the anger he felt at how shabby Pippa had been treated, saying.

'Oh Pippa, I can see your concerns over me being at The Marshman's and truthfully I wouldn't want to be there in these circumstances, and I wouldn't trust myself if he showed up.'

'Brendon, thank you for being so considerate, can we move on to nice positive things now, this is a start of a New Year. Bev will be pleased that you're coming back so soon, I'll quickly message her now.'

Brendon adding.

'You might want to ask her for a block booking.'

To which they both laughed.

The subject was quickly changed to the positives of Brendon's return trip. He suggested they take the train to London, stay two nights in a nice hotel and take in a show. As they were talking Pippa received a text and laughing said.

'Good it's Bev, she's obviously confirming our block booking request.'

Pippa was right, it was a text from Bev, but it read … are you decent? … Pippa read it out loud and they fell about in laughter … YES … she replied and with that there was a loud knock on the door.

Brendon instinctively jumped up and opened the door to a very excited Bev who walked straight in saying.

'What a wonderful year 2015 is going to be. Well done you two, we're absolutely thrilled.'

Desmond followed behind looking completely exhausted, which he put down to jet lag! Bev sat herself down, with a wrung out Des next to her.

'Of course, Brendon dear this place is yours for as often as you want. The truth is these days the only guest that ever stays here is Billy and he kindly lets Pippa come along too, don't your dear.'

Patting Billy squarely on the head. Bev was still furious with Henry the cat attacking him.

The four of them forged a very nice and genuine friendship, the guys had so much in common.

The time for Pippa taking Brendon to the airport came far too soon for them both. But they needn't have worried as they filled their time apart excitedly planning the time Brendon would be over.

It was arranged that Brendon would fly in on the Friday early evening flight. Their train to London was booked for Saturday morning, two night's dinner, bed and breakfast at a very nice hotel, they would see The Phantom of The Opera for the Sunday matinée and return by train on the Monday late afternoon.

Billy would stay with Eddie and Sophie, who would also act as taxi to pick up and drop Pippa and Brendon to and from the station.

The Friday flight to Norwich was on time and Brendon had arranged to hire a car at the airport, he wanted one with enough room for Billy and booked a large Audi estate.

Pippa arrived at the garden lodge before him, lit the wood burner and started preparing their evening meal. When Brendon walked in it was a scene of domestic bliss. Pippa rushed to the door, intending to throw her arms around Brendon. He let go of his case, raised his arms to cuddle her. They'd both missed one another so much. But instead of a romantic cuddle, it turned into a group huddle. Billy was as excited as Pippa to see Brendon and jumped out of his bed lumbering in the middle of them.

The meal was served, eaten and tidied away, and it was getting late so Pippa left for home with Billy. This left them little time together, which was probably a good thing as their desires for one another couldn't be contained for much longer.

As arranged Eddie and Sophie were round at The Marshman's to pick Billy and Pippa up and on to the garden lodge. Eddie made sure within the planning there was enough time for them to properly meet Brendon. They were thrilled that he was exactly as Pippa had described and they were so relieved he was nothing at all like Karl!

As they walked hand in hand through the station to the train, the happiness they both felt made them fit to burst. They were in first class and Pippa relayed about her last trip to London when she was staying at Stella's, her school friend's house, well not really at Stella's but her neighbours. Brendon loved listening to Pippa, her voice was so soft, and the stories were wonderful. From what she'd relayed of her parents they were both great storytellers, so obviously inherited from them. He thought it was her command of the detail and clear observations of things going on around her that made her stories so interesting and often hilarious.

They went for a bite to eat at an Italian restaurant in Knightsbridge before going over to the hotel across from Hyde Park.

They went up the lift to the top floor, with Brendon saying it doesn't matter what hotel or where you are in the world, you always need a decent view. As they entered it wasn't a room Brendon had booked but a suite, it was stunning. He was nattering away in his usual relaxed manner, hung up his coat and started to unpack his case and then realised Pippa was just staring out of the window, quietly taking in the view of Hyde Park. He gently asked.

'Is everything alright Pippa?'

Still taking in the view she replied.

'Perfect, it couldn't be better, thank you.'

She turned to him, still in her coat and he put his arms around her, and they gently kissed.

Pippa was grateful it wasn't a room but a suite, not just because it was big and posh, but it gave her personal space to get ready as she wanted to look her best. Brendon sat in the lounge area reading the paper and Pippa went into the bathroom to run her bath. As she went back through the lounge to get some things out of the bedroom. Brendon stopped her.

'I have something for you.'

He passed her a beautifully wrapped gift box. She sat down in one of the armchairs and slowly unwrapped her gift. It was a matching perfume, body cream and bubble bath. She squirted the perfume, it was divine.

'Oh Brendon, thank you so much but I feel bad as I haven't got anything for you.'

'Pippa, your being here with me is the only gift any man could ever want.'

Pippa collected her wash bag, and her new underwear from the bedroom and took them in the bathroom. She lay in the deep bath, with the bubbles around her, wishing everything to be just right, but she was worried, so very worried. What would Brendon think of her when she was naked.

Pippa was still haunted by the looks Karl gave her while the mass was taking over her tummy and if those looks weren't bad enough his reaction to the scar resulting from the incision to remove the huge mass was awful. No woman deserved to be looked at like that, ever!

For so long now, Pippa hadn't looked at her naked torso, even when she put on her body cream, she blindly rubbed it in as she dare not look. But she plucked up the courage and stroked the bubbles away until she could see her tummy through the clear water. Yes, she could see a neat line right down from below her rib cage to pubic bone, but she really had to stare to see it. She raised her tummy out of the water and was pleased that while the scar was obviously still there, it was difficult to see.

When Pippa finished in the bathroom, she went through the lounge wearing the hotel's complementary dressing gown and underneath her gorgeous new underwear. She blew Brendon a kiss.

'Bathroom's all yours'.

He smiled and blew her a kiss back.

Pippa straightened her hair and finished putting on her make up as Brendon came through from the bathroom, wearing just a towel wrapped tightly around his waist. He went over to Pippa and instinctively she stood up, untied the gown and slipped it off her shoulders. She was standing in front of the person she loved in just her underwear. Brendon took both her hands in his, raised them to her side.

'My God Pippa, you're so beautiful.'

With that he scooped her up and gently laid her on the bed, as the towel at his waist fell to the floor and began to make love to her and she to him. At that moment in time, they were one.

As they basked in the afterglow the telephone rang making them both jump. Brendon answered and Pippa listened as he apologised for missing their dinner reservation made at check in, saying he would ring shortly with a room service order. He reached over to return the phone to its cradle and they both dissolved into fits of laughter which wasn't long in turning into the lovemaking that neither could get enough of.

An hour and a half later, the call was finally made for room service.

They only just managed to get to Sunday breakfast. The show was wonderful, the perfect choice. The evening meal they sat down at eight and surprised themselves to be the last guests in the restaurant as they didn't stop talking. They knew the chance of making it in time to the restaurant the following morning was slim, so they were organised booking room service for breakfast.

Their whole time away couldn't have been more perfect and their bond continued to be forged stronger and stronger when they were back in Norfolk.

Dr Newcome said he was happy for Pippa to return to work, and she contacted Annie her manager and a return-to-work plan was put in place. Pippa was thrilled to be told that she had accrued the whole of her last year's holiday entitlement whilst she was off on sick leave and could she give some thoughts on when she wanted to use it. She knew this would come in useful what with the baby arriving in July and also to have time with Brendon when he was over at the garden lodge, plus, they had arranged for her to visit Brendon in Marbella.

The months were passing and while she had a sense of normality and enjoying life to the full, Karl would not acknowledge the divorce papers and the solicitor only confirmed what she already had been told. Unless they knew where he was at a certain time for a Process Server to issue the papers, he could just drag it on.

When she spoke with Brendon of her frustration, he confirmed the frustration was mutual, they couldn't work out what Karl was up to. On a few occasions when Brendon was over and she was at work he drove past Tracy's house and at no time Karl's car, or a car of similar status was on the drive. They thought he probably wasn't frequenting this address anymore.

CHAPTER 25

'To err is human, to repent divine: to persist devilish!'

It was early April, Pippa, Bev and Bella had arranged for a girl's night out. A table was booked at a restaurant in the center of Norwich that had a live salsa band, and a fun night was planned. They booked a taxi for the journey there and home so they could all have a drink.

But when the Friday night arrived Pippa was running late. She weighed up texting Bev and Bella to let them know that she wouldn't be joining them, or should she send a text to say she was running late. She decided she'd arrive late, drive herself, park and offer to drive them all home.

The trio were now all good friends and Pippa definitely didn't want to let them down. Much to both Pippa's and Bev's surprise it turned out Bella was a nice, genuine person and lost her title of 'Bella bloomin' Robertson' and was now known as Bella.

Pippa always made an effort with her presentation and just because she was late, knew that was no excuse to take short cuts. When she eventually got in her car, she realised she needed to get cash so would stop off in Bagby. She pulled into the bank car park, went to the cash machine and it was out of order. She turned to go across to the cash machine on the other side of the road and there was Karl's Jaguar car parked outside the pub.

Good grief she thought, he is still in the area.

She walked over to the cash machine to withdraw some money, as Karl and Tracy came out of the pub and walked in her direction, oblivious to her standing there. She stood looking at them. They didn't look close; Karl was a few paces behind Tracy. Pippa was surprised to see she now had very long, thick hair, so obviously had extensions put in. Tracy wore the facial expression of, is this as good as it gets. Without doubt, both their expressions were of a couple that had just had words, and not pleasant ones at that!

When they got closer Pippa took her opportunity.

'Hello, can you make sure you return the divorce papers.'

They were shocked to see her. Tracy was first to speak, saying to Karl.

'You said you returned them before Christmas, what's she going on about.'

He was not best pleased with Tracy for saying this or saying anything come to that and spat.

'I did, she's lying. Do you want a Pizza or not, make your mind up?'

Pippa got her cash and went to meet Bev and Bella. They'd delayed ordering their meal until Pippa was there but used the time to get through a bottle and half of wine and were well oiled by the time she arrived. She didn't mention who she'd bumped into she certainly didn't want to spoil the evening. The last thing Bev or Bella ever needed to be started on was a subject involving a wayward man!

When she was in bed she thought of bumping into Karl and Tracy at the cash machine. What on earth is wrong with him, why did he tell Tracy he'd returned the papers before Christmas when her solicitor had sent them out four times now?

On the Monday Pippa received an email from Karl asking if she could meet him for a drink, he missed her so much and could never love anyone else. When he'd seen her last Friday it just confirmed to him that he needed to be with his wife. He couldn't believe how awful he felt.

Pippa didn't rush with replying she gave great thought how to handle the situation. She decided to use the opportunity of a meeting to convince Karl they had to move on, and he needed to sign and acknowledge the divorce papers.

She agreed to see him. He suggested a drink on Friday night, the same pub in Bagby that she'd seen him and Tracy walking away from the Friday before! But she insisted a garden center on the other side of Norwich, and to meet the Friday afternoon not evening. Karl replied straight away that he suggested the evening as he hoped she would let him come home and they could go back together afterwards. But if it meant he got to speak with Pippa they could meet at the garden center.

Pippa didn't tell anyone of the meeting, she needed to grasp the nettle of dealing with Karl.

He was already at the garden center café when Pippa arrived. He looked different, he had lost weight, his hair looked thinner and had a lot of grey in it, he'd made an effort with his clothes, but then she thought he always had. She sat down and he started saying how much he'd missed her and was she coping alright with everything. Pippa was in two minds if she wanted to slap him across the face or scream that she would be getting on easier if he'd contributed to the bills. But neither would help, she didn't want to create a scene and she needed to keep in control.

'You've been living at Tracy's for six months now, this is the first contact you've made since threatening me with the police for stalking you. You haven't contributed anything towards the bills and you still take out half the rental money. You haven't acknowledged the divorce papers and by my solicitor having to send them out four times you've increased my divorce costs. So, what do you think? No, I'm not alright.'

Karl looked at Pippa with a very sad expression and a pleading tone in his voice.

'I've been to the doctor and he's put me on tablets. I've been on them two months now and they seem to be helping me so much. I didn't realise how ill I was, I'm starting to feel like my old self. We don't want a divorce that's why I haven't returned the papers. Think about how much you will be giving up. The properties would have to be sold and the future I have planned for you wouldn't happen. I love you totals, I could never love another. But you must understand when you were ill it made things so difficult for me, a man has urges that have to be met, that's all Tracy was. You've been ill. You won't be ill again. So you don't have to worry about that anymore. You are right, you need to move on to our future together. You've always said our vows were in sickness and in health, I've not been well.'

Pippa was taken aback! Karl carried on saying.

'Please Pippa, I love you, and I want to come home. I'll never treat you badly again, I promise.'

Pippa felt like crying she was so confused.

'I really don't know what to say Karl, this is an absolute mess, I'll have to think about what you've said.'

She stood up and left.

Pippa took Billy for a walk to try and gain clarity, the one thing she was certain of it was a complete and utter mess! All she kept thinking; I knew I shouldn't have fallen for Brendon.

Karl did appear more balanced, the tablets must be helping. It genuinely seemed as if Karl wanted to make it work, but what if it wasn't for the right reasons? She knew she couldn't speak to anyone about what to do, no one would understand. Oh God what am I going to do, poor Brendon. I love him. I've never had the feelings I have with Brendon for Karl. I don't know if I've ever had feelings like this in my life. I think I did for Matti but that was so long ago, and I was so young. I'm sure Karl is being genuine, but I can't give up what I have with Brendon, it's too real.

Pippa had a restless night and woke in the early hours in turmoil, she knew she wanted to stay with Brendon. She didn't care about all the money the divorce would cost her, but she was still married to Karl and their vows were in sickness and in health, he's been unwell.

She remained deep in thought and in the morning went to the graveyard to speak with Matti, they both kept their vows until death parted them. She knew she would have to try and make it work with Karl.

Her rose tinted glasses were firmly back and she really wanted to believe he was genuine this time, and hoped upon hope, she was doing the right thing.

When she got back home, she sat down and prepared herself for the awful call she had to make to Brendon.

He was devastated but so understanding and supportive.

'You're breaking my heart Pippa. Part of me wishes it works out for you, but a greater part hopes it doesn't. My darling Pippa you know where I am and always will be.'

With that he rang off.

Pippa sat and quietly sobbed for a long time. Then braced herself to let family know she was taking Karl back.

She phoned Eddie first and could hear Sophie crying in the background, then she phoned Ruth, none of them could believe it, but they would support her.

Bev was incandescent with rage, she screamed at Pippa.

'He's a salesman he just sees you as his next contract. As for those rose tinted glasses of yours, I feel like ripping them off your face and stamping all over them. Well don't expect me and Desmond to cut Brendon off, that won't ever happen.'

Pippa decided she wouldn't call Karl over the weekend but wait until the Monday to make him aware of her decision. She knew this would give her time to grieve for her loss of Brendon and she needed to be on her own without any interruptions.

First thing Sunday morning Eddie phoned on her mobile to say her landline had a fault. He'd reported it and a telecoms engineer would be there shortly. She thanked him for getting it sorted and within minutes of speaking, the doorbell rang.

It was the engineer. He informed her that the fault wasn't outside the property but in the house, could he come in and check it out. She showed him the two telephone points, one in the lounge and one in the kitchen, only to be told they were working, was there any other points in the house?

'Yes, there is one in the office but that hasn't been used for about six months now, I can't see that being the problem.'

But she led the way. The engineer unscrewed the plate on the wall, tested the wires and sure enough the fault was there. She said she'd leave him to it and took herself through to the orangery, hoping he couldn't tell she'd been crying.

It wasn't long and he called through.

'All sorted, you shouldn't have a problem with it now, I'll see myself out. Bye.'

She decided being on her own wasn't the best plan and phoned Eddie on the landline to say the engineer had been and gone, the fault was in the office. She offered as a thank you, would they like to go out for Sunday Lunch, which they did.

Before she went to work on the Monday Pippa called Karl to say she would try again but he must never lie to her again and he had to make a complete break with Tracy telling her the truth that they were finished. He agreed saying he would be honest he'd learnt his lesson and he would tell Tracy straight away that it was over, and he'd be home that evening.

Monday night as Karl's car pulled up on the drive Billy started barking a true German Shepherd bark, which was uncharacteristic of him. When Karl walked through the front door the bark was replaced with a low growl.

Karl ignored Billy's behaviour, simply announcing.

'Well, the dirty deed's been done, it's all over, Tracy's history.'

He stepped forward as if to kiss her on the lips, but she quickly intervened, gave him a tentative hug and kiss on the cheek, and timidly suggested that may be to start with he could be in the guest room to give her time to get used to him being back. Karl was clearly disappointed but agreed.

He brought his dirty washing in and put it in the laundry basket.

They sat in the lounge and Karl said.

'I can't wait to hear what you've been up to whilst I've been away. Not sure if you realised Peppa we should have flown to Dubai yesterday for that break. I cancelled it. That was to be a holiday for us, and I couldn't face going without you.'

Pippa thought of the date, yes, he was right. This convinced her that he was making a genuine effort.

CHAPTER 26
'On the ball, City'

In an attempt to placate Pippa and put her mind at rest, Karl suggested he would email his work itinerary for two weeks at a time over to her. His first week back at The Marshman's were detailed, showing he was to work from his home office all week until early Sunday morning, when he would fly to Germany for an exhibition. The flight numbers were listed, and it showed he would be back Friday afternoon. He reassured her saying for her not to worry, she could contact him whenever she wanted. He even went further saying in earnest, that even though he would be very busy at the Bautec exhibition in Berlin, he would answer straight away unless he was in an awkward position, and if that were to happen, he would call her back as soon as he could.

He placed a sum of money in the joint account, suggesting she transfer the direct debits for the utility bills from her personal account back to their joint account, again emphasising he didn't want her to worry about a thing. Pippa saying, it was a fuss to move the first time, she'd leave them where they were, but she'd transfer enough over to her sole account to cover the payments. When she later looked on the banking, she was surprised to see he had indeed placed a large sum of money there. She transferred monies for that month and all previous when he contributed nothing. When all said and done, that seemed only fair.

Karl did appear to be trying really hard, but he seemed terrified of meeting anyone. On his return he put his car away in the garage, something he never did previously. He'd always maintained it was a company car and not his problem. This change made Pippa wonder if he was scared of Tracy or anyone knowing when he was there, as with his car hidden in the garage, he could easily be Mr Elusive again to others.

Pippa thought she'd never known a week to drag by as much as this week and Karl had only returned the night before!

She was at work and Annie her manager called into the sub-office where Pippa was based and took her aside. Pippa could see she was fit to burst with excitement, as Annie burst into song.

'On the ball, City'.

Pippa through her giggles replied.

'Come on you yellows. Oh my goodness Annie isn't it fantastic news Norwich City are in the play offs, Eddie and Harold are going to the home game. As you know since Sophie's been pregnant Harold has gone in her place.'

Annie hugged her.

'We're going too Pippa, we've both won tickets to the game, we'll be in the Bank's corporate box at Carrow Road, we can each take a guest too. We'll be spoilt rotten with complimentary food and drinks.'

Annie explained Head Office had allocated each of the eight branches tickets for two members of staff, plus four tickets were reserved in a separate draw for retired staff, each winning person could bring a guest. The draw was simple and to make it fair, names had simply been picked out of a 'branch' hat by the Chief Executive. Annie was taking her husband and tentatively asked if Karl would be Pippa's guest. There was no hesitation in Pippa's reply.

'No, I'll ask Bev, she'll love it, especially if there's anyone from her days when she worked for the Bank.'

Annie was relieved that Karl wouldn't be there. She had never met him, but he didn't sound the sort of person she wanted to share a moment in the company of, let alone a fantastic fun day. Norwich would be playing their local rivals Ipswich and the winners would go on to the Championship League playoff at Wembley the following week. The winner would move up to the Premiership League with all its financial benefits.

Since Annie had transferred six years earlier from the Bury St Edmunds branch to manage the Head Office branch where Pippa worked at the time, they became good friends. During Pippa's time off sick, she would pay monthly home visits. She was one of the few people to be taken into Pippa's confidence on the Karl shenanigans. She could hardly believe her ears with some of the things she heard. It made her blood boil and wondered how on earth Pippa had managed to stay sane. On Pippa's return to work Annie was so pleased to see a positive change in her confidence. She adored the sound of Brendon and was totally gutted to hear she had taken Karl back. Pippa had been so happy right up to that moment and almost instantly lost her lust for life. Annie didn't pry. She was upset to witness this, but she knew Pippa well enough to know if she wanted to talk, she would, but in her own time.

When Pippa left for the day, she messaged Eddie and phoned Bev with the news. Bev was screeching with joy and confirmed she would most definitely join her adding.

'Don't you give my ticket away to that Karl, you may have taken him back, but I don't want anything to do with him, the lying cheat.'

When Pippa arrived home, she took Karl a cup of tea through to his office and heard all about his busy day. He felt he was the only person in the company that was doing any work. On top of all that he needed to spend time with the arrangements and preparation for the exhibition, he didn't know if he was coming or going. Pippa listened and made appropriate comments at the right moment and didn't share her good news. She changed out of her work clothes to take Billy for his walk.

They had just walked out of the driveway when they passed a chap new to the village.

She'd seen him a couple of times recently, acknowledging each other with 'afternoon, what a lovely day', but each time she had seen him she was preoccupied. Today was no exception she was deep in her thoughts. She missed Brendon so much and wondered if the pain she felt would ever subside. The doubt she felt for taking Karl back was gnawing away at her. It seemed a darkness had come over her from the moment he walked through the door. She really would have to try harder to accept her husband's return, when all said and done, he was trying to show he was a changed man.

Pippa forced herself to think happy thoughts and indeed she had so much to be grateful for. She would soon be a grandmother and Saturday at Carrow Road would be fabulous, truly a day to remember. But soon her thoughts drifted back to Karl.

She was determined he wouldn't know she was going to the match she would say she and Bev were going shopping. The fact that he had distanced himself from everyone, the chance of him finding out would be next to zero. If in time he decided to integrate back into her friends and family, she would just use the excuse it was too soon after his return for him to join her. She wondered if she hadn't invited him as her guest out of spite or guilt, or was it that she knew he would simply have to spoil anything nice or fun? She reassured herself her decision was right. Anyway, Karl supported Newcastle football club, not Norwich City. Yes, she was right, least said soonest mended.

Pippa didn't like the change in her, she was lying which normally didn't come easy to her. She also found she wasn't actually talking to Karl. The night before she listened as he spoke non-stop of his work, and what he and Tracy had got up to. Pippa had to stop him as she did not need to hear how 'enthusiastic' Tracy had been!

Karl asked what she got up to whilst he was away, and she replied.

'You know, all the normal things, work, saw family, friends, and walked Billy.'

But she didn't relay what friends or what she did!

He was particularly keen to know where she had been on holiday when she sent him the photo of her toes on a sunbed. It looked a lovely place, such a wonderful view, was it in Spain? No doubt she had gone with Bev. He really wanted to know so he could spoil his wife and take her back there. Finally, after his continuous badgering she said.

'You're so right Karl it was lovely, I didn't have to do a thing, just pack my case and crash. Goodness me what was the name of the place, it will come to me. Oh, that's right, I flew to Palma in Spain.'

Karl looked at his wife thinking, yes, he was right it was that bossy Bev had arranged everything for the holiday. That woman was trouble. How on earth had Pippa coped whilst he was away, Palma's in Majorca, not mainland Spain. It's a good job she never travelled outside Norfolk she'd never find her way back!

When Billy and Pippa got back from their walk, she prepared a salad for tea and extra for Eddie and Sophie. She then cheerily went into Karl's office and said his tea was in the fridge and with Sophie being pregnant she liked to help out as much as possible. While he was away, she had got in the habit of doing tea for them on a Tuesday and Thursday and didn't want that to change. She would have hers over at Eddie's that evening.

She was then about to leave, and Karl said.

'Yes, you are right you must continue with things you enjoy doing, the last thing I want is for you or anyone to think I'm a control freak. I've some good news, I thought it would be nice to go for a meal and with me being away at the exhibition next week I wanted to treat my wife. I've booked for us to go to that lovely restaurant you liked near the Cathedral, the Quayside, Saturday at two o'clock, we can have a nice meal and then get back here with enough time for me to finish getting ready for my trip away. Thankfully they've reserved a space in their car park as the City will be heaving with Norwich playing Ipswich in the playoff.'

Pippa was taken aback for a moment.

'The playoff? Oh, I'm sorry Karl I'd already arranged with Bev to go up the City to do some shopping and have afternoon tea, she's been looking forward to it so much I really couldn't let her down. Perhaps we could reschedule lunch at the Quayside for the weekend after you're back from the exhibition.'

Karl shrugged.

'Yeah, as you like, no skin off my nose, I just thought it would be a nice thing to do, you'll have to wait a couple of weeks though, I'll be too tired from the exhibition to go the weekend after, I don't think you realise how grueling it is on an exhibition stand.'

With that he got back to his computer, annoyed with himself for only minutes earlier saying she shouldn't change her plans for him.

Life before she kicked him out, her world revolved round him. But he'd come through the door the night before and she was different. It was hard to keep her attention when he was speaking to her, which wasn't good. He needed to work his magic and get her back in her proper place as dutiful wife. His plan was not going at all well.

Pippa and Billy arrived at Eddie and Sophie's before they were home from work. She went into the garden and picked some flowers which she popped in a little vase on the table, Billy needed to sniff the whole garden for any new smells and mark the boundary appropriately. Sophie was first through the door, closely followed by Eddie they both gave Pippa the biggest of hugs.

As they ate tea, their talk was plans for Saturday. Eddie offered to pick Pippa up on the way to Bev's with Pippa saying she had planned to get to Bev's earlier and it would be great if they could both be picked up from there. Goodness me thought Pippa, one lie leads to another.

Sophie was disappointed, saying.

'That's a shame you won't be able to take advantage of the banks hospitality and have a glass of wine as you're need to get your car back from Bev's. I'll be driving home so Eddie and my Dad can have a pint at half time. It's going to be a one-off event if I was you Pippa, I'd enjoy every minute. Let us know if you change your mind.'

Pippa gave thought of how she would get round this problem. She had told Karl her and Bev were going into Norwich to do some shopping and afternoon tea, she hadn't wanted him to be suspicious with Eddie giving her a lift, but as Karl himself had said the City would be heaving and parking a problem. He knew Eddie and Sophie were Norwich City season ticket holders and Eddie always parked in his work's car park, a five-minute walk from the ground. Yes, that would do, and if Karl asked, she would just say she was worried about parking with the City being so busy and it gave her the opportunity to join Bev with a glass of fizz with her afternoon tea.

As she left, Pippa said she would love if she could be picked up on the way to Bev's.

Surprisingly what had started off as a week dragging, suddenly sped by. Sophie lent Pippa a Norwich City top from the previous season. She also offered to lend Bev her previous season's away top but try as she might Bev couldn't get the top over her ample bosom, so Eddie lent Bev his previous year's top. Pippa and Bev were excited, they would be together in the corporate box in matching Norwich City football tops.

When Pippa woke on Saturday at her usual early hour the weather was beautiful. She walked Billy then showered and dressed but she knew she couldn't put the Norwich City top on, that would give the game away to Karl. She popped the football top in her bag and was wearing a white tee-shirt with a sleeveless vest under. She prepared a cooked breakfast for her and Karl which they ate at the kitchen table.

She was being more friendly to him, trying really hard all week to accept Karl. This didn't go unnoticed, and he was feeling quite smug with himself, hopefully not too much longer and she couldn't resist him and become a proper wife again. Him having to be in the guest bedroom was not helping him woo her, plus he needed his ego and other things massaged!

When half past ten arrived, she kissed Billy and shouted bye to Karl who was holed up in his office. He was in a panic that he wasn't going to have everything ready for the exhibition. As she walked down the driveway she thought, I've done Karl a favour not going for the meal today, if he'd gone that would have left him even less time to prepare.

She stood at the end of the drive on the side of the road waiting for Eddie, when a young woman in walking attire went past on the other side of the road, they smiled and acknowledged one another. As Pippa waited, she thought how popular the area had become for walkers lately. Just then there was a hoot, hoot, hoot, of a car horn and it was an excited Eddie, Sophie and Harold. The Range Rover had green and yellow football scarves hanging out of the windows and it made Pippa laugh.

'Not wearing your football top Mum?'

Eddie asked disappointedly, and Pippa produced it out of her bag.

'I thought I'd leave putting it on until the last minute, I don't want to mess it up and get anything down it.'

When they got to Bev's, she and Desmond were waiting outside. If Pippa thought Eddie, Sophie and Harold were euphoric they were subdued compared to Bev. Desmond was quietly pleased when Eddie drove off. Since Bev received the message she was going as a guest in The Eastern England Bank's corporate box she had not stopped talking of her time when she worked at the bank.

Eddie pulled on to his work's car park. Sophie took herself in the direction to the shops to look at baby clothes with the rest of them starting the short walk to Carrow Road football ground. The happy carnival atmosphere was wonderful.

When Bev and Pippa arrived at the entrance of the corporate box they were greeted by the Bank's Chief Executive, a waiter at his side with a tray of champagne glasses. Many of the winning staff and their guests had already arrived, including Annie and her husband. One of the retired staff was the manager of Pippa and Bev from when they started at the bank. The girls had thought he was ancient back then, but he had only turned forty, so now he appeared surprisingly spritely for being in his eightieth year.

There were many people Pippa didn't know from branches further afield, Ipswich, Colchester and Bury St Edmunds. Just as they were about to take their seats for the kickoff, two women arrived, they were obviously twins. The game was nerve racking and when the whistle for the first half was blown the score was level at 0-0 or 1-1 on aggregate from the first leg held the previous week.

Bev looked exhausted.

'Oh Pip, I'm out of breath I feel as if I've made every kick of the ball, certainly time for a drink. I don't know if my nerves can take it.'

The buffet was splendid as was the waiting service, they were truly being spoilt. Bev quickly filled her plate with food and was back reminiscing with their old manager, leaving Pippa still selecting from the buffet. The twins were next to her and Pippa introduced herself. The women were Kelly from the Colchester branch and her sister Katy. When Pippa heard the name, her thoughts went straight to Karl. Pippa asked Katy if she also worked for the bank and the twins laughed with Katy answering.

'Oh, I wouldn't have lasted a minute in a bank, I work selling beauty products.'

Pippa was complementary of both the girls' complexions and wished she'd had a sister in the beauty industry, she would love all the free samples. She then plucked up courage to ask what was on her mind.

'Kelly, I think we've met before at one of the bank's award dinners.'

Kelly at first looked perplexed and then said.

'Oh, I did go to one, quite a few years ago now, but I didn't see much of it as I wasn't very well. I'd just sat down to eat and got the most terrible migraine, so I spent the rest of the evening in my hotel room.'

Pippa quickly changed the subject to how surprised she was when Annie her manager told her that she had won a ticket.

Kelly was agreeing with her.

'Me too, I never win anything, the bank has even paid for our train tickets and a taxi at the end, they really haven't skimped on making this a day to remember.'

Kelly looked in the direction of Annie, saying.

'I used to work with Annie. Before she was promoted to manage the Norwich Head Office, she was based at the Bury St Edmunds branch and would act as the Colchester branch relief manager. Everyone thought she so deserved the promotion, but we were sad to see her go, she's such a wonderful person, everyone loved her.'

It was time for everyone to take their seats for the second half and it turned into a brilliant 4-2 on aggregate win for

Norwich. The atmosphere in the whole ground was euphoric, well obviously not the Ipswich end. The walk back to the car took them longer than on their arrival as the throngs of people didn't want the day to end.

Sophie was waiting in the car and diligently drove them back home. They pulled into Bev's driveway and Desmond was waiting with a bottle of champagne. He popped the cork as Eddie hopped out to open Bev's door. Everyone except Sophie indulged in a celebratory glass of bubbly on the lawn.

Pippa had been thinking how on earth was she going to change out of the football shirt back to her white tee-shirt. Her mind was going overtime, and she realised this scheming and lying couldn't continue. She needn't have worried, as Bev unknowingly came to her rescue. In her excitement she went to take a glass from Desmond to pass to Pippa and her hand slipped on the wet flute champagne glass, tipping it straight down the football shirt.

'Oh no' Pippa said with a laugh, 'wet tee-shirt party again.'

This gave her the opportunity to change back to her white top. Bev was beside herself and even offered to wash the top before it went back to Sophie, so Pippa didn't even have to take the champagne-soaked football shirt back to The Marshman's.

When Pippa was finally dropped back, she let Billy out and was disturbed to see that he acted as if he were bursting for a pee. She assumed Karl would be in his office, but he wasn't. She went to the garage and his car wasn't there, he'd obviously gone out. Her only thought was how long had Billy been on his own, deprived of going in the garden.

Pippa was in bed when Karl came home, he knocked on her door, saying.

'I'm back, I'll be off early in the morning for my flight.'

To his surprise, Pippa opened the door.

'Safe journey, I hope the exhibition goes well, you've put so much effort into it. See you Friday.'

She then gave him a peck on the cheek. She could tell he'd been drinking.

Karl suddenly felt that he had to offer an explanation for going out. Pippa knew he was nervous as he had reverted to his Geordie accent. He said he had gone to a pub to watch the Norwich, Ipswich match and a couple of the guys there supported Newcastle. He felt happy in their company and had a great time, the three of them went on for a kebab. They exchanged mobile numbers and arranged they would share the journey when they next went to a match to cheer on the Magpies. He was so pleased to have finally found friends in Norfolk after all these years.

When Pippa woke on the Sunday morning Karl had already left. He messaged her from the airport saying he had arrived safely, and his plane was about to take off.

She had a nice day planned, she would get on with the project she was working on, lining a Moses basket ready for her grandson's arrival. There was only six more weeks until he was due. Every stich was filled with love. Her and Sophie chose the material together and she was thrilled with how it was turning out.

On Monday when Pippa got in from work, she went to her jewellery box to look at the beautiful infinity necklace Brendon gave her for New Year's. She thought of her handsome First Footer. She was struggling with her emotions, she felt wretched without him being in her life and hoping he was alright. She put the necklace back and opened Matti's grandmothers ring box, it was empty. Oh no, where could it be, she looked through the jewellery box. Where was the sapphire and diamond ring, she religiously put it back in its box? It was nowhere to be found!

Pippa was on annual leave from the Thursday lunchtime and all the following week. The time had been booked before she broke up with Brendon for her to fly to be with him that week. She'd asked Annie if she could change the time off but was diplomatically told that since Pippa had accrued so much holiday while on sick leave, it would really mess the work schedules up, which she understood.

Pippa arranged to have lunch with Annie when she finished on Thursday. They took their packed lunches as they often did and walked through the lovely old streets in Norwich, between the large outdoor market with its colourful stalls and the City Hall with its impressive bronze lions, over to the Chapelfield Gardens, only a short distance from the branch. Annie wondered if the time was right for Pippa to talk about what was going on with Karl and in a roundabout way Annie was right.

As they walked Pippa was saying that Karl was away in Germany at an exhibition, she had messaged him every day and he had messaged only once as his plane was about to leave the airport on Sunday.

As they sat on a park bench Annie asked if Pippa had second thoughts about taking Karl back.

Pippa did her normal thing when she was upset of not making eye contact and continued to look at the sandwiches in her lunch box. Then taking a deep breath, emotionally said.

'Second, third and a thousand thoughts. I complicated things falling in love with Brendon, I still miss him terribly. I'm trying really hard with Karl, but I just feel suspicious of him all the time, my gut feeling is he has a plan. I don't even like leaving Billy in the house with Karl. It's almost as if Billy can't stand being in the same room as him. Karl's just got to pull on the drive or come anywhere near me and he puts on this low growl. I know it sounds daft but it's as if Billy senses something and is trying to warn me.'

Annie quickly reassured Pippa.

'I don't think it sounds daft at all, it's obvious to me it's Billy's animal instinct kicking in and it would be strange if you didn't feel suspicious of Karl. You've got to admit it Pippa, he did some very odd things, even when you were unwell!'

Annie offered Pippa a kindly look and continued.

'Brendon was a breath of fresh air. Have you spoken to him to let him know your feelings are still so strong for him?'

Pippa slowly finished her mouthful.

'I haven't contacted Brendon, I said I would give Karl a chance and I need to try to do that.'

Then she quickly changed the subject to the wonderful day they had on Saturday.

'Those twin sisters, Kelly and Katy they were so nice. Kelly said you used to be the relief manager at her Colchester branch. She really sang your praises.'

Annie confirmed that Pippa's instincts of the twins was right, both lovely girls. Their parents owned the three beautiful Saunders department stores, one in Ipswich, Colchester and Bury St Edmunds. Katy managed the beauty departments for each of the stores. Kelly had been working at the bank's Colchester branch since leaving college having decided she didn't want to go into the family business. Poor Kelly had an awful experience with a horrible guy, who left her with huge debts and managed to get quite a lot of money out of her before he disappeared. Kelly's father was furious that one of his daughters had been treated this way and vowed if ever he saw him, he'd kill him.

Pippa listened in silence then said.

'Poor Kelly Saunders, she came across as such a nice person I'm not surprised her father wanted to have his pound of flesh, what an awful experience.'

'Kelly's no longer Saunders her surname is Masters, she and Gareth were only married for about a year before he cleared off. I went to the wedding it was a really lavish affair. She looked stunning, well as you can imagine, both her and Katy are natural beauties. It was horrible to see Kelly suffering, and from what she said the entire dirty episode of Gareth took its toll on the whole family. Obviously, it goes without saying Pippa this is confidential

I shouldn't really tell you, but I know you won't say anything to anyone. But if it hadn't been for her parents stepping in to bail her out, she could have lost everything. It all centered around France, Kelly loved holidaying there and that's where she met Gareth. He worked in the wine industry. Shortly after they were married, he convinced her to take out a mortgage on her home and buy a place in Dordogne. To help with the purchase he would put a large chunk of money in and transfer monies monthly towards her mortgage. I saw photos of the property it was beautiful, if truth be known we were all a little bit envious, hate to say it but I was.'

Annie pulled a guilty face, shrugged and continued.

'As he supposedly was over in France with work, Gareth offered to deal with the solicitor. But there was no solicitor and no sooner than the mortgage monies were released to Kelly in the UK, she transferred them over to what she thought was the solicitor's bank account. Yes, you've guessed it, the monies and Gareth disappeared. She obviously contacted the police but that got her nowhere as she'd voluntarily made the transfer. The French bank washed its hands of any blame, insisting the account opening process for this Dupont guy had been followed correctly and anyway they couldn't help as the account was now closed. It turned out the same day the monies hit, they were removed by a large cash withdrawal from the branch in Bergerac. Kelly's father contacted Gareth's work, but they'd never heard of him and any leads quickly dried up.'

Whilst Pippa met Kelly Masters very briefly on Saturday, she was saddened to hear how cruelly and dishonestly she had been treated.

As they walked back, they were chattering only stopping when they needed to go their separate ways, Pippa to the car park and Annie to the branch on Castle Meadow. Pippa jokingly saying.

'I'm really pleased you didn't change my annual leave now Annie, what with it being bank holiday it will be hellishly busy next week. Seriously though Annie thank you for your broad shoulders, I'm sorry to offload on you, but at the moment I can't speak to family about my concerns over Karl, and goodness me I most definitely can't speak to Bev. She's still furious with me for taking him back.'

Annie hugged her.

'Don't be so silly Pippa, I may be your manager, but we will always be friends, I'll always be here for you. All I will say though, and please don't take offence from this, but I really think you should contact Brendon sooner rather than later.'

On her drive home her thoughts were of poor Kelly Masters and she started questioning herself. Why had she been suspicious of Karl just because he had been with a girl that used to work at one of the Colchester branches called Kelly who had a twin. That didn't mean it was the same person and apart from anything else the girl that lived with Karl her twin had died! Talk about adding two and two and getting to seven. Pippa knew her mind had gone overtime and the Kelly she met on Saturday had been married to some horrible guy called Gareth!

She was grateful to Annie not only for telling her about Kelly but having someone to speak privately, was a huge relief.

But she knew Annie was wrong, she couldn't contact Brendon, that would just complicate things even further, and would be so unfair to him.

All of a sudden, her car was stuttering. She looked at the engine warning light and that didn't show a problem. She knew she was distracted and not concentrating on her driving.

The following day she was on her way back from the Diet What Diet classes and her car started playing up again. It was nothing to do with her concentration, there was something wrong with the car. She managed to get home and called the small garage Murray and Son she always used. John the garage owner reassured her that if she could get it to the garage next morning, first thing when he opened, he'd give it a look. She needn't worry, he knew her car inside out, he'd get it sorted for her.

She still hadn't heard from Karl but messaged him saying her car was playing up and asked if he could help her drop it off in the morning. He replied a couple of hours before he was due back, assuring her of course he would help. The message went on how much he missed her, he couldn't wait to get home, the exhibition had been very busy, and he was exhausted.

When Karl pulled on the drive, Billy did his new intruder alarm bark and she went to open the front door thinking this may reassure him, but it didn't. They stood at the door and Billy reverted to the low growl. Karl got out of the car, straightening up as if after a very long journey, he went to the boot to get out his case and walked towards them.

'Hello you two, have you coped alright without me?'

Pippa just stared at him and with total surprise in her voice said.

'You've got a full-blown tan!'

'Yes, it was scorching in Berlin.'

Pippa served up dinner and listened to Karl saying how great the company's stand looked, they were expecting a lot of business coming their way it was worth the effort putting up with the intense heat.

Pippa said she couldn't find her sapphire and diamond ring. She had gone through everything. Karl didn't look that interested so she changed the subject to her car and the arrangements for getting it to the garage. She was asking if in the morning he could follow in his car and bring her back, they didn't need to collect her car later as John the garage owner had made arrangements to drop it back to The Marshman's. She was about to sing John's praises but stopped herself when she recalled Karl's poor opinion of Murray & Son, or Grease Monkey's R Us as he would refer to them.

Karl was keen to help his wife and suggested as her car was faulty, he would drive hers and she could drive his. So that's what happened.

They left just before eight, Pippa in his car and he followed behind in hers. They both had their mobile phones with them just in case Pippa's car broke down.

As she was driving with the radio on, the Bluetooth picked up a call on Karl's phone and Pippa heard a woman's voice saying over and over.

'Where are you, are you out, where are you going, I didn't know you were going anywhere, where are you?'

Pippa was shocked, she pushed the radio to turn it off, but being unfamiliar with the car all that happened was the volume went louder, the voice was breaking up now and again, just repeating.

'Where are you, where are you going, can you hear me, this is crap?'.

Pippa got to a roundabout and as she went round, Karl wasn't behind her anymore and the message cut out. Pippa noticed the mobile number ended 329.

She carried on driving and then just before arriving at the garage, she could see in the rearview mirror Karl was right behind her again. The Bluetooth kicked back in and the number ending 329 connected. The same woman's voice was speaking.

'Can you hear me? This is a crap line I can't believe this! You need to get that phone sorted, or is it that precious Jaguar of yours that's crap. Can you hear me?'

Pippa said clearly and loudly.

'Yes, I can hear you, you're speaking with Phillipa Taylor, Karl's wife.'

The call cut off.

Pippa worked out the calls came through when Karl's phone in her car behind was close enough to the Jaguar and the call would be picked up by his Bluetooth as it had been programmed to accept calls from Karl's phone.

Her car was dropped off at the garage and they returned to The Marshman's, she didn't say much on the journey as she was deep in thought. She'd heard the voice before but couldn't recall where, she knew the voice wasn't Tracy's. She made them a cup of tea, handing him one saying.

'Oh, by the way, you had a couple of phone calls, they kicked in through the Bluetooth in your car. The mobile number ended 329.'

Karl didn't hesitate, he looked at his phone and said straight away.

'Yes, I can see that was Carol from work, I'll call her later she's chasing a tender document.'

Pippa repeated what she'd heard and added.

'Chasing a document on a Saturday? Goodness me this Carol from work sounds awfully common, if she's talking like that. Crap this crap that. Very inappropriate.'

She looked at Karl and he sighed, looked back at her, shook his head and gave her a look as if to say what's your problem!

Pippa's car was brought back to The Marshman's and later in the afternoon she was sitting in the garden reading her book. Billy laying in prime position on her left with Daisy and Gertie at her feet contentedly preening themselves. Karl brought them a glass of wine, she thanked him, and he sat down to join the happy little group.

He knocked his wine back quickly!

'Peppa, are you listening I need to come clean? I said I would be honest with you. I need to tell you something that happened Easter weekend. Hew invited me and Tracy to his as Jeanette was away looking after her mother. We had a threesome. Tracy was in her element, Hew liked it more than me, I just went along with it but Tracy kept getting messages from him asking for us to do it again. He's done the dirty on me, keeping in touch with her, I'll never speak to Hew again, the dirty snake in the grass.'

Pippa sat taking on board the disgusting comments she'd just heard. She knew what Karl said was a lie because Hew and Jeanette had been in Gran Canaria over Easter. Jeanette had sent though photos of their holiday.

She took a deep breath, got up from her chair saying.

'Karl, I've really had enough.'

She walked over to him and tipped the contents of the wine glass over his head.

Karl was screaming like a Banshee, shouting.

'What have you done, how dare you. I'm calling the police. You're not right, there's something wrong with you.'

'Karl I've heard enough of your lies. You weren't at an exhibition in Germany. I checked, the Bautec exhibition took place in February. You'd moved the Dubai holiday on two weeks and went with Tracy. As if you'd get a tan on an exhibition stand. You must think I'm daft! As for that disgusting orgy story that's another lie. Hew and Jeanette were in Gran Canaria at Easter, she sent me photos of their holiday.'

He was furious.

'How dare you have contact with Jeanette, she's nothing to do with you, Hew's my friend.'

She calmly replied.

'Well from what you've just said he's not your friend anymore is he? And I'll be friends with whoever I want.'

Turning to Billy she asked.

'Did you want a walk old chum?'

She picked up his collar and lead and they walked out.

They'd only walked a few minutes and the man new to the village passed her, they exchanged 'afternoon'. She didn't know how, but she managed to keep herself together until it was just her and Billy. She sat on a fallen tree stump and sobbed for quite a while. She knew she had to pull herself together, gave her nose a good blow and phoned Brendon who answered straight away. Through a wobbly tear-filled voice, she managed to say.

'I have to ask Brendon, you said you'd always be there for me, are you?'

'Where else could I possibly be. What's happened?'

She blurted out, there was no stopping her.

'He's pure evil, I hate him and what I hate most he came between us. He's a complete nutter. I'm divorcing him, whatever it takes I will not be married to him one moment longer than necessary.'

'Pippa you will be free quicker than you think. I'll be there on Tuesday, my flights already booked as I need to finalise certain things in Norwich and I'll explain all when I get there, but for now you have to trust me. I'm going to ask you to try and carry on as normal, but if it's too difficult or you feel you're in any sort of danger promise me you'll go to Bev's?'

Pippa promised, she trusted him fully and couldn't wait to see him.

She wondered why he needed to be in Norwich, but it didn't matter, just hearing his voice knowing he was in her life and they were a couple gave her such strength. Her voice was still wobbly, but she managed to tell him she was still on annual leave the following week. She'd busy herself the next day and then Monday was a bank holiday, and it was already arranged she would go over to Eddie's for a barbeque and to watch Norwich at Wembley on TV. She would make sure that her and Billy were there as long as possible. She would pretend to Karl that she was going to Ruth's on Tuesday and work out other excuses for the rest of the week for her and Billy to be out.

Pippa walked through the back door at The Marshman's, half expecting that Karl would have tried to lock her out. He was watching the telly in the lounge, having changed out of the wine soiled clothes but his thinning hair was still wet and randomly stickling up in all directions.

Determined to keep the pretense of not being in Dubai, he said.

'I'll be working from here this week. I'm totally exhausted from the exhibition in Berlin. Shall I go and get us a

Chinese take away for tea? That will save you cooking, you look tired.'

She didn't know how she managed to answer with any form of normality in her voice, but she did.

'OK, if you can get me a mushroom chow mein and then I'll have an early night, I think the stress of my car has worn me out.'

CHAPTER 27

'All good things come to those who wait.'

As soon as Brendon finished speaking with Pippa, he phoned Desmond.

'Go ahead and put your side of the plan in place. As arranged I'll be there on Tuesday to deal with my bits. I'll put Pippa in the picture then, I thought it best to do that in person. You might want to bring Bev in now, but make sure she doesn't spill the beans.'

'Thank God Brendon, that's brilliant news. Bev's been an absolute dragon to live with over this mess, the sooner it's sorted the better for all of us.'

'Too right my dear friend, I'm so grateful for all your help.'

He rang off quickly before Desmond could detect the lump in his throat.

On Tuesday Pippa couldn't wait for the afternoon and the arrival of Brendon. She wondered what he needed to finalise in Norwich and what his cryptic words meant. She popped her head in the office first thing, saying.

'We're now off to Ruth's, see you later Karl.'

She got Billy in the car and drove to the shops at Bagby to pick up food for Brendon's stay and then on to the garden lodge.

She could see both Bev's and Desmond's cars parked at the main house but didn't want to disturb them. She was feeling foolish and embarrassed for the hurt and stress she had caused her dear friends and family by allowing Karl back into her life. She just wished the time would fly by. She couldn't wait to see Brendon.

When he arrived at the lodge she ran out to the car and as soon as he held her in his arms she burst into tears.

'I'm so sorry, I love you so much.'

'Pippa I've been so worried for you my love, believe me when I say it is all OK now. Let's go inside, you need to be sitting down to hear what I have to tell you.'

They went in and Pippa sat down. Brendon produced out of his flight bag a thick file and sat next to her.

'Pippa my darling this is going to be a big shock to you. All you have to do is sign one of these papers, it will go in front of a judge tomorrow and you will no longer be married. Even better for you, it will be as if the marriage never was.'

He relayed a private detective had been hired, whose full report came through the week after she announced she was taking Karl back.

Brendon carried on.

'Please don't think badly of them but your friends and family have told me more than you have. They didn't do it as gossip, they did it as they love you and wanted to protect you. Desmond has been such a star, I had the private detective and the lawyers, but he brought in an ace barrister.'

He reached over, taking Pippa's hands into his.

'Karl is a criminal, he's committed bigamy and his wife Helen is in on the game. If you sign this first paper I have here, I will witness it and Desmond's barrister has an appointment with the Crown Court Judge at ten o'clock tomorrow and your marriage will be annulled.'

He passed her the document and a pen, without hesitation she signed.

'So does this mean, I don't have to divorce him?'

Brendon reassuringly squeezed her hands.

'Pippa your husband died, you are a widow. You were never legitimately married to Karl. There are a few more documents that you will need to sign but I think we should go and see Desmond and Bev now, they're waiting for us.'

Pippa was dumbstruck she didn't know what to say, she wanted to cry, she wanted to laugh, she wanted to scream for the hurt Karl had caused but most of all she just wanted to forget it all and curl up in the safety of Brendon's loving arms.

When they walked into the kitchen Bev started crying.

'Thank God Pip, finally that monster will be out of your life and out of ours too. I hate him. I hoped something positive was afoot when Desmond said last week that Brendon was flying over and needed to stay at the lodge and to keep it quiet from you and everyone at all costs. I assumed he was coming over to convince you to take him back. But when I was told on Saturday of the detective's report, I couldn't believe it, I still can't believe it. What a disgusting con artist, the sooner he's behind bars the better.'

Pippa was still speechless, she just hugged her friend, she couldn't believe she was going to be free. She had so many questions, but she didn't know where to start.

As if reading her mind, Brendon said.

'My darling you must have so many questions, Desmond will be better explaining this to you than me.'

Desmond sat her down.

The Marshman's will transfer into your sole name. Karl will be removed from the rental agreement for the Pride and Joy. I hate to say it Pippa but as that property was bought in your sole name you could have changed the agreement to just you at any time, Karl had no rights to any of those monies. There will be an injunction that prevents him from coming near you or going to any of the properties, its commonly called a restraining order. The last document is the criminal complaint. Eddie, Brendon, Bev and I have already filed ours, so you don't have to. I say you don't have to Pippa as there are things in it that we know to be true, but you will find disturbing.'

Pippa needed and wanted to see everything and without hesitation said.

'Thank you let me see the papers.'

As she read, she felt her strength growing with each word. The criminal complaint was truly damning, and the amount of detail unearthed by the detectives was breathtaking. Karl's real name was Michael Wilson and was known by several names, Gareth Masters being one of them.

He worked at Building For The Future for just under a year and was sacked for poor performance. The business cards and all the paperwork in his home office were purely a false front and contact information doctored, she now understood when she called the number on his business card why it went straight to an answer machine. He hadn't had a job in over seven years, he didn't need one his lucrative income came from his conquests to which he devoted all his time and energies. He owned two houses, was mortgage free and both properties were in the joint names of Michael and Helen Wilson, an impressive house in Dedham which was the family home and a holiday cottage in Aldeburgh.

Kelly Masters was mentioned as one of his victims along with two other women. Pippa hoped Kelly's father would finally have his long-awaited pound of flesh!

Karl hadn't lived at Tracy's, he stayed occasionally when he wanted to be in the area to keep an eye on his investment, The Marshman's. He spent at least three nights a week at his latest target, Arlene Hipperson a wealthy widow in Cromer, she knew him as Frank Smithson.

He hadn't taken Tracy to Dubai, his wife Helen accompanied him.

Without hesitation she signed the papers, turned to Brendon, saying.

'Where's a bottle of champagne when you need it, I feel we should be celebrating. I love you all so much.'

Desmond smiled opened the fridge and pulled out a bottle of Pol Roger, saying.

'Brendon had a case delivered this morning.'

'Oh, I was only joking, I have to drive me and Billy back later and for the time being keeping up this charade.'

Brendon looked sheepish and gave a little cough.

'Pippa my darling, that's not a problem. The private detective will be driving you home, he and his team will continue to look after you until this is over.'

Pippa worryingly asked.

'But what if Karl sees me being driven by a strange man?'

She was quickly reassured. Out of sight from The Marshman's the detective would hop out at the bottom of the drive allowing Pippa to continue and park in her usual spot. This also ensured the detective was close to hand should he be needed. Brendon quickly returned to the matter in hand.

'What we need to know is when Karl will definitely be at The Marshman's. We need to arrange for the papers to be served and the police will be there at the same time to make the arrest.'

Pippa gave a little thought.

'It's his birthday this Friday, I can say I'm preparing a lovely meal, will six o'clock be OK, that would be a time he would normally expect to eat?'

Both Brendon and Desmond in unison said.

'Perfect, Friday at six it is.'

Pippa turned to Brendon.

'Of course, the meal I'll prepare will be for us and if these two haven't scoffed it all by then, bring a bottle of the Pol Roger with you please.'

Brendon gave a heartfelt sigh, saying.

'You're being very brave my darling now might not be the right time, but we have a few of the recordings from telephone calls Karl made from his home office, and his side of the conversation of calls on his mobile while sitting in his office. When you are ready it might help you understand what his game plan was.'

She took a deep breath.

'If it's alright with you can we listen to them now. Come Friday I hope never to think of that evil man again. How did you get recordings of his phone calls?'

Brendon explained Eddie was kept fully informed of everything, he was also a crucial part of the decoy to bug the phones as they needed to find out what Karl was up to. When Eddie phoned Pippa to say her landline was faulty and a telecoms engineer would be with her shortly, there was nothing wrong with the line. The engineer was one of the detectives and had placed two bugs in Karl's office and one on his landline.

The recordings were played. Pippa quietly listened and spoke only once when she heard Helen's voice.

'That's the woman I heard Saturday on the Bluetooth in his car. I knew I'd heard that voice before, it was the same voice on the answer machine when I called the office number on his business card.'

Bev screamed, 'What, heard her on Saturday, you never told me!'

'Sorry Bev, but the last few days life's been a bit hectic to say the least!'

The recordings certainly did give clarity. There were various conversations of Karl and Helen conspiring how to get more money from Pippa. But the scariest recording was when they were plotting to fix her car. Helen saying. 'I can't believe how badly you've cocked up on this one. Why the hell you couldn't convince her to buy that big house so she didn't have such a major share in it, I'll never know. Then if that weren't bad enough, she goes and buys the rental bungalow in her name, nought to do with you. As if a little bit of rental's gonna go far. I think you're losing your touch. I've really had enough, make sure she's a gonna, time's running out, we need to move on, just get on and deal with her but knowing that bitch she's got nine lives so make sure you do it proper. No one will suspect anything with her car being at the garage yesterday.'

Bev burst into tears. Pippa went over to hug her, trying to make light of the awful situation with a 'meow' noise, causing Bev's tears to flow more.

The doorbell rang, Eddie walked in. He hugged his Mum.

'We've been so worried about you Mum. You won't know how many times I wanted to take my cricket bat and smash it round Karl's ugly face. Thank you Brendon, you're a top guy for sorting this so the only person that goes to prison is Karl and hopefully his skanky wife Helen.'

He went over and shook Brendon's hand. Eddie couldn't keep the emotion out of his voice.

'I only popped in Mum, sorry I can't stop. I've arranged for Harold and Sally to come to tea as I felt it important to have their support when I break the news to Sophie. I just hope when she hears Karl is out of our lives doesn't bring the baby on early, she hates him as much as I do for how he's treated you, he's not human.'

Up to hearing this Pippa had managed to be strong but she now had the biggest lump in her throat and no amount of hard swallowing would shift it, so taking a sip of champagne she raised her glass.

'Well my boy thanks to Brendon he most definitely will be out of our lives, drive safely and huge hugs to Sophie and the bump.'

Brendon walked Eddie out, grateful for the opportunity to bring him up to speed with where they were with the legal proceedings, together with the arrangements for Friday when the police would make the arrest. He emphasised the need for the continuance of secrecy and everyone keeping a low profile, not only as they didn't want to spook Karl off, but Brendon was concerned for Pippa's safety. He reassured Eddie that the detectives would be close at hand, but Friday could not come soon enough for any of them.

Pippa was not in any great hurry to get back but knew she couldn't leave it too late as didn't want to cause any suspicion. When she walked in Karl was watching telly and quickly stood up saying.

'You're late.'

'Yes sorry, it's George's birthday, Ruth put on a little impromptu party for him.'

Karl excitedly said.

'Never mind that, you're here now, guess what I found under the bed in the guest room.'

He produced Pippa's sapphire and diamond ring, she knew straight away that was a lie, she suspected all along that he had taken it. She managed to bite her tongue; she was just so grateful to get Matti's grandmother's ring back. She took it from him, put it straight on her finger vowing never to take it off again.

'Oh Karl, thank you I'm so grateful, I'll have to think of a way to say thank you properly.'

She went through to the kitchen to make them a cup of tea thinking this is a heaven scent opportunity. Karl just made getting through to Friday evening a doddle.

Taking his cup through to the lounge, she was looking at the sapphire and diamond ring on her finger.

'I'm so pleased you found my ring, how about as it's your birthday Friday, I'll fix a very special meal.'

Then looking at him in a saucy flirty way continued.

'Plus, I'll have a couple of little surprises for you. I really can't wait for Friday to be here now.'

Karl stood up and moved toward her.

'Why wait Babe, I mean Peppa.'

She stepped back, smiling saucily.

'Steady on, good things come to those who wait, and I've been waiting a long time.'

Karl couldn't believe his luck, finally he was going to be back on top.

Wednesday first thing to avoid any suspicion she took Billy for his morning walk. She'd only gone a few yards when she spotted the man she had seen recently walking round the village. As usual he was dressed to fit in, this time in well-worn walking boots. He was walking in the same direction on the other side of the road. Pippa realised, he was following her. It was the private detective that had driven her the night before! She hadn't recognised him then, he had been wearing a suit, the evening light was poor, and Pippa had other things on her mind. She now understood the influx of new faces she noticed around the village. She couldn't wait to tell Brendon how good they were. She thought this private detective protection lark was a bit of overkill when Brendon told her, but now she felt so safe.

When she got back from walking Billy, she popped her head round Karl's office door, chirpily saying.

'Just to remind you, I'm over at Eddie's today and tomorrow helping get the nursery decorated. Your lunch and tea are all ready for you and plated up in the fridge. I've let Amy know I won't be at the Diet What Diet meeting this Friday as I've a very special meal to prepare. I hope you're looking forward to your birthday as much as I am. See you later.'

With that her and Billy went off to meet Brendon.

She arrived at the garden lodge and changed out of her scruffy decorating clothes and Brendon drove them to Norwich as they needed to do some shopping.

Thursday, she drove straight to the garden lodge, and it was no surprise that just as the day before it was time to head back before she knew it. She loved being in Brendon's company and he in hers. Tonight, she had trouble getting Billy into the car, clearly, he didn't want to break up their happy family.

Pippa reassured him.

'Not long now Billy, it will all soon be sorted, and we won't have to see that vile man's ugly face ever again.'

She approached the drive to The Marshman's with trepidation, but that feeling vanished when she saw the private detective in the shadow of the hedge, he'd stepped far enough out for her to see him when he recognised her car. She was so grateful to Brendon for making sure she was protected, and this protection had been lavished on her even after she'd sent him away. She was so lucky to have Brendon in her life.

Karl's day hadn't gone so well.

Since Tuesday Tracy had left various voice mails, saying he had to phone her, she was so stressed. Finally, and very begrudgingly he called her, listened first to her moaning why had it taken him two days to call her back and then she was crying. She'd got home Tuesday from her job as a hotel cleaner to find the beautiful sapphire and diamond ring he'd bought her gone; she couldn't find it anywhere. She knew her insurance cover wasn't enough to replace such an expensive ring, especially as Karl had told her it was an antique.

He finally got a word in.

'I'm really up to my neck in work. I can't believe it, Doug is expecting me to even work on my birthday and he knew I had plans to see you. I was going to surprise you Babe and take you for a lovely meal Friday night, but I won't be back in Norfolk until after the weekend now. Tell you what we're go for a meal on Monday, just book somewhere nice, you choose.'

This calmed Tracy a little over him never responding to her texts or calls but when she asked what was going to happen to replace the ring, he just suggested she might need to look closer to home and ask her daughters or their boyfriends where her ring was.

CHAPTER 28

'Revenge is a dish best served cold.'

Pippa was up early Friday morning, she showered, dried and straightened her hair. Karl walked past her bedroom, looked in, and she was sitting at her dressing table putting on her make up.

'Morning Peppa.'

'Happy Birthday Karl. Don't worry when you hear any noise today, I've bought a new bed and its being delivered this morning. I think it's important to draw a line and put the past behind me for my fresh start.'

Karl said with a smirk.

'I knew you would come around to my way of thinking, I'm looking forward to this evening and the surprises you've planned.'

'And so you should, you really do deserve them Karl.'

Pippa was amazed the way she handled the response, she knew her role was to make sure Karl was there for six o'clock, so many had put so much into this, she couldn't let them down.

The new bed was delivered, it was a navy wrought iron frame with black iron finials, and a deep sumptuous mattress. The old bed was taken away. She went to her car and brought indoors the new pillows and bedding that she and Brendon chose together when they went up the City on Wednesday. It was beautiful, antique silver coloured satin damask. She enjoyed taking her time ironing and organising it all, determined to make sure everything was dressed perfectly. She then added the finishing touch by draping a sensuous midnight blue negligee on her side of the bed, and on the other side, matching midnight blue pyjama bottoms. The room was transformed, even Billy's bed had a new cover.

Later in the afternoon Karl walked past the bedroom and looked in, he couldn't believe his luck. He walked through to the kitchen and the smell was wonderful. It was a mixture of the delicious food and Pippa's heady natural scent. Sitting back in his office he could barely concentrate, he loved it when a plan came together, he was so looking forward to telling Helen how well this was working out. All the setbacks Pippa had created by not dying on the operating table were being put right. Soon it would be time to put the final piece of the plan into place, literally the last nail in the coffin. Helen might think she was the brains behind everything, but it would never work without him. He had a few more conquests in him before this stud would be ready to be put out to pasture.

As arranged, at four o'clock Pippa sent a text to Brendon, simply saying 'ALL GO FOR 6.' She then went through to Karl in his office.

'Hi, sorry to disturb. As you know I've put so much into planning this evening, but obviously it's not about me, it's you, it's your birthday. Please give yourself enough time to freshen up and get ready for your evening. I really want to give you the first of your surprises at five minutes to six. Hate to be so pedantic about timing.'

'No probs Peppa, I'll be on time. Love the look of the bedroom, that bed will get a good breaking in tonight.'

She threw him a flirtatious smile saying.

'You bet it will.'

That excited Karl and he found it uncomfortable to sit with the twitching that was going on between his legs.

As the time approached Pippa surprised herself, she wasn't nervous. She put Billy in the kitchen, popped on the radio to act as a distraction for him and shut the door before going through to the lounge.

Karl walked in at the appointed time, he could see Pippa was looking very happy. She handed him a small gift bag. Karl was already beside himself with anticipation and hastily tore open the bag, there was a glasses case inside. Expecting a pair of expensive sunglasses, he was perplexed as he found himself holding a pair of glasses with a rose tint. He looked at Pippa and silently mouthed the word 'what'?

She smiled sweetly.

'They were mine, they're yours now, I've a feeling you're going to need them.'

Karl didn't know what she was going on about, and before he could respond the doorbell rang and still smiling sweetly, she said.

'There you go, that's for you. Happy birthday.'

Karl thought, those glasses were a silly joke, this is my real present.

Eagerly he opened the door to a man in a suit with some sort of an ID on a lanyard around his neck. The man handed Karl what he believed was his present and as he took the large thick envelope, the man said.

'Karl Taylor you've been Served.'

As the man turned away another man slipped by him and went to stand next to Pippa, taking her hand into his. Karl's head naturally turned to follow this man inside, but before he could react, he caught movement from the corner of his eye and turned again to the door. Karl was confused and then fear set in. Another man in a suit was holding up a warrant card and next to him a tall police constable in uniform. The man in the suit said in a clear strong voice.

'Karl Taylor I'm Detective Sergeant Gordon, we would like you to come down to the station to answer a few questions. It would be best you came quietly sir, let's not have a fuss.'

Karl exploded as he waved his arms around, screaming obscenities to the man holding Pippa's hand and also at the police officers. DS Gordon turned to the constable, nodded saying.

'OK Sam, if you would secure the suspect please.'

Sam took a step forward, Karl turned to run away and before he knew it found himself face down on the floor with his hands cuffed behind his back.

DS Gordon knelt on one knee beside Karl.

'Michael Wilson, also known as Karl Taylor, Gareth Masters, Hercule Dupont, Stephen Butterman and Frank Smithson, I'm arresting you on suspicion of bigamy and offenses under section 76 of the serious crime act. You can add resisting arrest and affray for your conduct tonight. Anything you say or refuse to say and later rely upon for your defence may be used against you.'

Sam helped Karl to his feet and led him out to the police car.

As DS Gordon turned to follow, he looked back at Pippa and Brendon saying.

'What a nasty piece of work, that's the last you'll see of him.'

The front door was still open, but Brendon could wait no longer, he scooped Pippa in his arms they kissed passionately unaware that as the police car drove off with Karl handcuffed seated in the back, he was witness to their embrace.

EPILOGUE

At the same time as the events at The Marshman's a certain property in Dedham was visited by the Essex Police. This was no coincidence. The neighbours gossiped but no one really knew why Helen the woman that had lived there for years, was taken away in handcuffs by the police. All they knew for certain, the property was seized under the proceeds of crime act and subsequently put up for sale.

COMING SOON
FROM MON A JOHNSON

Accident of Consequence

It's not only the beautiful Norfolk countryside that's discovered by a group of walkers. To their horror, they stumble upon a woman's body in a shallow grave. Perhaps the area around Hepton-On-The-Marshes isn't so sleepy after all.

Pure Poison In Three Acts

From the comfort of her Norfolk country house in the picturesque village of Bagby, Lisa finds herself in a complicated situation with a tricky question on her hands.

Is it best to let the sleeping dog lie or rouse the beast from its slumber?

After careful sleuthing her decision is made. When all said and done, this sleeping dog has had his day.

Keep up to date with future books
@ www.mon-a-johnson.co.uk